LUCINDA, DARKLY

THE *demon* PRINCESS *chronicles*

SUNNY

"Fans of Laurell K. Hamilton
will love Sunny."
—*New York Times* bestselling
author Lori Foster

*For every pain—there will
be pleasure…*

BERKLEY SENSATION

$7.99 U.S.
$9.99 CAN

ISBN 978-0-425-22870-8

5 0 7 9 9>

S > EAN

continued . . .

"[A] superb fast-paced urban fantasy in the tradition of Laurell K. Hamilton."   —*Midwest Book Review*

"One of those books that grabs you and won't let go! Such an incredible start to a series, *Lucinda, Darkly* simply has it all. Each turn of the page will take you step-by-step into this intricately fascinating world. Sunny's ingenious imagination captivates . . . Both erotica and paranormal readers alike will be engrossed by the story as Sunny introduces a place where pain brings pleasure and blood is an aphrodisiac."   —*Two Lips Reviews*

"*Lucinda, Darkly* is . . . spellbinding. Sunny tells a wonderful story that is very intense, emotional, and sexually charged about a demon dead princess who finds romance and a part of herself that she was missing."
    —*Night Owl Romance*

"Full of paranormal passion, Sunny's fast-paced first in a new erotic fantasy series, the Demon Princess Chronicles, introduces Lucinda, a six-hundred-year-old demon princess who's getting bored with her long unlife."
    —*Publishers Weekly*

"Sunny is a wonderful writer that has created characters that readers will demand to learn more about and whom they will enjoy reading as the characters find their way to happiness. A captivating series."   —*A Romance Reader*

LUCINDA, DARKLY

SUNNY

BERKLEY SENSATION, NEW YORK

THE BERKLEY PUBLISHING GROUP
Published by the Penguin Group
Penguin Group (USA) Inc.
375 Hudson Street, New York, New York 10014, USA
Penguin Group (Canada), 90 Eglinton Avenue East, Suite 700, Toronto, Ontario M4P 2Y3, Canada
(a division of Pearson Penguin Canada Inc.)
Penguin Books Ltd., 80 Strand, London WC2R 0RL, England
Penguin Group Ireland, 25 St. Stephen's Green, Dublin 2, Ireland (a division of Penguin Books Ltd.)
Penguin Group (Australia), 250 Camberwell Road, Camberwell, Victoria 3124, Australia
(a division of Pearson Australia Group Pty. Ltd.)
Penguin Books India Pvt. Ltd., 11 Community Centre, Panchsheel Park, New Delhi—110 017, India
Penguin Group (NZ), 67 Apollo Drive, Rosedale, North Shore 0632, New Zealand
(a division of Pearson New Zealand Ltd.)
Penguin Books (South Africa) (Pty.) Ltd., 24 Sturdee Avenue, Rosebank, Johannesburg 2196,
South Africa

Penguin Books Ltd., Registered Offices: 80 Strand, London WC2R 0RL, England

This is a work of fiction. Names, characters, places, and incidents either are the product of the author's imagination or are used fictitiously, and any resemblance to actual persons, living or dead, business establishments, events, or locales is entirely coincidental. The publisher does not have any control over and does not assume any responsibility for author or third-party websites or their content.

LUCINDA, DARKLY

A Berkley Sensation Book / published by arrangement with the author

PRINTING HISTORY
Berkley Sensation mass-market edition / September 2009
Berkley Sensation trade edition / August 2007

Copyright © 2007 by DS Studios Inc.
Excerpt from *Lucinda, Dangerously* by Sunny copyright © 2009 by DS Studios Inc.
Excerpt from *Dragon Moon* by Rebecca York copyright © 2009 by Ruth Glick.
Cover photograph of woman wearing red robe by Paul Vozdic/Getty Images.
Cover design by Monica Benalcazar.
Interior text design by Kristin del Rosario.

ISBN: 978-0-425-22870-8

BERKLEY® SENSATION
Berkley Sensation Books are published by The Berkley Publishing Group,
a division of Penguin Group (USA) Inc.,
375 Hudson Street, New York, New York 10014.
BERKLEY® SENSATION and the "B" design are trademarks of Penguin Group (USA) Inc.

PRINTED IN THE UNITED STATES OF AMERICA

10 9 8 7 6 5 4 3 2 1

ONE

NIGHT FELL SOFTLY with purple fingers of dusk. An ending of the day for many, just the beginning of mine. Crisp New England coolness flowed like silk across my skin. Massachusetts air. Fresher than New York; far less crowded to my senses. But even here in the Berkshire Hills, there were still so many.

So many of them. So few of us.

Heartbeats pulsed around me like the drips of a thousand leaky faucets. None but I was aware of those precious beats of life, like a constant drumming in the background. Aware of what I, myself, no longer possessed.

My heart did not beat. I did not breathe. Yet I walked and flowed among them, but was not one of them. Apart. Not alive but dead. Demon dead, to be specific. But what was dead, really? I'd had over six hundred years to roll that word, that elastic definition, round and round in my head, and had found it perpetually stretchable. Was I alive? By human definition, no. But was I dead? Also no, by their definition. For I spoke, I thought, I bled, I wept. I existed thinly in between.

Eyes fell upon me like invisible touches, gazes drawn to my lushness, my petite beauty, the golden hue of my skin, the mauve redness of my lips. Nothing unusual to stand me apart from others but for the long, curling strands of my golden tresses. Not blond but true gold. As if a million silky strands, gossamer fine, had been spun from a spider. Floating behind me, ethereally light, as I walked—spanning the colors from auburn red to honey blond, somehow blending together and becoming one. The rolling sway of my hips was natural, fluid, and feminine. Quintessential woman. Ironic, really. Because that was something I had not been for so many years, decades . . . centuries. A woman. Just a woman.

I laughed softly at how deceiving looks can be, and it drew the eyes of yet more humans. Let them look. Let them pay their silent homage to this false goddess of femininity. Perhaps had they seen my nails, razor sharp, discreetly covered now by gloves . . . but, no. Even then they would not have known of their significance. Only someone like us . . . ah, that word again—us. Even now, after so long, I still betrayed myself. No, not like us. Someone like what I had once been. Only they would truly know what I was now.

As if my thoughts had conjured him, the slow beating of one heartbeat called out to me in the freshly fallen night. Slow, so slow. Inhumanely slow. Beating at half the speed of all others, its distinct, sluggish pace blared like a trumpet's blast in my ear.

Slowly I stopped and looked around, searching for its origin. It came toward me then. A man tall, with shoulders broad, hips trim, and legs long. Skin pale beneath the silvery caress of moonlight, hair raven black. Lips full, sinfully red, as tempting as Eve's apple. *Come taste me*, they beckoned. And, oh, how I yearned to abide that silent plea.

He moved with lithe grace, drawing wakes of appreciative yet ignorant eyes. His sweet beauty, as false as mine, beguiled innocent souls. He was a dangerous predator . . .

like me. The tingling awareness of his presence was unmistakable. A Monère warrior.

He was dressed like a human, his hair cropped short and styled in their manner, and he was in the company of a young human male. A boy, really, no older than eighteen or nineteen, as tall as the warrior but with the leanness of youth. He chattered animatedly and familiarly with the warrior.

What was this Monère doing here, alone in this leafy townlet, far removed from the normal territory they patrolled, the big cities and bustling metropolises?

Our gazes touched, met, and held for a long moment that spun out in time. He smiled innocuously, casually, in passing, stunning me . . . and hurting me. Not the smile itself but the unconcern, the unawareness. His heart did not speed up in fright but kept to its slow, pulsing rhythm.

He knew not who and what I was—that surprised me. My lack of answering spark—that was what hurt me. Even now, centuries later, I still mourned that loss: the innate, powerful draw of a Monère male to a Monère Queen. What I had once been before I had died and become demon dead. Now they sensed me, but barely. What had once been a strong and irresistible tidal wave of a pull and swell—my aphidy—was now only a faint stir. Silly to mourn what had been lost so long ago. But that which you no longer possess often becomes what you then most desire.

Tears stung my eyes, blinding me for a moment, so that I sensed rather than saw him turn his head, his eyes still following me as he passed me by. And that puzzled me. Why did he look at me if he thought me human, as his slow beating heart proclaimed he did? There was no reason to draw his attention then. Monère gained no pleasure from mating with a human. Even this dead Monèrian still remembered that.

The soft whisper of the young man trailed sharply and clearly into my ears. "Stefan, is she like me?"

The man, Stefan, looked away from me, his attention

drawn back to his companion. "Hush, Jonnie." His voice came softly, sweetly, a warm and vibrant baritone.

I searched harder with my senses and felt it then: the faintest hum of the boy's presence, a pale shadow of the Monère warrior's vibrant power.

Ah. The boy must be a Mixed Blood. Half human, half Monère, the resultant product of a passionless and irresponsible mating—a Monère woman's desperate need to bear life, but not wanting to raise an impure one. Because human blood tainted the Monèrians' essence, rendering them essentially human without the powers or privileges of our mother moon's gifts. That was what we—*they*—were. The Monère, children of the moon. Supernatural creatures that had fled their dying planet over four million years ago. The genesis of the legends of werewolves and vampires.

A Mixed Blood—is that what they thought I was?

I almost laughed. It had to be the oddest thing to happen to me in more centuries than I could recall, being mistaken for a Mixed Blood! Had times changed so much? What did they teach their people nowadays? Or perhaps it was the unexpected locality of our meeting. Demon dead, after all, weren't expected to be seen roaming out and about. If we'd passed each other at High Court, he would have known immediately what I was with my skin dark and golden among the lily whiteness of the Monère. Here, among the humans, I just looked tanned or Mediterranean in flavor. It was almost nice that he didn't know. A novelty. Amusing.

Ah, child. How wrong you are. And how young you both are. Yes, even you, my warrior, even though your power thrums strong and vibrant against my senses.

He could not have been more than a century old. But what was a hundred years?

Sadness swept over me, and remembered loss. All whom I had known in my old life were dead and gone. Only a handful of my Monèrian friends had been spared, powerful enough to make the transition and become demon dead. And most of them now were faded back into the darkness as the centuries marched by like relentless soldiers of time.

When time stretched long and endless, and all that is familiar and dear to you falls away into dust and darkness— all but my brother, my only constant—then time no longer is a blessing but a foe. Something to be endured. And anything that breaks that boredom is something to be treasured.

His blood sang to me in tempting beats, this Stefan, who- ever he was. But I would not have touched him, for I still remembered those stringent rules of Monèrian Queendom— that messy bitchhood. You did not taste the property of an- other without sought permission or given grant. I would have left him and journeyed on my way, continuing in my aimless travel to seek out wayward demons and return them back to Hell, as my official duty charged me to do, had I not noticed three humans following furtively behind Stefan and the boy, Jonnie.

Three swarthy street men dressed in long winter coats shadowed them, stopping when their prey stopped, con- tinuing apace when they walked on. The Monère and the Mixed Blood remained unaware.

Intriguing.

I followed them, a block behind, not needing to see them, just smell them, their sweaty tang, eager and anxious; their hearts beating faster in the excitement of the hunt.

Do you foolish humans know who you hunt? I won- dered.

I watched as the three stalkers shortened the distance, as they suddenly snatched the boy, dragging him into a dark alley. Stefan, alert now, turned, chased after the men. He was a fast blur, disappearing into the alley, but still moving only human fast. The sound of grunts and thuds came loudly to my ear from the alleyway.

"Watch out!" I heard the Mixed Blood cry.

I slid into the dark shadows of the building across the street just in time to see one of the men lift a crossbow to his shoulder and let fly a sharp stake through the air. Stefan snatched it with his hand before it could whiz past him and endanger the boy. With a quick toss, he threw it back, the blunt end striking the shooter in the face, causing the man to drop the bow.

"Throw the holy water!"

A vial of water was splashed upon Stefan's face, but no cry of pain, no stench of burning flesh filled the air. Just a look of disgust on Stefan's face as he advanced upon the men. "Enough!"

They backed up, even though they were three to his one. One man fumbled out a silver cross, holding it out in front of him.

"I am not a vampire!" Stefan said.

When the third man pulled out a gun, though, the amusement left me.

"What are you doing, Clarence?" one of the men hissed. "He don't seem to be no vampire like you said he was."

"Well, he ain't human!" Clarence snarled back. "No human can snatch a stake out of the air like that." His breath came too fast, and the gun trembled in his hands. "But you fast enough to stop a bullet?"

"Man, I'm outta here." Disquieted, the other two men fled the darkened alley, leaving Clarence alone.

Stefan stood quietly, making no move to dodge or rush Clarence. "You've made a mistake. Or is it money you want? You can have my wallet, gladly."

"Shut up! I ain't no thief. You ain't human and I'm gonna prove it." He pulled the trigger. I moved then, but it was too late.

"Jonnie, get down!" Stefan cried. Bullets whined and blood blossomed red like a crimson stain across Stefan's white shirt as he closed the distance in a blur, snatching the gun from Clarence and crushing his hand. Clarence's screams of agony rent the air as I rushed past them to the figure crumpled on the ground. The smell of fresh blood filled my senses long before I saw it spurting like a tiny oil well, pumping from a hole in the boy's side where a bullet had pierced him. A severed artery, leaking away his life with gushing gusto.

"Oh, blessed Goddess. Jonnie!" Stefan dropped to his knees beside me, heedless of his own spilling blood. He ignored his own wounds, but I could not. I remained sharply aware of it—the even richer smell of his blood.

"Jonnie . . . I have to get him to a hospital." Moving in a kind of shocked daze, he bent to gather the boy into his arms.

"Wait."

He looked at me then, almost blindly. "I can't. He's dying."

My hand held him back and I watched as he became aware of my strength—as great as his. No . . . even greater.

"His life bleeds out from him. We must stop it now," I told him. "Even a minute more will be too late."

"I can't. I have no healing gift." Then more softly. "What *are* you?"

What. Not who.

I smiled. Saw the realization bloom across his face as I removed the glove from my right hand and let his eyes fall upon my razor-sharp nails. "I can stop the bleeding if you will allow me."

He swallowed. Raised wide, desperate eyes back up to mine. "Then do so quickly, I beg of you."

It pleased and surprised me, that plea. I would have helped, regardless, even had he fought me. But it was good not to have to waste time and energy restraining him. And the sweetness of his unexpected trust was . . . nice.

I let it rise in me then, my power. A calling from deep inside, a quickening surge pulled from the core of me, of who I was and what I am. I felt it bubble up like hot lava to the surface. Felt it throb up from deep within, fill my chest with a hot tingling rush, and travel down my arm, my hand, in a fiery spilling stream. I trickled that molten power carefully down into just my forefinger, pulsed it to the very tip of the nail, and inserted that glowing tip gently into that flooding spill of blood, sizzling it until I searched out the flesh beneath. With my senses thrown wide and open, guiding me, I found where the nicked artery pulsed, and touched Jonnie there, letting my power flow, cauterizing the wound. Black smoke rose, and the caustic smell of burnt flesh and blood stung my nostrils.

I removed my finger from Jonnie's wound, withdrew and cooled my power. He lay there, still and unconscious, but the bleeding had ceased.

Stefan swayed suddenly, like a toppling tree. I reached out, steadied him with my unbloodied hand, and caught a glimpse of his back. The bullets had left small holes in front, much larger ones in back, each exit wound at least two inches in diameter. A large chunk of him had been blown away.

"Hollow point bullets," I observed.

"He missed the heart. I will be fine," Stefan murmured, but I realized the truth. He could have died had Clarence, the gunman, aimed a little higher. The hollow points might have taken out his heart—one of the ways to kill a Monère. He'd stood there and let the bullets strike him when he could so easily have dodged them.

I frowned. "Why did you risk yourself?"

"I am harder to kill," he said, and I realized then that he had tried to act as a human shield for the boy, protecting him with the barrier of his own flesh. But the bullets had gone through him and struck the boy anyway. And Stefan had let Clarence run away. A pity, but a prudent move. The human's death would have stirred up even more trouble.

He puzzled me, this warrior, with his mercy for the shooter and his care for the boy. Monère usually treated Mixed Bloods as a lesser breed, inferior stock. With contempt instead of care. "Is the boy of your blood?"

"No, but he is all I have. He is like a son to me."

"Your Queen?"

"I serve no queen. Have no brethren other than Jonnie. I am a rogue."

A rogue. A Monère warrior driven out by his Queen. Or fled from her before she killed him because he had grown too strong for her, become too much of a threat. Such waste. But it explained much.

Stefan swayed. "Please, I beg of you. He must be brought to a hospital—"

"I will see to it," I assured him and moved swiftly down the alley. A small crowd had gathered at the entryway, drawn by the gunfire. An older gray-haired man dressed in a business suit and a light wool coat talked rapidly into a small phone.

"Call for hospital transport," I told him crisply. "A boy has been shot."

He nodded. "I'm on the phone with the police right now."

I turned to another tall onlooker and captured his eyes, flexed my will. His eyes glazed, bespelled by me. "I have need of your coat."

The man took off his long, black leather coat and handed it to me.

"Thank you," I murmured. Never hurt to be polite. "You will leave now and be on your way." Eyes fixed and unseeing, he obediently left.

Returning to Stefan, I lifted him gently to his feet and helped him into the coat, buttoning it completely, hiding his wash of blood. The wail of sirens sounded mournfully in the distance as I propped him against the alley wall. "You should leave before they arrive."

"I can't leave Jonnie—"

"I'll see that he gets to the hospital."

"Why are you doing this? Helping us?" he asked, his voice suddenly fierce.

Because you interest me. Because you break the boredom of my ageless, endless wander. Because I still see you as my people.

But I said none of these things. I smiled instead with the sultry wickedness that was my natural wont and desire. I let it fill my voice, my face, and said instead something he would more easily believe. "Because I shall return to collect payment from you."

He paled even more, his heartbeat fluttering like a sparrow finding itself suddenly captured. "I will gladly pay it. Thank you. Thank you for saving Jonnie."

His gratitude touched me oddly. To cover it, I leaned into him, pressed the generous swell of my breasts against his chest, and purred, "Don't thank me yet. Later, after I've collected my due from you." I smiled, allowed my fangs to emerge. Allowed him to see them. "Save some of that precious blood for me."

He stared at my mouth, transfixed for a moment. Then, swallowing, he gave me his address, an apartment complex several blocks away.

"I shall await you there," he said and stumbled away.

Two

S TEFAN HAD HEARD of the demon dead before, but had never seen them. Most Monère never did unless they went to Court and glimpsed the High Prince of Hell, Prince Halcyon, a High Council member who attended the parliamentary sessions frequently. But the scant times Stefan had been to Court, he had not glimpsed the legendary prince that all of their kind knew and spoke of with fear and respect.

They saw demon dead rarely because few were powerful enough to cross over from that other realm, Hell. And all spoken about had been male—the Prince, the High Lord whose picture hung at Court, and the few demons over the centuries who had crossed the portal and rampaged mad with bloodlust, ravaging Monère blood. But never a female.

Demon dead were the stuff of legends and nightmares, the Monère's bogeymen. What mothers taught their young children to fear and avoid. *Beware the demon dead.* They were either ravaging beasts or dangerous seducers, trading pleasure for blood, stronger even than their Warrior Lord.

Only, she had not seemed a beast or a monster, as the

legends declared. Stefan didn't even know her name. She was so petite in size—five foot two, or three at best. And so beautiful, such radiance. Hair of spun gold, skin dark like ripe honey. Lush, with full hips poured into leather pants, generous breasts straining her silk burgundy shirt. A waist tiny, wasp-small. And the way she moved, so fluid and graceful. She was sex incarnate, with an almost touchable sensuality.

In all the warriors' talks and fears about the demon dead, they had said nothing about kindness. Perhaps that was what threw him off most, her kindness, even after he knew what she was. She had been benign with him and gentle in her care of Jonnie . . . until he had demanded why. Why was she helping them? Then the dangerous hardness, the fiery hunger, had spilled into her eyes. But still he did not fear her. He wanted to fuck her, please her . . . how could any man not, even one wounded such as he . . . but fear her, he did not.

Only it was not sex she wanted. It was blood.

Stefan staggered along the darkened streets until he reached his apartment, located on the third floor of a ten-story complex. He shrugged out of the leather coat, heavier now with the weight of his blood, but better soaked in the garment than leaving a bloody trail for someone to follow. He had been careless enough, not realizing he had drawn the attention of human hunters. His daytime sleeping habits and pale skin had attracted Clarence's notice and made him think Stefan *vampyre*. He snorted.

All these years since Stefan had fled his Queen, he had worried more about the danger of stumbling across other Monère warriors who would not hesitate to kill him, a rogue, had they come across him. He had overlooked the threat humans might pose.

He had abandoned his former life when his Queen had started cleaning house again, killing off her strongest warrior, Geoffrey, her captain of arms. Using Stefan as her instrument and Geoffrey's replacement. He'd beheaded his friend because he'd had no other choice; he'd been ordered to do so in front of her. And then he'd fled because in a few more years, it would be his turn. His death on a pretext or a whim. He'd fled because if he'd stayed, he might have killed his Queen instead of serving her. His friend's death at his hand had been the last straw.

She had been neither cruel nor kind. Just ruthless. Her strongest warriors were killed off every ten years or so. He had not loved her. He had come too late and too old to garner any bed interest. But he had not hated her before. Now he did. So he had fled come the dawn, with sunlight burning his skin, and his brothers in arms all fast asleep.

He'd fled across the country, traveling along the fringes of territories, areas less frequently patrolled, hiding among humans in small towns, not the forests where they would have hunted for him. He'd traveled like that for one year, growing to understand human ways, picking up jobs here and there that allowed him to work at night.

Being alone had almost killed him. It had stifled his spirit, made listless his heart. Having no purpose, no meaning, serving no honor—that, more than no longer being able to Bask, to drink in moonlight . . . that had slowly leeched away life and the will to live. Until the day he'd heard a cry late at night on the way to work, and had found a newborn babe abandoned near the back of a hospital. Its faint familiar presence had drawn Stefan to pick it up. He'd held the babe in his arms and had known that both human and Monère blood mixed within it, and that it had been discarded because of this impurity of blood. He'd looked into those innocent brown eyes, and had felt love and purpose stir anew within him once more.

Jonnie had been his reason for living since then. And now this woman, this demon. Coming across her tonight was like how he'd felt holding that newborn babe. Something stirring. Something being brought back to life.

He closed the window curtains and showered quickly, bandaging himself tightly to stop the bleeding. This blood was not his to waste so freely anymore, it was hers. So he did his best to conserve it. Crawling into bed, he lay there still and unmoving, letting his body begin to heal. Waiting patiently for her to come.

Hours passed in healing slumber before the doorbell chimed, waking him. Upon opening the door, Stefan noticed what he had failed to notice before—the absence of a beating heart. No stirring sound of deep, slow breathing. All the things a Monère relied upon to detect the presence of others venturing into their space. There was nothing to warn him of her arrival but for a whisper of her faint presence.

She entered silently, moving in that languid rolling grace, hips swaying softly, sensuously. "Jonnie is well. Lost a lot of blood, but the doctors are replenishing that. No major organs damaged. He'll be fine."

Relief and gratitude flooded Stefan, weakening him, while desire drew him nearer to her, as if she were a flower blooming and he a famished bee. He wanted to touch her, see if she was real, tangible. If she felt different from his kind. So much myth and mystery, fear and fright associated with the demon dead, those mythical beings from another realm.

He touched her then, as he wanted to. Captured her hand and held it in his. Her skin felt warm and soft against his fingers. She was real, as tangible as any of them, save for a darker skin, a richer hue. Shades of shiny brown and gleaming gold.

"You were kind to have stayed longer than you needed, to see that Jonnie was well."

Gently she eased from his grip. Moved her sharp, lethal nails away from the brush of his skin. "The police. Had to answer all their questions without mentioning you. They have a good description of the three men." She smiled sharply. "Especially gun-happy Clarence. Then there were all the bloody forms at the hospital. Piles and piles of them to fill out. I made up most of the information. Hope you don't mind."

He shook his head. "It does not matter. I shall settle their bill, then we will leave this place when Jonnie is better."

"Is it safe to remain here that long?"

He shrugged. "As safe as any other place for now. I crushed the attacker's hand. I do not think he will attempt anything further until he has healed. We will be gone by then."

"Jonnie was worried about you when he roused. I told him you were injured and could not be there, but that you were fine."

"I am in your debt," he said formally.

"Yes, you are," she purred and gazed about the apartment curiously. It was a home filled with the comfortable clutter of living, books lining the shelves, CDs stacked neatly by a stereo. A basketball, a baseball bat and glove piled in a carton by the door. Signs of Jonnie all around, speaking much of the importance of the boy in Stefan's life.

"How can I repay you?" Stefan asked.

She blinked those dark sultry eyes, focused on him. "I'm thirsty."

"What can I get you to drink?"

She smiled slowly. "Blood."

He answered calmly, "My veins are open, awaiting your first bite."

Her smile grew, stretching her lips until he could see her small, white even teeth. No fangs yet.

"Good," she purred, leaning against him, "you remembered your pledge." Her breast and hip brushed his uninjured side, and the sharp tips of her nails rested on his bare chest. He made no move to draw away from her, nor did his heart speed up in fright. He just stood there willingly, like a silent lamb, waiting for her to pierce him, to puncture him.

"Let me see your wound," she said, stepping away. He obeyed her silently, unwrapping the bandage.

She frowned. He had begun to heal, though not as much as she would have expected for someone with his power. Even so, what had been two large gaping holes were now knitting flesh, shrunk to a third of their previous size, but still raw with juicy wetness.

She sniffed lingeringly at the wounds, the sanguinary

aroma tempting her, making her wonder what he tasted like. Would he be honey sweet? Or more citrus tang?

"Come into the bedroom." Taking her hand, Stefan drew her to the bed and sank down upon the mattress, lying on his side. She stretched out behind him, pressed her fingertips lightly into his flesh. Gently scraped her nails down his back.

He shivered at her touch. Not in fear but in pleasure. "Tell me your name, please."

"Why? Never been bitten by a strange demon before?"

"I want a name to remember you by."

"A sentimental fool," she murmured, and dug her nails lightly into his skin.

He unleashed a small cry.

"Name is Lucinda."

"Lucinda." He rolled the name upon his tongue. "My name is Stefan."

"I know." She pressed her lips to the curve of his back, flicked her tongue out to taste the skin. He gasped, his muscles tensed, but in suspenseful waiting rather than in fright.

So white, so tender his skin. She wanted to see it glow against hers in brilliant light. But he was weak, he was wounded, and healing slowly. So she decided not to use any of her powers, to spare him the shock and the thrill of it. She brushed him lightly with her hands, played upon him with her lips. Tasted him with her tongue, her mouth. Rimmed the edge of his wounds in back, licking, lapping. Finally tasting his blood.

This one was sweet. Honey sweet.

Lucinda felt the punch of his thrumming power seep into her with his taste. She sucked and suckled him, her heart sweetened by the teasing taste and power of him. Ah, what a feast he would be. But all she intended to do today was play with him.

Her fangs emerged, her savage hunger roaring to life like a living, breathing thing. But she reined it in, held it tightly to its leash keeping the monster at bay—he was too

weak to feed her today—and continued to lap delicately at
the burgundy nectar coating his wounds, licking it clean
with her tongue. Drawing shudders from his body and delicious sounds from his throat.

"Am I hurting you?" she asked in a throaty purr.

"No . . . yes. I don't know. Somehow it feels good."

She lifted herself over him. Lay in front of him so that
she could see his face, watch his eyes. They were hazel in
color, a warm mix of rich blue and vivid green.

"There is a healing element in my saliva," she said, running the tips of her nails down the side of his face in a dangerous caress. "It eases the pain, stops the bleeding if I so
wish."

"And if you wish otherwise, could you increase the
bleeding?"

"Good guess."

"Is that unique to all demon dead?" Stefan asked.

"Most have that ability."

He smiled, a crooked, little uneven smile lifting up
only one corner of his mouth, an endearing imperfection. It
warmed her, stayed with her as she scooted lower until her
face was level with the two entry wounds in his belly, still
visible when they should have been almost completely closed
by now. Daintily, she put her mouth over one tiny hole,
licked her tongue over it, felt him draw in a deep breath. Lips
sealing over it, she sucked tightly on it for a moment—not
quite gentle, not quite rough, dancing that delicate line in
between. He trembled as she moved on to the second little hole and laved that, too, in a delicious swirl of tongue.

He gave a shaky exhalation. "Oh, Goddess."

This close to his lap, Lucinda could not fail but notice
his risen bulge. An almost shocking surprise because she
had used none of her powers upon him, nothing but her
simple touch. He was swollen and full, rising in silent homage, begging for her touch. She looked up into those sea-
swirling eyes, saw the heat there making his eyes gleam
like precious gemstones. Touched upon his flushed cheeks,
his flaring nostrils. Drew irresistibly back down to that

lovely, long male ridge. Unable to resist, she pressed her cheek against him, rubbing and purring like a cat against his hardness, his moans and shuddering groans trickling like an unexpectedly sweet song into her ears.

She drew back with surprise. "You want me."

"Yes."

"You are wounded, injured."

His eyes seared her with heat. "I feel much better."

She laughed, rubbed her face once more against his swollen thickness. "I guess you do."

"It has been so long since I have been with a woman . . . May I touch you?" he asked, and caught the briefest glimpse of something in her eyes—surprise? Surely not—before she shuttered them.

"If you wish."

"I do. Most fervently." His hands lifted and alighted softly on her hair, fingers sifting through her long tresses. "So silky and fine," he discovered. "Like spun gold." He twined the long locks about his fists, squeezed them tight for one crushing moment, then let the silky strands slide free. His hands slid down to brush the bare skin of her neck. The feel of his callused fingers gliding over her there sent a delicious shiver tripping down Lucinda's spine.

"Does it please you?" he asked. "The touch of my hands upon your skin?"

"Yes." Again that flash of emotion in her eyes.

"Why does it surprise you? Has no other touched you like this?"

She smiled, that slow stretching of lips—wicked, wanton, wry. "I am usually the one touching them while they are stiff with fright." Or later, greedily grasping her desperately in the throes of their enthrallment and pleasure as her magick played upon them, as she seduced them for a drink of their blood. Never this gentle, simple, voluntary stroking. He touched her as if she were lovely and delicate. Something fragile. Something to be cherished. Everything she was not.

She drew back in confusion.

"No, please, don't pull away. Let me touch you. Let me please you."

"Why?" Her dark eyes searched his face.

"Because I want to. Because you helped us when you did not need to. Because it would give me pleasure to give you pleasure. To touch a woman once more."

Touch. *How long has it been for you?* she wondered. For her as well. The voluntary touch of someone wanting to bring her pleasure?

She sighed in soft acceptance, unable to refuse the gift he offered her. Not just of touch, but of his trust that she would not hurt him. That was far sweeter, more precious. She slid up with slow, sultry ease. Settled herself soft and full against him. "Yes, touch me."

It was like a feast suddenly presented to a starving man. Stefan's heart leaped, his hands shook. With his touch gentle, if unsure, he lightly stroked his fingers over her shoulders. When she did not protest, just blinked those dark cinnamon lashes at him, his hands moved in a firmer caress down the sleek slope of her back, making her arch a little so that her full breasts caressed his chest, releasing a sigh from him.

Ah, the treasure here. Greed for more sprung up hotly. But Stefan kept it leashed, his hands gentle, the course patient, sliding over the flare of her hips, such curves. Dipping and gliding in front then to back over her rich femininity, cupping the generous mounds of her bottom—lush, abundant. Soft, succulent, and firm. He squeezed them, filled his hands with her ampleness then dipped into the valley between, sliding from the top of the crevice down, down below, almost to where she lay hottest. Stopping just there, hovering. Feeling the heat, the building warmth down below, savoring the ripening fruit of his labor.

His hand retreated, making her wiggle in small outrage, in tiny disappointment, her eyes flashing with that echoing heat building slowly within. Stefan smiled and wandered his fingers back up, caressing the dipping indenture of her waist, so small. "Let me feel your skin."

With her dark chocolate eyes languid, opaque, and unreadable, she nodded. He grasped the silk of her blouse and pulled it from her waistband, making vulnerable the soft flesh beneath that he so craved to feel and explore.

Finally . . . bliss. The silk of her skin beneath his rough hands. He had to see what his hands enjoyed. Had to lift his head so that he could feast with his eyes as well as his touch. Slowly he pushed her shirt up, a silken tease, exposing increment by increment the naked, golden skin. His hands trembled at the sight gradually revealed, the soft feminine flesh, the wonder of touching it, caressing it. The contrast of his white hands against her honeyed darkness. The tenseness of her belly as he glided his hands over her, finding her responsiveness more precious than the moon's renewing rays.

"How soft you are," he murmured in pleased wonder. "Soft and fine. Firm yet fluid. Lovely, so lovely."

The shy dip of her belly button drew him and he followed its silent calling, tracing one finger down around its rim, then dipping in deep to search out its hidden secrets. She gasped, the golden goddess, as he pierced her in this small way. Her hand flew up to cover his like a sun-kissed benediction, tawny skin over white, the long sharp curves of her nails gleaming like elegant ivory. Another difference to explore.

Leaving one hand captured beneath hers, he lifted free the unfettered one—how nice to have two—and stroked along those slender fingers, so tiny, so much smaller than his. Slim and elegant, yet capable and strong.

He lifted her hand, drew it to his mouth, kissed the silken skin on the back, inhaled her soft subtle fragrance. His to do with what he willed, that lovely hand. To turn it and press his lips into her palm. Firmer skin here but just as fine. Smooth, unblemished by calluses, soft and yet hard. A lady's hand. A warrior's hand, too. He tasted it with his tongue. Stroked along the lines of her palm. Pressed his tongue, surging its thickness between her fingers, felt her gasp and tremble as he pushed deep. His lips slid up her elegant finger and traced the smoothness of her nail with his sensitive tongue. Freezing her into stillness as he delicately explored its pointy tip.

Despite Stefan's care, its razor sharpness pierced his tongue, and the sweet metallic tang of blood filled the air, fresh against the scent of old blood. Her eyes drew irresistibly to his mouth.

"Kiss me," he said. "Taste me."

He watched as another hunger filled those dark, lovely eyes. Watched as her mouth moved toward his. Then he could only feel: the sweet press of her soft lips against his; the wet stroke of her tongue against his seam, asking for entry. He parted his lips and opened to her. She entered, seeking, finding his bleeding tongue. Guiding it into the warm, wet cavern of her mouth. Sucking upon it gently at first, humming her pleasure with that initial taste. Then drawing upon it more ravenously. Fiercer, harder, with almost painful suction.

A sound came from him—pain or pleasure, even he could not tell—and she relaxed with a shudder against him. Stefan's arms came around her, so small and tiny in his arms, the softness and fullness of her body pressed lusciously against the hardness of his. He stroked his tongue against her own, delicately explored the sharpness of her fangs. Traced along the soft, pillowy fullness of her lips, enjoying the tangy tart flavor of her.

It was the most exquisite tease, that tongue, giving Lucinda a tiny potent taste of him. Drawing her hunger suddenly, sharply, to the fore. Submerging, for a moment, that other hunger he had unexpectedly drawn out—skin hunger. The need to feel another's body against your own, the press and rub of naked flesh to naked flesh.

"Drink from me," he urged against her lips, pressing kiss after kiss upon her mouth. Learning the shape of her bottom lip, the upper peaks, the hidden corners. "I offer it freely. Drink from me."

All the most dangerous parts of her he deliberately sought out, not shying away from them. Making love to her there. It made Lucinda tremble against him—his voice, his words, his hands upon her waist, splayed across her belly, touching her skin intimately as he kissed her lips, traced her fangs with his tongue. The memory, both visual and tactile, of him drawing her finger and its sharp lethal nail into his mouth . . . all flooded her mind with rich stimuli.

"No," she said against his lips. "A taste of you is enough."

A soft kiss pressed to her lips. "Why?"

"You are wounded." Then because he was so tempting she said, "Perhaps later, when you are well."

His lips inched outward to explore the sweet curve of her cheeks, to nibble the soft lobe of her ear. "Will there be a later?"

The feel of his breath blowing softly across the shell of her ear made her shiver. "I don't know."

His wet tongue delved into her ear's tantalizing canal with a delicate probing stroke, making her squirm against him. "You are hungry," he said. "Let me feed you."

A part of her marveled at how he could make her tremble like this, offering freely what she usually took. "No. You test my control, and that is not a good thing to do. You taste so good, so incredibly good. If I start, I won't stop until I've taken more blood than you can afford right now."

"Do I?" He sounded pleased, silly man.

"What?"

"Taste that good?"

She smiled. "Yes, Stefan. Deliciously potent with power, rich and sweet."

"Lucinda." He said her name like a caress. "Tomorrow. Take from me what you need tomorrow. I will be more healed by then."

She sent him a slanted look, eyes smoldering, cynical and puzzled. "Why?"

His long lashes lowered, fanning across his cheeks. "Because it would please me to give you what you need. To serve you in this small way."

"Why? Why would that please you?"

His eyes lifted back to hers, lost and sad. "Is that not what is bred into every Monère warrior? The desire to serve his queen?"

The words thrust sharply into her like a knife. She rolled away from him. "I am no longer a Monère Queen but demon dead. I cannot be your queen."

"No, please. Don't move away." His arms came around her, held her from behind. "I'm sorry."

She could have easily broken free, but she didn't, staying there for a moment in the bittersweet comfort of his embrace, in a fragile, brittle silence.

"Forgive me, I spoke without thought." His lips pressed against her hair, and he rubbed a penitent circle on the back of her hand. "If you will not let me ease your hunger tonight, allow me to please you another way," he said in a husky murmur.

Ah, what words that came out of his mouth. What desires he stirred. But the things one yearns for are not always possible. "Perhaps we are not compatible, without chemistry, like a human is to a Monère."

"I do not think that is the case. I know that my touch gave you pleasure." His voice sounded sure, arrogantly male.

She rolled to face him, aggrieved and amused by him at the same time. Moved by him. "But will my touch give you pleasure in turn? Just my simple touch, unadorned by my magick or any enthrallment."

He gave that endearing lopsided grin again. "I am most eager to find out. It is a question worthy of pursuit, in the name of science, of course."

Lucinda smiled slowly, wickedly, a smile touched with both mischief and sultry promise, hinting of both torment and bliss, stealing his breath, hardening his body with anticipation.

"Ah, yes. Our duty then, such hardship." She stroked him boldly with her hand, grasping him, measuring his length. Feeling him leap and pulse eagerly in her tight, squeezing grip. "Such terrible, terrible hardship."

"Mother Night," Stefan gasped, and found himself suddenly on his back with her crouched over him.

"Don't move." Delicately she hooked the zipper with one sharp nail and pulled it down.

Looking at those nails poised so intimately close to his groin made Stefan shudder, made his eyes dilate with both pleasure and fear. But it was eagerness that rode his movements as he rid himself of his pants, baring himself to her.

He was lovely. So pale that he was almost luminous in his fairness. An exquisite blend of power and grace, of beauty and masculinity. Creamy white skin framed by the raven darkness of his hair spilling out about him. Eyes gone dark, burning with heat and excitement, framed by long sooty lashes. The splashing redness of his lips, full and swollen from their kisses. Blue veins tracing over the marble white perfection of his skin like the most delicate of etchings.

Lucinda lowered down to his neck. Breathed in the pounding life that ebbed and flowed just beneath that thin layer of skin, concentrated most tantalizingly over the pulse point that throbbed with each heavy beat of his heart.

The scent of blood rode thick in the air and the lingering taste of him was full in her mouth. The press of his invisible power was sweet against her skin as she took in his scent so rich and full of life. It almost made her drunk, the potent punch of him, as she followed those marbled veins down the swell of his chest, the ridged flatness of his belly. Coming finally to his potent manhood standing flushed and darkly swollen with blood.

She rubbed her nose along the velvet length of him. Caressed him against her cheek, bare skin to bare skin. How lovely he felt. Soft but full, hard but tender. So potent, so rich. So vibrantly tempting she had to run her lips over him, make him cry out and lift up and press himself against her. His scent, his pulse, his vitality so incredibly, incredibly tempting that she shook with hunger and restraint with him so close to her mouth.

A taste. Just a small taste.

Almost against her will, her tongue swept out, licked over that round head. And Stefan's skin began to glow softly with that beginning kiss of light, like the moon rising up in the night. As if their lunar home was captured within him, and a part of it was. He was a true child of the moon—Monère. Descendants of another race, another world. They were a people who glowed only in pleasure; they did not shine with humans. But this one shone for her.

"Please," Stefan said, voice strained.

Lucinda knew what he wanted—for her to take him into her mouth. What she most desired, too. She trembled with the control she had to exert not to do so. "My fangs . . ." she said thickly.

Stefan became aware then. Aware once more of her blood thirst. And of the blood filling him down there, swelling him up in that place where a man was most strong and vulnerable. The realization dilated his eyes even more until they became like a sea of blackness, swallowing up the blue green rim. "Can you taste me as you did with my tongue? A small prick?"

Lucinda shuddered violently at what he was offering. "You would trust me? You would allow this?"

"Yes. Please."

Dear Goddess, Lucinda prayed. *Help me control my-self. Let me please him. Not hurt him.*

THREE

KNEELING AT HIS side, I grasped him carefully, my hand closing around his thickness, my nails carefully held away from his tender flesh. Aware, so aware of the pulse that beat there against my palm, a living throbbing thing, calling to me.

"You must not move," I said as my other hand clasped his hip, securing him.

He nodded, face grim, breath coming fast, the lunar glow of his skin intensifying as he watched me lower down to him. Watched me open my lips, lap him in one wet swirling caress. Then with my pink tongue wrapped around him, guide him carefully into my mouth. His belly tightened beneath my hand, and a tremor passed through his body as my fangs brushed against his succulent flesh, scraped over its firmness. I heard his breath catch but he did not move. He lay there, still and trusting, my nails upon his skin, my fangs against the most tender part of him. And even that part of him glowed with a rosy white-ness, light shining from within.

Oh, how sweet he was. Long and thick and hard, thrumming in my mouth. I explored him with my tongue, rimmed the head of him. Swept under the bumpy ridge, delved into the little hollow behind that helmeted head. Traced those veiny ropes of life that pumped his shaft with life, and watched him watch me as I savored him, that shiny long length of him. I could only take half of him in before the press of my fangs against his flesh became too dangerous. I slid him out, suckled along the side of him, nibbling, scraping, running my lips, teeth, and tongue along him in long sure strokes, testing his thickness, measuring his length. Enjoying the feel and play of him in my mouth until that ultimate taste of him became a calling too strong to resist.

I moved back to his tip, and there at his taut shiny head, I nicked him. Watched as a drop of crimson welled up like a cherry red beauty mark, a colored twin to the clear drop of fluid oozing like a tear from his little slit. I put him back in my mouth carefully, just the head of him, and lapped at the twin juices—liquid life, liquid desire. The two flavors twined within me, filling my senses. And the taste, the scent of him sliding down my throat triggered a burning hunger for more. I closed my mouth in a tight seal over the head of him and sucked hard. Long deep pulls, milking blood and desire's seed both from him as frantic little sounds escaped his throat. His head thrashed, his hands fisted in my hair, and his body shone brilliantly bright as if he had swallowed down the moon. He was a beautiful, glowing thing stretched out for my pleasure upon the bed and in my mouth, his body held still as I sucked upon him, as I felt the twin nectars flowing down my throat.

A tiny taste of him.

So little blood for such abundant pleasure.

I squeezed and pumped him hard with my hand. Felt him swell more, becoming even thicker, even longer. His blood ran down my throat in a steady trickle as I milked him with my hand and milked him with my mouth. As I sucked upon him with my lips. Lapped and laved him with my tongue.

"Ah, Lady." He shimmered like a beautiful unearthly thing, casting shadows upon the wall, so brightly did he glow. He cried out, jerked against my hand, and only my pinning hold upon his hip held him down. His length leaped like a living creature in my fist, and he spurted like a geyser, bursting forth a rich bounty of fluid and blood, filling my mouth.

I swallowed him down. Savored his last ebbing pulses. Sucked upon him sweetly now, gently. Finally released him with a last healing lick that made him shudder in satisfaction. He lay limply on his back, gasping, his eyes heavy lidded and slumberous as the light faded slowly back into him, a pink flush tingeing the whiteness of his skin, making him look like a pale rose stroked by dawn's first crimson rays.

"Lady," Stefan sighed and smiled. Slowly, languidly, he rolled to his side invitingly. "Let me hold you."

The barest, briefest hesitation at the odd request, the first time it was ever made, and I lowered myself down beside him. I felt his arms close about me, draw me full against him. Felt him sigh in peace and contentment, my head resting on his shoulder, his chin spooned over the top of my head. And I found a pleasure in that firm, gentle hold. In bringing him such ease.

His hand stroked my back for a quiet moment, rubbing over the silk of my shirt. "You have too much clothes on," he murmured. "Take it off. Let me see you unclothed. Let me feel your bare skin against mine."

I smiled against the smoothness of his silky skin. Brushed my hand over the soft fur arrowing down his midline. "You wish for more?"

"Oh, yes." He rubbed his chin over the top of my head. "You have had your wicked way with me. Now it is my turn. Allow me." His fingers slid around my waist to rest on the lowest button of my shirt. When I made no protest, he slipped the button free. When I still made no murmur, he moved up swiftly and surely until the last button was undone.

"Take it off," he said softly and watched, face tense, eyes unsmiling, as I slid free of the shirt. His nostrils flared.

"You are so lovely," he said. "So lovely. Your pants . . . take them off."

He watched me with an almost unnerving intensity as I yielded to his words, to his desire, and slid my pants free. I lay naked and bare before him, feeling strangely shy. It felt odd to have a man, unbeguiled, desire me so without fear. Seducing the seducer with nothing but his words, the look in his eyes, his needs, his wants. With me lying before him with no intent of drinking of his blood, no intent to beguile. Just us coming together for the sake of coming together. So terribly unusual.

Mix in a little blood and I was your girl. But having sex with my prey . . . that was rather unusual for me. For him, too, come to think of it. Monère males could gain power mating with a queen. He would get nothing but pleasure, however, in joining his body with mine. Oddly enough, he seemed more than happy with the deal.

His eyes burned bright and hot upon me, but it was from simple desire and simple pleasure, not that inner lunar glow yet. He ran his eyes upon me, over me, and it felt as if he were drinking me in. As if *he* were the one sipping from me with those hot, burning eyes, almost feverishly intense. Devouring me without a touch.

He lifted his hands, lay them upon my collarbones like butterflies settling upon their chosen flower, readying to sip the nectar. The first gentle stroke upon my skin and I shivered beneath his hands. He smiled down at me, so male that look. Slid those rough, callused hands down my arms in a gentle abrading caress that prickled my skin and tightened my nipples. He found my hands and slid his fingers between mine, sliding back and forth, back and forth, letting my slender fingers sheathe his thicker ones. A moment to savor the sensation, the foreshadowing of what was yet to come, then he moved down to cup my hips, to splay a hand over the smoothness of my belly.

I lowered my gaze. Saw the contrast of our skins together,

dark and light. Like moonlight falling upon earth's rich
soil. His hand so large, spanning my entire waist with fingers long, strong, and elegant. Resting there for a moment,
making me tense. Making me wonder if he would choose
to go up or down . . . both places yearned to feel his touch.
My nipples peaked, rising up, while down below moistness
gathered, softening me, preparing me for his coming, filling
the air with my wet fragrance, my desire as keenly evident
to his senses as his body's reaction was to my eyes. Eyes
that fell upon him and watched him as he lengthened and
swelled, grew full once more, filling again with that wondrous blood and desire.

His hands moved up to glide over the delicate ridges of
my ribs, coming to rest beneath my full mounds, stroking
there softly. Cupping me with his hands, squeezing lightly,
testing my weight before gliding up to brush over the peaks.

His light, searching strokes and the rough pads of his
fingers scraping over my sensitive tips closed my eyes,
arched my back. Pressed me more fully into his wonderful
hands. His fingers closed around my jutting points and
pinched me lightly.

"Oh!" My eyes opened to see his face lower to my rosy
tips, pebbled tight like jagged mountain peaks. Almost too
late, I found my voice, my reason. "You must not bite me.
All else you may do, but do not take my blood or you shall
die. Do you understand?"

Stefan nodded. "Yes," he said, his voice a husky rasp. He
opened his lips and took my nipple into his mouth. I don't
know which burned me more, his eyes or the feel of me in
that wet cavern. Moisture and surprising warmth. Silky lips,
luscious red, the color of blood, engulfing me. The rough
hard rasp of his tongue across my tender nipple. His hair
falling forward in a black silky wash, stroking over my skin
like a thousand tiny caresses.

A hot jolt of pleasure arrowed down from my nipple,
shooting straight to my groin, clenching another part of me
deep inside, making me suddenly feel so empty. Aching.

My thighs pressed together, my hips moving restlessly

as his hand squeezed my other nipple. He feasted upon me, sucking hard, pressing my ripe tip up against the roof of his mouth with his tongue. Tugging with his mouth, making me cry out, arc up against him.

My hands reached up blindly to hold him. Almost touched him before I remembered my nails. He'd made me forget. Another tug, another pinch almost painfully hard. Another hot wash of pleasure flooding me, making me writhe. I plunged my hands deep into the comforter, piercing down to the mattress beneath, anchored myself safely there. Then I yielded myself fully to the pleasure. Let myself go mindless, becoming nothing more but a creature of sensation, wave upon wave of sensation. Giving up total control.

He milked and squeezed my breasts, feasted upon my nipples, then moved down greedily to where my hot fragrance filled the air. He spread my thighs with his strong hands and held me open to him as he licked me.

I gasped. I moaned. I writhed beneath him, opened my legs wider to him. He rewarded me by spearing his tongue in deep, a sharp hard probe, filling me for one blissful moment. Then pulling out, making me cry out at the loss.

"So warm here." He swirled his tongue up and over my hidden pearl, drawing another cry from me. "So sweet," he marveled, and sank a long slender finger into me, making me groan with aching pleasure.

"Oh, Stefan!"

"So wet, so soft, so warm. Are you ready for me?" he husked, his breath fanning across my curls.

"Yes . . . Oh Goddess, yes."

He rose above me, his skin shimmering with a soft luminescent light, his inner glow starting to come forth. A shiny perfection marred only by the two dark holes where the bullets had pierced him.

"Your wounds."

He lifted up my hips, pulled me to him. Poised himself there for one suspended moment with his tip nudging my portal. Then he began to enter me.

"I'm fine," he said, his voice taut and groaning as he found me snuggly tight. Teeth gritted, he pushed gently but insistently forward, moving into me with small incremental surges. His head pushed through.

"I'm good," he grated, sliding in another inch, shuddering at the feel of me swallowing him up while I shuddered at the sight and feel of him, his glowing light, his hardness entering me.

"I'm bloody wonderful . . . *Ah, Goddess!*" He shoved in all the way until he was fully hilted, and held himself there trembling, gasping, muscles straining in imposed stillness.

"You hold me so sweetly," he panted, lowering down over me, sinking onto my chest, caressing me with his body while bracing the bulk of his weight on his elbows "Are you well? Am I hurting you?"

My nails flexed, pierced deeper into the mattress. "Only by not moving. Move!"

He smiled, burning brightly, a radiant creature surrounding me with that cool shimmering light, making my skin glitter like gold dust beneath his shine. I looked down and saw my womb glowing with his light where he filled me, where he lay buried deep inside me. And I watched with awe and wonder that dance of iridescent light play upon my dusky skin, lighting me from within and without as he began to move. Then I could only feel him, sliding within me. Filling me, stretching me. Rubbing, gliding, sliding. A sweet rhythmic surging like the relentless tide washing upon the shore. A natural force of nature, a building tempo. A tightening crescendo within me as pleasure wound me higher and higher until I could no longer contain it. It spilled out of me in a powerful convulsive release that bowed my spine, lifting us both up, throwing back my head, tearing a harsh raw cry from me as I spasmed around him, my inner muscles clenching him tight as he continued to drive within me.

I knew he'd been holding back only when he stopped doing so. When he suddenly started thrusting with full stabbing force and building momentum, going deep, so deep inside of me. A long relentless plunging of his hips, a strong steady pounding into me.

"Come for me again," he urged, his eyes locked with mine, glowing almost blindingly bright as I continued to shake and quiver beneath him.

"No." I shook my head, still helplessly caught up in the last ebbing washes of my release. "I can't."

"You can." He drove deep into me, rocking me with his force. "Again. Come for me again." Face hard and intense, determined, he adjusted his hips and thrust, eyes fixed upon me, catching every little nuance that crossed my face. He made another incremental adjustment, plunged into me at a slightly different angle, and my eyes widened in surprise at the new wash of sensations.

"Oh, Goddess," I breathed as he hit a spot that threw back my head and opened my mouth wide on a soundless cry. That caused my inner muscles, already tight and clingy, to squeeze even tighter about his surging hardness that drove into me in a steady unhurried rhythm now that he had found his spot. Patiently, ruthlessly, he lifted me higher, wound me tighter, taking me somewhere I did not want to go again. Taking me up there whether I willed it or not with that steady thrusting and coiled driving of his body in and out of mine.

"Please," he gritted, pressing heated kisses against my opened lips. "Let yourself go. Give yourself to me."

Was it the sweet yearning in his voice, the need burning in his eyes, or the hot filling friction of him moving within me? Perhaps all of it combined. Whatever the reason, I found myself suddenly flung up high again, shattering once more. So completely this time that I was blinded by the light, by the overwhelming onslaught of bursting rapture. So that I became only a creature of the senses, ripped apart and put together again by an explosion of pleasure so intense that it bordered on pain.

I felt him drive one last deep time into me. Felt him finally give himself over to his own release, shuddering and spurting within me, a convulsive burst of wetness. Saw the brilliant light ebb, slowly recede. And smelled the fresh scent of newly drawn blood.

I couldn't move. Could barely speak. "Blood . . . what did you do?"

His hands stroked over me with lazy languor as he lay sprawled atop me, soothing caresses down my side and over my hips. "I couldn't bite you," he said, breath coming fast and ragged. "So I bit myself."

A love bite left upon one's partner. A sign of a most wondrous lover. He'd felt the urge to mark me, but had marked himself instead because I had told him he could not taste my blood. It was the highest of compliments among the Monère to be so marked. And so dangerous. So terribly dangerous. But he had heeded my words. Kept us both safe. While I'd totally forgotten, caught up in the throes of my own pleasure.

Sweet Mother, what he had made me feel . . . Was this what it was like for those I fed upon? Had they felt like this afterward? Shaken, unsure of their own bodies?

When I stiffened beneath him, Stefan lifted himself off, moving carefully, gingerly. His wounds. I started to roll off the bed but was stopped by his hand upon my arm. "Lucinda, wait. What's wrong?"

I shook my head, my face turned away. I didn't even know, myself, how could I answer him? All I felt was a terrible need to get away. But I didn't break free as I could have so easily done because I didn't want to jar him with unnecessary force. I was trapped by my own desire of not wanting to hurt him. A constraint I had never felt before. Shit.

"Lucinda, what did I do?" His arm slid tentatively around me, drew me back against him, holding me, cradling me. "Please tell me what I did wrong?"

What could I say? *You made me feel too much. You sought my pleasure first, not your own. You asked me to belong to you . . .*

His words had pierced my heart like an arrow striking its target true.

"Did I hurt you?"

Yes. Yes, you did. But not the way you mean. "No," I said, choosing to answer his meaning, not his words.

His hand stroked up and down my arm with a tenderness that pained me even more. "I'm sorry." His voice was soft and unsure. "It has been so long for me. Forgive me for my clumsiness."

I laughed raggedly. "You were far from clumsy. And you pleased me greatly."

"Then why do you wish to leave me?"

"Why did you want to please me so?"

Stefan took a deep breath, released it. "I had hoped that you would want to stay with me."

His answer shocked me, so unexpected it was. "You wish me to be your lover?"

He turned me gently in his arms and looked into my eyes. "I want you to be my lady. I want to please you. I want to serve you. I want to belong to you, and have you belong to me."

I shook my head. "I cannot be what I once was. I cannot be your Monère Queen."

"Not my queen, no. But you can be my lady. I have been alone for so long, and better than most rogues, with Jonnie to care for. But I was dying slowly inside in exile, dying in spirit if not in flesh. All Monère males have that great need and desire to serve a powerful female, to be in her presence. Being with you fills that terrible hollow emptiness in me, an emptiness almost worse than death. You make me feel more alive than I have felt in over two decades."

"I am demon dead." My voice was flat and dry. And if there was an echo of pain, only I heard it. "How can something dead make you feel more alive?"

"I don't know. But you do. Let me feed you, let me please you. Let me be with you. Let me be what I was born to be."

His plea quivered in the air.

"So you would donate your blood and your body for my pleasure. But what would you gain in return? I cannot Bask. I cannot draw down the renewing rays of the moon to prolong your life as a queen can. You cannot even gain power by mating with me. There is nothing, nothing to your benefit."

"I would gain your company, a purpose and fulfillment to my life." He smiled, his teeth white. "And the sex is spectacular. You cannot argue that."

Unwillingly, my own lips curved up. "Yes, the sex was wondrous. Would that be enough for you?"

"Oh, yes. I don't know how to explain it, but being with you not only soothes me, it gives me great joy. Something I have not felt for decades far longer than my exile."

"That is such a human outlook, Stefan. Not Monère."

He shrugged. "I have lived for over twenty years among the humans. There is some wisdom to be learned from them."

Oh, the yearning in his eyes. It could not be greater than my own. I wanted. Oh, how I wanted what he offered. But . . . "You have not fed me. I have not truly taken your blood yet. You may not like it."

"Drink from me now. Let us see," he said eagerly.

"No. I explained why before. Do not press me on this. You do not really know what I am."

"You are demon dead."

"But you do not fear me when you should. You do not truly know what I am." I drew away from him and started to dress.

"I know you are kind," Stefan said. "That you are strong. Stronger than I."

"I am not kind. Nor will I always restrain my strength or power." With a thought, a bare flexing of will, I let power flow from me and gave him a taste of what I had withheld. He froze, unable to move, his limbs bound by the force of my invisible bonds. His muscles strained and trembled. But they were chains he could not break, restraints he could not even see.

"And that is but a small taste," I said, tucking my shirt into my pants. I allowed the power to trickle into my voice, to coat it with a thin layer of darkness and touch him with it. "There are reasons why we are feared."

He shivered as my voice stroked him, feathered over his skin.

"You are what we prey upon. That is our nature."

"Then I would be your willing prey," Stefan answered calmly, no longer fighting the bonds.

"Why?" I snapped and released him with a thought. He staggered, suddenly free. "That is not natural."

"What is natural?" Stefan asked, hands spread. "Not my exile, not our meeting here in this sea of humans. Not having you restrain your hunger because I am hurt. But because it is not natural, not usual, can you not see that it is even more precious, what we have found between us?"

Now it was I who trembled in his calm. He stood there naked while I was clothed, strong and sure in his belief. In what he wanted—me.

"I have to go." I turned to leave.

"Will you return?"

A breath of silence. "I don't know."

"Think on what I have said."

"I doubt I shall be able to think upon anything other."

"I will wait for you here until Jonnie is better. A week, no longer. Then we will have to leave this place."

Without turning, I said, "I cannot be long away from my realm. I would have to return there often."

"I would not mind as long as you returned to me."

I left without making any promise, without glancing back. Afraid that if I did, I would not leave him at all.

FOUR

THE OTHER REALM, Hell, was a landscape of muted colors. Sweltering in heat that was dry and scorching. Only plants that bloomed in darkness grew here under the three moons that marked our days and nights. Three moons that nourished us, renewed us. No sun. But no full moon here, either.

The most shocking and wondrous thing about roaming Earth was seeing once again the full moon in her round and brilliant glory. Walking the bright light of day. Sunlight did not burn the demon dead as it did the Monère. The children of the moon were not like *vampyres* of human legend, burning and bursting into ashes at the first touch of sunlight. But legends of old are usually based upon a kernel of truth. Monère skin burned after several hours under the sun's direct rays.

Becoming demon dead had some compensations—we didn't burn. But we paid for wandering under the sun's brightness. It weakened us greatly to spend hours in its unfiltered light. It softened our flesh, made it tender, over-ripe, as if ready to spill at the slightest touch if we dared its rays too long. It drained us of energy to the dangerous point where we might not be able to cross the portal back into Hell.

That was what happened to Halcyon, my brother, the de facto ruler of Hell. Blaec, the High Lord of Hell, had ceded the reins to Halcyon long ago. Or rather, Blaec had fallen prey to the condition that oft afflicted those who existed too long—world weariness. Mixed in with betrayal, bitterness, and sorrow, it had led to apathy and withdrawal.

One woman, my mother . . . or perhaps two, if you counted myself . . . had driven the High Lord into that state. It had taken another woman to bring him back out of it. Mona Lisa. Not the human painting, although she was human, in part. Mona Lisa was a new Mixed-Blood Monère Queen, the first ever. She had come down to Hell— another first, that something living could survive in our realm—accompanying my love-struck brother who had risked himself in the first place because of his foolish fascination with her.

Halcyon had been greatly weakened by the sun before and after he had been captured by a cunning, evil Monère Queen—someone who had known far more than she should have about the demon dead. Mona Lisa had rescued him and brought him back to Hell to recover. And in doing so she had helped father as well as son. An encounter with her, a quick trip back to the human realm for satisfying blood-rendering vengeance, and the High Lord was said to be all perked up now. Men, as with women, I guess, had to be needed. To have a purpose.

I thought yet again of the purpose that had just been offered me. *I want to belong to you. Have you belong to me.* Living words that had haunted this dead demon for the past four days since I returned. Ironic, wasn't it? Our family seemed to have a penchant for those lily-white Monères living in that other realm. Unnatural . . . and yet I could no longer berate my brother for his foolish infatuation. I understood it now, I sadly realized as I raised my hand to knock on the front door of Hallowed Hall, my brother's private residence. The perimeter wards would have warned of my approach. No surprise, then, when the tall door swung open before my hand even touched the carved wood. A dour-faced little demon stood before me, not much taller than I, her dark hair streaked with pure silver, keys jangling from her belt. The *gouvernante*, or housekeeper, of Halcyon's remote castle residence. She still grumped about missing the two most talked about occurrences in Hell—a Mixed Blood walking this realm, not just a living creature but Halcyon's sweetie, and the challenge Halcyon had accepted from another demon, and fought, because of her. The two thrilling events had happened during her annual ten-day leave from Hallowed Hall.

"Princess Lucinda."

"Jory." I nodded to the little demon. Asked politely, "Is Halcyon in residence?" He had better be after summoning me here.

"Aye. He be waiting for you in the downstairs study."

My brows lifted. It was the room he used to conduct formal business while in residence. So. This was about an official matter.

I stopped before a closed door at the end of the hallway. Knocking perfunctorily, I entered the simply furnished chamber. No need to try and impress: the power that filled the room was impressive enough. The ruler of the realm sat perusing some documents. He was plain like the room he inhabited, of average height and leanish build, with dark hair and eyes. He wore a simple shirt of white silk and black tailored pants, diamonds glinting discreetly from the cuffs, looking more elegant than handsome. A portrait of the High Lord, his father, hung above the mantel of the fireplace, the crackle of the flames from the burning hearth adding warmth and sound to the room.

The portrait of the father above. The son sitting below. They looked almost identical except for the silver that burnished the High Lord's temples, and the black shirt that he wore like his name, Blaec, which meant darkness. But whereas the High Lord's skin was a deep bronze, the hue our skin would eventually attain if we existed long enough, Halcyon was golden skinned like I.

The High Lord's stamp was strong upon my brother's face. His parentage would never be questioned, unlike mine.

"You summoned me on official business?" I queried.

"Lucinda," Halcyon said, greeting me. He set down his pen and leaned back in his seat. "Yes, official business. Regrettably so. There is a Monère rogue that the High Council requests your assistance with."

I stiffened. "The rogue's name?"

Halcyon's brows slanted upward. "The warrior's name is Nico. Do you know him?"

For one horrible moment I had feared they wanted Stefan. "No, I don't know him. Nor do I wish to hunt him, poor bastard. Send another guardian." If I returned to that other realm—to him—and with each passing day it seemed that I would, it would be for an entirely different reason. Stefan . . . he haunted my thoughts even now.

"Would that I could. You have just returned. In this particular case, however, only you will do. He has settled into your province, and none of the Monère warriors tracking him dare enter into it."

Wise of them. I would not have tolerated any trespass lightly. "Is he causing trouble? Did he harm his Queen?"

"No."

"Then if he is simply fleeing her and causing no problems, why don't they just let him be?"

"An oddly tolerant view of rogues you've suddenly developed, sister. Unfortunately, he's chosen a bad time to take flight."

"I didn't know there was a good time to do so," I returned dryly.

"A good time would have been anytime before Sandoor and his band of rogues upset the entire Monère society," Halcyon replied.

Sandoor had faked the death of his Queen and had held her captive for over ten years. An unheard of atrocity, breaking one of their greatest taboos. It had unsettled the whole Monèrian race, a delicately balanced matriarchal society built around their precious queens. Only queens could call down the life-renewing rays of the moon. And Mona Lisa had been the one to stumble upon this poor Queen and rescue her while liberating herself, sending ripples throughout their entire world. For a little Mixed Blood, she sure was shaking things up, above and below.

"A bad time is now, just after this unfortunate occurrence," Halcyon said, his hands folded together on top of the desk with his nails sharply displayed. "The rogue's Queen demands his return, and the Council, in this case, supports her petition. They wish the rogue punished to serve as a public warning, and to reinforce the queens' powers. No doubt so that mistreated warriors do not try to do a 'Sandoor' themselves."

Hunting a rogue would not have mattered to me before. But since meeting Stefan, I was more in sympathy with those who fled their queens. "Frankly, if they just treated their men better and found something other to do besides killing their most powerful warriors off, they would not have this problem."

"True," he said. "Sadly what this Sandoor fellow did not only argues in favor of the current system, but the dead bastard's set off a bloodbath that will likely not abate for years. Many powerful warriors will be slaughtered as a result of this. As a part of the Council, though, we have a duty to help reinforce their wishes and help them keep order."

"You are part of the Council, Halcyon, not I. You may have a duty, but I do not."

Halcyon just looked at me. I hated when he did that. So calm and reasonable.

The High Lord had been one of Hell's more civic-minded rulers, concerning himself not only with matters of this realm but of the one we had left behind. He had raised Halcyon in that tradition. Myself, I was generally more self-serving. My existence was easier that way. But in this matter, I yielded to my duty, unpleasant though the task had become. It seemed I had no other choice.

"Very well," I said. "I shall return this wayward rogue to his Queen."

And then . . . then I would go claim my own rogue.

FIVE

M Y PROVINCE WAS in the human state of Arizona, sandwiched between the gorging Grand Canyon and the university town of Flagstaff. My territory was comprised of a handful of townships, the largest numbering a few thousand residents, the smallest, a few hundred, if even that. Located in the remote Arizona strip to the far north, dotted with canyons, plateaus, and volcanoes, it was a wilderness area that many travelers had yet to discover. Which suited me just fine.

One traveler, though, was making himself quite at home at Smoky Jim's, the bar-restaurant I had tracked him to. Finding him, in this case, had been ridiculously easy. Just listen for the slow, slow heartbeat. He was sprawled cozily back in his chair propped against the far wall, surveying the room like a lazy lion overlooking his domain. He didn't look like a rogue . . . and, no, rogues don't have a particular coloration or build. But one thing they were not was relaxed . . . happy, even. Those two words, for that matter, weren't something that could be applied to Monère males in general, not once they had passed their puppy-fresh virgin state, that blissful time in life when first entering a queen's bed.

This one was far from a puppy or a virgin. He thrummed with power that could only come from years of Basking—a hundred years, at least—and years of mating with queens. If he had frequented less in his lady's bed, been wisely doled out, as it were, for greater longevity, perhaps he might have even reached over two centuries of life, which would put him in his prime.

He was neither the most handsome Monère male I'd ever seen nor the ugliest. More ruggedly attractive, with a square jaw and a bold, beaky nose, saved by plainness by stunning heather gray eyes fringed with long thick lashes, and hair as fair and bright as sunshine—that rarer, more coveted coloration among the more commonly dark-haired, dark-eyed Monère. But even the ugliest among us—there I go again . . . among the *Monère*, drew a human's eyes. And he was no exception. Three women—three!—sat gathered around him, gazing adoringly at him as if he were their bright and shining sun. Hah! Not likely. He sat there beneficently soaking in their attention and spreading his own around, rubbing a dark Mexican flower's shoulder, playing with a freckled redhead's long curls, laughing richly at something his third companion said, a handsome Native American Indian woman.

My brow winged up. How nice. An equal opportunity playboy. Then I frowned, pondering over his odd behavior. For it *was* odd for a Monère to act so comfortably in the company of humans, unafraid of drawing attention to himself. Odder still to lavish his attention on their women. Because Monère did not gain pleasure from sexually mating with humans. They were of a different chemistry, a different species. Their skin did not glow—yes, yes, I know what you're thinking, but demon dead and Monère *are* alike enough to share pleasure, that I knew for certain now. Not so with a human. Making love to one of them was, frankly, a tedious and unpleasant chore, usually forced upon a warrior if his queen desired business or monetary concessions from one of them, and usually requiring the aid of a potent aphrodisiac to stiffen that which needed stiffening. I smelled no such scent upon him. Why, then, was he troubling to be so charming to them?

He laughed again and my eyes narrowed, feeling a distinct and growing irritation within me. He did not look like a rogue desperately running for his life. Not in the least. The bastard was clearly enjoying himself here in my town.

I wondered if he had trespassed knowing who ruled this small province. Or had he stumbled into my sanctuary unknowingly, and then stayed when no warriors pursued him here? Had to be the latter; he could not have known who ruled here, for he was not scanning for the absence of a heartbeat or he would have noticed mine.

Still, as seemingly relaxed as he was, he was alert enough to note my entry. His eyes widened appreciatively as he caught sight of me, and his lips curved upward, blossoming into a wide, flirtatious smile that issued a clear invitation: *Come play with me.*

Nope, definitely didn't know who I was.

Another rogue who thought me human. It was becoming almost tedious. And this one was acting like the Goddess's gift to women. Who the Darkness did he think he was? Powerful though he was, he was no Warrior Lord, ruler of his own lands.

That inviting smile settled it. It was off with the gloves, literally. Not what I had originally planned, but it would serve the same purpose of getting him outside where I could take him. The other options were to wait for him to leave or lure him out. His human harem, and the smile he had still aimed my way, greedy bastard, decided me on a more quick, direct route.

Yes, I'd be happy to play with him.

I met those lovely gray eyes, held them. Let a sweet, savage smile shape my lips. Let heat burn in my own eyes. Heat that glowed in anticipation of the coming hunt.

I stroked the leathery tip of my glove across the lower fullness of my lip. Pushed it inside my mouth with tantalizing slowness. Circled my red mauve lips around it, and sucked it in deeper. Across the room I heard his lungs expand in a deep, involuntary breath. Heard his heartbeat pick up. And I issued a soft hum of pleasure, the barest sound, but one he heard. The black centers of his eyes grew, expanding like dark flowers unfurling their bloom at night. His hands stilled, as if he had forgotten the human flesh he was touching, stroking.

I opened my encircling lips and set my teeth delicately on the leather tip, and gently . . . and not so gently . . . tugged, pulled, and nipped as if something else was at the portal of my mouth. Slowly, I removed the leather glove, unveiling increment by increment the golden nude skin of my hand. A teasing disrobing as if I were uncovering more than just my glove. Off it finally came. It took him several seconds before he focused on what had been revealed.

I knew the exact moment when he finally took note of my long, sharp nails. When his heart stuttered a beat then sped up to match that of his human companions. When his face, which had slackened as he had watched the play of my lips and teeth, lost that easy congeniality and became as hard as granite. I knew then that he was focused fully upon me, and that he saw me not as a woman, but as a hunter.

His power flared out over me, seeking, searching, testing mine. Meeting only that faint, barely there presence that those who came from Hell emitted. Noticing, finally, that no life-pumping organ beat within my chest, that no air filled and emptied my lungs. Unless I deliberately chose to do so, as I did now . . . to smell and taste his fear, and roll it on the back of my tongue.

"Run," I whispered, soft enough that no one else heard me. No one but him.

Deliberately, he removed his hands from all that feminine pulchritude, and pushed back his chair, an unhurried controlled moment.

"Ladies," he said, his face calm, his eyes locked upon mine. "Forgive me but I must leave you now."

Truer words than they realized. All had noticed where

his attention rested. Correctly concluding that he was leaving because of me, but utterly wrong in their assumption of why. He watched me now because he was afraid of taking his eyes off me. Because I could strike that fast and take him out, though I would not. Not here in front of so many human witnesses. We both knew that. We both still played by the rules. Yet he did not leave me unwatched. Prudent of him. Not as dumb as he had first seemed.

"Don't go, Nicky," the Mexican flower pleaded, grabbing his hand as he stood up.

He turned his palm and brought her brown hand up to his lips, lightly kissing the back of it. A gesture that almost made the recipient swoon, I observed. I smiled with a soft curl of my lips, tinged with both amusement and disgust.

"I'm sorry but I must," he murmured, a pleasing Continental lilt to his words. "Thank you, ladies, for your delightful company."

Then he was walking boldly toward me, and past me, as human men parted way for him. He strode out the front door, with me right behind. The muttered comment of one of those men sounded softly in our ears. "Lucky bastard."

"For a time," Nico murmured. "For a brief, lovely time."

SIX

THE DEMON DEAD—shocking to think of it as a *her*—walked beside Nico until the din and noise of Smoky Jim's faded. He felt as if he were towering over her, and he was not an unusually tall man. On the shorter side, actually. But she was so small.

No matter the size, though, it was clear who was the hunter, and who was to be the hunted. By mutual consensus, they headed for the dark woods opposite the crowded, well-lit parking lot, fading like shadows into the leafy darkness, both of them natural predators of the night.

Nico's heart pounded but his resolve did not waver even though he cursed himself for a fool. A woman! Dear Goddess, she was a woman when he had been expecting a man. And a beautiful, stunning woman, at that, so lush and so tiny. Still, what did it really matter? She had to be powerful, more powerful than he, or she would not be here.

When they had treaded far enough into the forest, he stopped. "If your offer is still open, milady, I would like to take you up on it." His words fractured the tense silence, although the tension was more on his part. She seemed just . . . eager. Which was actually good for him. She wanted a true hunt or she would have taken him already.

Her dark chocolate eyes flashed at him in the rich, silvery moonlight. The near perfect roundness of their mother planet shone over them in benefic glory, bringing tears to Nico's eyes; making his heart yearn unexpectedly for an anguished moment. A full moon had recently passed, the traditional time for Basking. One he had missed yet again.

No more would its renewing rays dart like quicksilver into him, making his skin glow, making his senses tingle and feel so alive. So blessedly alive! No more would a queen call down its rays and share them with him, for he no longer belonged to any queen.

Nico wanted to lift his eyes one last time to the glorious round orb, their source of life and power, but dared not take his eyes from her. He would die, yes. But he did not want to die too soon or too easily. A matter of pride for him. Silly, perhaps. But precious when that was all he had left. No home, no queen, no brothers. Not even this precious human haven anymore.

"What offer? And do not call me 'milady' when I am not," the demon snapped. But even when the tone was hard and unhappy, her voice was as rich and softly sensuous as her body, her face, that striking hair that gleamed like metallic gold in the silvery darkness. When death came for you, Nico thought with an odd pang, it should not be this beautiful.

"To run. That is what you wish, is it not? A chase, a true hunt." With effort, he pulled a light, mocking smile onto his face, hiding how effectively she had already shattered him. He wanted this chance. Dear Goddess, how he wanted it. One last chance at life. At escape.

She turned, gazed upon him fully then. "Yes," she purred, and deliberately removed the remaining glove, dropped it to the ground, stretched out her fingers. Curled them into claws. Her teeth flashed ivory white, lethally sharp, as she smiled at him, fangs fully extended, her dark eyes growing almost black in her excitement, her anticipation. "Run."

He ran. For his very life, for his freedom. As if a demon chased behind him. And one did . . . one truly did. He sprang full out, leaping with that inhuman strength and graceful speed all children of the moon were born with. A fast blur springing into the forest, dodging trees, jumping over bushes, flowing around obstacles with instinctive ease, with swift silence. Behind him, she followed without sound: no rustling of leaves, no cracking of twigs, no heartbeat thundering in his ears, no breath, no life, no emotion when he felt bursting with it.

She tackled him in midair, slamming him down hard upon the shrub-covered ground, sending birds screeching into the air at the sudden graceless disturbance. Yes, she was strong. But still, greater strength notwithstanding, she was smaller, lighter than he. With a writhing twist, a hand and knee carefully placed, Nico sent her soaring over him, using her own coiled momentum to throw her off him. He sprang away and ran with every ounce of strength, every force of his will, a part of him sure he could not possibly escape her, another part still hoping. A terrible thing that can be—hope. You never knew how strong that flickering emotion was until it was fully extinguished.

Nico flowed, almost floated over the ground, cutting through the air, so free. A last taste of freedom, of life, and then he—it—all came crashing down again. She brought him harshly down to Earth with slamming reverberation. His arm was twisted back in a joint lock, her left hand grabbing his hair, arching his head back. "Playtime's over. Yield."

"No," Nico grated and fought with the madness, the desperation of no hope at all. He bucked and twisted, tried to roll her off, unable to, fighting with despair, with the bitter dredges of dashed hope.

Agonizing pain shot through him as she jerked his arm up to the point of breaking, stopping and teetering there on that painful edge. "You have lost. Yield."

"That," Nico said, panting with exertion and pain, "is why I cannot yield." And he continued to struggle against her hold.

A tiny force more and his arm broke. Searing heat flashed through him, followed by a brief numbing lull, as if his shocked body had yet to realize what had happened. Then the hot spilling agony of pain washed over him like a baptism of fire. He felt something hard and metallic encircle his wrist. More wrenching misery as his broken arm was straightened, as he was rolled over and the other end of the silver handcuffs snapped onto the opposite wrist and secured in front.

Looking down, Nico saw that what bound him were thin silver handcuffs, almost flat, easy to keep upon one's person, and more incapacitating to him than the thicker, stainless steel ones the humans used could ever hope to be. That touch of silver against his skin drained him of his Monère strength, made him only human strong. But that was still strong enough for what he had to do.

Gritting his teeth against his body's weakening distress, he got to his feet slowly. Pushing away the aching pain, he sprinted forward. No more than three paces, and a foot sent Nico crashing to the ground. A guttural cry escaped him at the blinding wash of pain that shot through him as he landed hard, face down.

"Don't fight me anymore, you fool," the demon snapped.

Nico rolled onto his back. Fighting nausea, he sat up. Biting back a whimper, he knelt and with trembling care, slowly climbed to his feet once more.

"Walk straight ahead," she instructed coolly.

He turned left and ran. Without a sound, she was before him, a golden roadblock. He veered right. Again she blocked his path. Before he could turn again, she reached out and with casual strength put a hand on his injured right forearm. A slight downward pressure and she dropped him to his knees, sheet white with blinding pain.

"You stink of agony and defeat, and yet you still run."

Her eyes were grim, hard as ice. "Are you too addled by fear to understand what I wish of you?"

"You stink of bloodlust," Nico shot back. "You are the one afraid of me. My blood calls you, the pounding in my chest, the rush of it in my veins. You smell me, hear me—fear, pain, desperation, struggling prey. A heady perfume for you. You yearn to sink your fangs into me. I threaten your precious control, don't I?"

She grabbed him by the throat, squeezing it, a blatant warning, the sharp nails sliding like knives into his skin. Only a tad more pressure to crush his windpipe, or rip it out.

"Incredibly stupid. How did you manage to live this long?" she wondered.

Nico looked up into the eyes of death and taunted it more. "I live while you do not. Who is the stupid one, demon?"

With a snarl, she threw him from her. He sucked in a breath as he flew through the air and crashed against a tree, the force of it jarring his injured arm again. White-hot pain seared him, made him see stars.

The air shivered, trembling for a moment with the demon's anger. With a quick downward slash, both sets of nails buried themselves in the thick trunk behind him, a whisper away from his ears, pinning him there. The smell of weeping sap filled the air.

"You wish me to feast upon your blood?" she whispered, her mouth a hairbreadth away from his own, her voice sultry but her eyes cold.

"Yes," he breathed and moved up into those sharp fangs, baring his throat.

She stopped him with a word. "No."

"Why not?"

A simple flex and push, and the tree fell back away from him, groaning and crashing to the ground, its waist-thick trunk breaking beneath her strength as if it were a twig snapped. "Because you are my prisoner, not my food."

"What's the difference?"

"I treat my food better." She lifted him to his feet, and turned him around. With a push, she started him forward. Through the teeth-clenching haze of pain, Nico reached down deep inside and found the strength somehow. Jerking right, he broke into a stumbling run.

Like a haunting specter, she appeared before him again. "Unbelievable," she said as he staggered sharply to the left, away from her.

"I will not return with you," he said, forcing his hurting body to continue running, one foot in front of the other, even when screaming agony blurred his vision. "I will fight you as long as I yet live."

"Why?"

"Because you will not give me what I want."

"And what do you want, rogue?"

Nico came to a reeling halt. Turned to face her. "I want to die here. I do not care how, by your hand or beneath your teeth. I will not return to her."

"I'm sorry." With a gentle blow to the head, she knocked him unconscious. "You have no choice."

SEVEN

T HE WILL WAS a curious thing, I found. Some men's wills were fragile things, easily breakable like fine china. One drop of pain, one slap, and it cracked. Others' wills were stronger, more enduring like tempered steel. These did not break, but they bent. Oh yes, they bent beneath my will. Most warriors were intelligent enough to realize when they were defeated. They stopped fighting because it was useless to continue doing so. They had lost to a stronger foe and became resigned to their fate. I had to luck out with the exception to this rule.

This one's will was a fearsome thing, unbreakable and unbendable. He did not stop fighting or struggling, and he was far from resigned. Hot vitriolic words—and "blood-sucking demon bitch" was the mildest term among them—spewed out unending abuse in a malevolent tide from the backseat of the car where I had chained him. His wrists were anchored to the customized door fastenings I'd installed, with his knees secured at the other end. That's right, his knees. Why had I cuffed his knees? Because securing his ankles had left him far too much leeway. He didn't curl up on the seat like a good little defeated warrior. Oh, no. He'd flailed me with his words, and then flailed me with his body, throwing himself against the front seat again and again until his ankles and wrists had become not just raw and abraded but had torn through his flesh, spilling hot blood in a burgundy gush and filling the car with the stink of fresh blood. I'd had to stop the car and roll down all the windows, then lick his blood clean from his ankles and wrist, letting the healing properties in my saliva stop the bleeding. Had he been grateful? Nope. The bastard had struggled and jerked away from me, making helpless frightened sounds deep in his throat, trying to trigger my predatory instincts.

"It might have worked on another demon dead, playing the helpless struggling victim," I told him as I tied a rag around his left wrist to cushion the wound before clamping the silver cuffs over him once more. Hell, it probably would have worked on me . . . before I had met Stefan. It sure as Darkness triggered my hunter instincts. Had not my pity— yes, pity . . . Had that not been stronger than the hunger he triggered, I would have sunk my fangs deep into him and drunk down enough blood, not to kill him as he wanted, but enough to weaken him sufficiently so that he wasn't as much trouble. To do so now, however, seemed distasteful.

"But you picked the wrong demon to play your games upon," I informed him. "I am centuries beyond losing control like that."

He stopped playing the victim and started back up with the foul insults, the noxious threats, anything he could think of to trigger my anger while I tied a rag around his right wrist. Not because he was bleeding. Nope. His skin there was intact, unripped, unchafed. I tied the cloth there more as a preventive measure, so that his wrist wouldn't start bleeding when he thrashed himself around. I'd left that right wrist free because of his broken arm. They say no good deed goes unpunished. Ain't that the lousy truth? He'd struck the back of my head with that broken arm, even though it had to have hurt him far worse than it did me, which was not at all. It had simply been more of an annoyance, really. But he'd continued at it until the car stank not only of blood but of pain, his pain. Man, this Monère certainly knew how to yank a demon's chain, got to give him that. He was smart, but lousy with luck. The poor rogue bastard had gotten stuck with perhaps the one demon it just wasn't going to work on.

I snapped the silver cuffs around his right wrist. If he drew in a sharp, painful breath as I pulled his broken arm up and over his head to secure it to the door fastening, I knew that it was less painful than what he had purposely inflicted on himself. Frankly, it was more of a measure to protect him from further damage. Holy Hellfire, he healed fast, much faster than Stefan did even though they felt of similar power. If he hadn't been bashing his arm around trying to anger me enough to kill him, it might have been halfway healed by now.

I'd had to dig out my largest pair of handcuffs from the back of the trunk to find a pair that would squeeze tight around his thighs just above the knees. They dug deep into his soft flesh, and his legs were bloodless white below the kneecaps, but at least it secured him right and tight, leaving him no room to toss himself about. I gazed down at him all trussed up like that with the satisfaction of a job well done.

"Now, if you will only shut up," I murmured.

His maddened, rage-spilling words suddenly stopped and the intelligence I had first seen at Smoky Jim's shone once more in those remarkable gray eyes. He could not anger me enough. Could not tempt me enough to break my control. He had tried, oh how he had tried, and it hadn't worked. So now he tried a different tact.

"Please," he said, his hoarse voice calm as I bent over him. "Just end it here. It will be a kindness to me, in truth." He tried something that no other Monère warrior had ever thought of trying—appealing to a demon's mercy. "Please, I beg of you."

Oh, crap. Those few words, humble, calm, and pleading,

flayed me worse than the hour-long verbal and physical abuse he had just heaped upon me.

My fist flew out, clipped his jaw. Knocked him unconscious once more. And if I was completely honest about it, the act was more of a mercy for me than for him.

EIGHT

❧

I WAS IN a pissy mood. It grew even darker when the rogue began to stir as we entered Mona SiGuri's domain, the territory he had fled from. Revived, no doubt, by the feel of the Monère guards we passed as we slowly made our way up the side of a mountain. They knew who we were because they sensed my captive's presence and my lack of presence, my lack of heartbeat; it was as effective as if a loud clarion had trumpeted our arrival. I sensed one guard shift form and wing off into the night to warn the others of our approach.

A small crowd of solemn faces had gathered by the time my car crawled halfway up the mountainside and pulled to a stop before an old weathered hunting lodge. *Secluded* would aptly describe it. No human neighbors in the near and not-so-near vicinity that I could detect. *Creepy* was another good word for it. The lodge was a large, three-storied dwelling that once might have been grand, but no longer. And the sad, neglected air of the building was reflected in the people themselves—a score of men, and a glimpse or two of women, their curious faces peeping out behind ragged curtains. They gawked not so much at the rogue as at who was returning him.

My lips thinned with displeasure as I unfastened the cuffs around my captive's knees. He didn't even try to kick me although he was fully aware, his eyes opened and unblinking.

"No more struggles?" I said as I roughly rubbed his lower legs to restore circulation.

"What would be the purpose now?" he answered. "My chance . . . your chance . . . both have passed."

I leaped over the car, startling some gaping warriors, and opened the other door. The rogue didn't even move his hands as I freed his good arm's restraint from the door fastening. I snapped the free end of it onto the wrist of his broken arm, and removed the second pair, no longer needed now. Gently, I lifted him out and set him onto his feet. Watched him swallow back a groan as he lowered his arms down in front of him.

"A thinking man now. I liked the wild one you portrayed much better," I taunted, wanting to get a rise out of him for some reason.

"Me, too."

His soft reply only made me madder.

Four warriors advanced. The lead man dared reach out to take Nico from me.

"Back off," I snarled, flashing fang.

The dark-haired warrior gasped and fell back a pace as his men drew swords and daggers.

"What is this circus?" I growled. "Don't you know anything about the proper etiquette?"

"Etiquette?" the warrior asked, clearly bewildered.

The circle of onlookers parted and a woman, a Queen, came forward. She was tall, thin, and beautiful in a cold sterile way, dressed in a long black gown with her chestnut hair long and loose down her back. But it was her strong presence, distinct and different from that of her men that really proclaimed who and what she was.

"You mean the one that has us say, 'Greetings, Guardian. You have returned one who has wandered back to us.'" She smiled unpleasantly as she said the words.

"Yeah," I gritted, my voice low and rough with displeasure, "that custom."

Her tinkling laughter floated in the cool night air. "You must forgive my men. They are too young to be aware of such archaic protocol."

My eyes glinted near black in anger. "It is not their lack, but rather yours for not teaching it to them. And allowing them to gather like this to watch and gape as if my prisoner and I were a circus come to town. Very poor form for one who knows better."

There were indrawn gasps of shock. Fear and expectancy scented the air like a fine and sweet perfume as all eyes were drawn to their Queen and to her reaction of my public reprimand.

No tinkling laughter now. Her dark brown eyes narrowed and her lips firmed thin and cruel. "Beware, demon. This is my land."

Perhaps had she been grateful, followed custom and procedure. Or maybe even then it would not have mattered. Because somewhere on that long drive up the mountain, I'd unconsciously already decided what to do.

"This is my prisoner that I have taken the trouble to return to you," I said as our custom dictated. "I have done so, my duty accomplished, my word kept."

"So formal," Mona SiGuri said with delicate scorn.

Here was where I departed from custom. "Now I claim him as my own." I turned to the stunned warrior beside me. "Nico, get back in the car."

All froze. They looked at me as if I were mad, even Nico. I gave him a soft nudge. "Go on."

Mona SiGuri's eyes narrowed into slits. "Do not be any more foolish, Nico, than you have already been. Do not make your death even more painful." It was a clear warning. A clear choice.

Like a sleepwalker suddenly rousing to his surroundings, Nico looked at his Queen then glanced at me. He made his choice. He took a step toward the car.

"Stop him," Mona SiGuri commanded, her voice shrill and strident. "Stop them both."

I smiled and my fangs flashed in sharp amusement at the wall of warriors who jumped to do her bidding. "You can sure try." A blink, a fraction of a moment in time, and her men, over a dozen of them, were spilling onto the ground, eviscerated, their guts bulging out of their bellies, wounds I had sliced open in fast ripping tear, right on down the line. When they saw me . . . when I *allowed* them to see me again . . . I stood, almost in the same spot, looking as if I hadn't moved at all, licking the blood off my long nails, which had grown even longer. Into razor-sharp talons.

"Umm . . . yummy," I purred. "Monère smorgasbord. Anyone else?"

"Spread out, you fools!" Mona SiGuri screeched. "Stop them now, or face the consequences."

The consequences must be pretty dire because her few remaining men instantly obeyed her, their fear of their Queen even more than their fear of demon dead. They sprang at me one at a time, or so it seemed. In reality, they converged on us all at once from different angles. But they went flying out individually, one after the other, just a grab and toss. The fifth and last one I grabbed and took a munch on before tossing . . . one quick ruthless plunge of my teeth deep into his white neck, one deep sumptuous drink while he screamed . . . before I tossed him out to pile with the rest, his gushing blood spraying in a crimson arc from his ravaged neck. No clotting agent for him.

"Thanks for the snack," I said. "But gotta go."

"Talon!" Mona SiGuri screamed.

"Yup," I said, waving my curved claws at her. "Neat trick, huh?"

"Hurry," Nico urged from inside the car where he'd run. "Hurry before he comes!"

"Before who comes, darling? Men, always in a rush." I

vaulted through the open window into the driver's seat and started the engine. From the corner of my eye, I saw something not just dark but black appear next to the Queen. And sensed something that threw me, confused me for a moment because it could not be, not here in this realm. But it was, I realized. And knew that I had realized it too late because the creature had opened his mouth.

As the sound of his unearthly scream rent our ears, the devastating echolating force of it hit me full blast. And darkness took me.

THEY WERE IN big trouble, Nico acknowledged as waves of devastating pain inundated him. Even worse than the wagonload of manure he had been floundering in before, because now he had dragged someone else into his mess.

Chained to the post next to him was the demon. First his hunter, his captor, and then for one glorious moment in time, his savior. *Now I claim him as my own*, she'd said. He didn't know what "my own" entailed. My own meal, my own slave, my own guard? My own lover? A tantalizing thought, that last one.

She'd called him darling. Facetiously. In play. But it had plucked a chord deep within, that resonated still. He would have liked to have been her darling. He had feared her, respected her—her strength, her intelligence, her force of will that had held even when he had pushed and pushed against it. But that wicked, dark, playful side of her amidst all the chaos, the danger, the thwarted escape . . . that had drawn him irresistibly. None of the queens he had ever served had been playful. They had all taken themselves far too seriously for that.

Nico would have liked to have served her. He would serve her now, in what little time remained. And if the Darkness was merciful, it would be little time, and not drawn out and protracted as Mona SiGuri usually liked. Surely not with this dangerous demon huntress she dared hold captive. But then, Mona SiGuri had not always proved herself prudent or wise, and this demon was a small female, not a tall, frightening male. And beautiful, unfortunately. More so than the Queen.

Mona SiGuri liked to ruin beautiful things. To destroy them slowly, painfully.

He gave an inner sigh as the demon beside him finally stirred. The crowd watching them stirred as well—sullen injured warriors angry at being bested by a woman, demon though she was; quiet, subdued females who were glad it was not them looking so lovely . . . and the object of the Queen's petty ire tonight. A keen collective anticipation thrummed the air as if to silently say: *Alas, the show begins.*

How much of it the demon felt and was aware of was hard to say as she lifted her head and looked unerringly to the nearest blood source—him, strung up naked and bleeding beside her.

Nico hung suspended from chains, with his toes barely touching the ground. Just enough to brush it, to feel the whisper of solid earth beneath him, but not enough to help bear any of his weight, so that the full burden of his bulky mass was heavy upon both of his arms, ensuring that damage was done, or rather redone. His mending arm had rebroken beneath the strain.

Whenever his left arm muscles bulged, whenever he tried to ease some of the agonizing weight with his uninjured arm, the whip sang through the air and cut into his flesh. He was neatly patterned with raw lash marks down his front, back, and sides. Fully tenderized, ready to eat, with waves of enticing pain perfuming the air along with his blood. A silver-braided whip had been used, ensuring that the wounds would not heal so quickly, if at all. Not before he died, that is, beneath the demon's fangs, which were growing frighteningly long and sharp before their eyes. But that was not why everyone gasped. Not because of her teeth. Most of them had fangs in their other form. No, what was so shocking and disturbing was the way her face morphed a little, bones shifting, broadening, thickening, forehead bulging, like something pushing beneath it, wanting to come out. And the way her eyes suddenly burned red with flickering flames. Like the fiery hunger that must be consuming her . . . because they had bled her nearly dry. They'd sliced open her wrists and let the blood run in a trickling stream into the earth to weaken her and drive her into bloodlust.

With startling suddenness, the demon jerked against the chains, peculiar black ones, not silver. But the chains held, and all of them—even Nico—breathed a sigh of relief.

He would serve her in whatever way he could, even if it was as a one-time meal. And yet, even so determined, he could not keep his heart from beating faster in apprehension as he watched her—demon changing. Her skin rippled as bones moved beneath her flesh. But she was too weak, her blood and her power too little. The eerie morphing subsided and she remained as she was, caught in the beginning of change, unable to complete it.

Mona SiGuri's disdainful voice sliced through the air. "Foolish Nico. Bold but never too bright. You ran, turned rogue. And then you chose her, this demon, over me. Let your fate be an example to all of what such unwise choices lead to."

"I still choose her over you," Nico said. "Even when she hunted me, she showed me more compassion and care than you ever gave me as my Queen."

The stunned silence was broken by the crack of Mona SiGuri's hand against Nico's face, whipping his head back with the force of the blow. Then as if that were not retaliation enough, she snatched the whip out of the guard's hand and struck Nico full in the face with it. Silver braided leather lashed through the air and sliced open the left side of his face, dispersing the smell of more blood into the air.

A deep echoing growl spilled out like ominous thunder from the demon huntress's throat, making the Queen fall back a step before catching herself.

"Look at you," Mona SiGuri sneered, regaining her composure, "more animal than woman." She turned and shot a poisonous look at Nico. "So be it. Enjoy your chosen fate. Loosen her chains." She stepped back from him. They all did as a guard freed up ten more feet of chain then quickly darted out of reach himself.

Slowly, carefully, like a sinuous snake gathering itself to strike, the demon advanced step by careful step, chains rattling, until she stood swaying before him. Saliva glistened from her fangs, and hunger, ravenous hunger, burned red and hot in her eyes. Sweat dampened her face, darkening strands of her flaxen hair, and the obvious restraint she exercised not to pounce on Nico made her visibly tremble. Her arms came up and around him, and he felt and heard her inch-long nails sink into the thick post behind him. She looked up, found his eyes. And as he stared down into the red wildness of hers, into that half-morphed, beastly face, he still found his words true. He did choose her.

"It's all right, milady. I offer my blood freely."

She shuddered against him in their near embrace, and closed her eyes for a second, her fangs a kiss away from his neck. She pulled back and caught his eyes with her own.

"Be still. Be at peace," she said, and he felt a whisper of compulsion push at him. But she was too weak; it was not enough to make him submit. Nico did that of his own free will. Her effort to try and make it easier for him, though, melted his heart and made him truly hers—body, mind, and soul. He bent his throat down to her, relaxed into her bite. Welcomed the small stinging pain as her teeth pierced him, as she drank him down fiercely and urgently. And pushed something in turn into him—pleasure like nothing he had ever felt before. Like warm bursting sunlight. Like heavenly ambrosia. It came spilling into him in an overwhelming wash of sensation that flashed over him, filled him up with aching quickness. Exploded out from him in almost painful ecstasy. In waves of powerful release. In a burst of blinding light called forth from his body. In cries of shuddering satisfaction.

It must not have been quite the show Queen Mona Si-Guri intended. "Enough," she cried.

He felt the demon release him, lap his neck gently one last time. A final taste of him as his light faded and absorbed back into him.

When she spoke, her voice rumbled deep and full like the sound of echoing thunder. "Yes. It is enough."

She pulled her nails out of the wooden post, and Nico felt the air between them stir and swell with power, with a sudden wash of energy that rippled over him. Before his eyes, he watched, felt her change.

Nails thickened and darkened, pushed out of her fingertips until they were great hooking claws half a foot long. It was one of the first things to change, though not the most impressive. Her face completed the transformation it had started, her forehead shifting, becoming wider, thicker, coarser, jutting out. Her body swelled, too, in width and length, with thickening bones, with dense rippling muscles, with towering height. Growing from a stature no taller than his chin to way over his head. Buttons popped, though a few strategic ones held. Her clothes tore, ripping along the seams, and not only cloth gave way. With a stretching groan, the dark metal shackles broke apart beneath the dense, growing flesh, falling away from her wrists and ankles. And she became demon unleashed.

Women screamed. Men ran away while a handful stayed behind to guard their Queen. With easy strength and almost no effort, the demon beast ripped down Nico's silver chains. Mercifully, she still held the broken ends of the chain up and gently lowered his numbed arms down instead of letting them drop. Even so, searing pain screamed from his broken arm at the movement of it and at the blood rushing back into it. The weight of the shackles still encircling his wrists with their dangling links was excruciating, and spots whitened his vision. Desperately he fought off the whirling faintness. Too much pain, too much blood loss.

"I'm sorry," he gasped. "I'm not going to be much use to you in this fight."

Those terrifying fangs lifted up into what he interpreted as a grin. "Just stay behind me," she rumbled.

"Talon!" Mona SiGuri screamed, and her sinister creature came running, a thing small and thin, the color of darkness, his head too large for the short slender body, his black hair bound back in a long plaited braid. An unearthly creature like the demon, with no heartbeat and no breath. He was slim, graceful, and weak but for that formidable cry, and of so delicate a build that you could not tell if he was male or female at first. But Nico knew what he was—a boy becoming a man.

Talon opened his mouth and emitted that loud echolating cry. But the demon was prepared for it this time. She shielded herself and Nico, and he felt the force of it pass them by.

"Again!" Mona SiGuri cried. "Hit them again."

"Enough." This time it was the demon that said it. Stretching her hand out, she circled her long taloned fingers.

Talon gasped . . . or tried to. He seemed unable to draw breath.

"Come here, little flower," purred the demon. "You're just what I need."

Against his will, Talon came, his jerky legs propelling him forward, unable to resist the compulsion in that voice.

"Stop her, attack her! Make her bleed!" Mona SiGuri commanded. And her poor men obeyed. Silver knives flew through the air. Had Nico not been there, she could have dodged them easily, but he was obediently behind her, protected by her immense mass. She didn't move.

He felt a push of power, and the blades were deflecting to the right, whistling by harmlessly. Two warriors, his former brethren, Karpon and Joffrey, leaped for her from opposite sides, their swords drawn. She pushed Nico back with a gentle nudge and her claws sliced up in a quick, singular motion. The swords flew into the air in a gush of blood with the two warrior's severed hands still attached to them. Screams tore from the maimed men's throats. A downward swipe of those great claws, and those horrified cries became rattled, broken sounds as Karpon and Joffrey landed in crumpled heaps across from where they had launched, their chests torn asunder.

But it was her back side—his area—that proved her weak spot. A third warrior, stealthy and silent Timor, came at her from behind with sword in hand, and glee in his eyes. With the demon's attention occupied by the other two, and Nico injured and unarmed, his Monère strength dampened by the silver manacles, rendering him only human strong, Timor had, in essence, a clear unhindered shot of her. That is, if he discounted Nico, which he clearly did. But after spending a great deal of time with humans these past few weeks, Nico had a greater appreciation of their strength. And his determination . . . well, his determination was still Monère strong, silver chains notwithstanding. Or in this case, hopefully, withstanding.

Amidst the tumult of blood and the maimed warriors' cries of pain, Timor sprung into the air and attacked, his sword slashing down, aiming for the demon's neck. Leaping up, Nico met him in flight, and metal rang against metal as the sword struck Nico's silver shackles and cut into the flesh of his hands. But that sting was like nothing compared to the overwhelming pain that burst through him as his good arm—and his broken one—absorbed the full force of the powerful blow, and deflected it. Gripped in agony, utterly frozen by it, Nico could do nothing against the dagger Timor drew with his other hand. Could only look into the eyes of his former brother as Timor plunged the knife into his belly. Not a killing blow, but an eviscerating one. One that crumpled him to the ground, soundless.

METAL STRIKING METAL rang loud in my ears behind me. And the call of pain, such terrible pain, rang just as loudly. I whirled, and in that slow way time had of stretching out during a fight, I saw my rogue, the man I had claimed, the man I had tried to protect—Nico—fall to the

ground, blood blossoming from his belly like a liquid
flower. I saw the bloody, guilty dagger clasped in the attacker's hand, the sword he swung at me. And rage . . . hot
scalding rage . . . boiled up within me and slipped free. A
cry, a roar, a shock wave of sound and energy and power
burst from me and trembled the air, widening the warrior's
eyes in primal fear—his last expression, as I stopped playing nice. In quick succession, I severed his arm holding the
sword, the hand holding the dagger, and then his head.

The body parts fell away, metal struck the ground, and
cool light, the moon's vital energy, flowed free from the
beheaded warrior . . . and into me as I drank it down. Flesh
melted into ashes, puffing the air, dusting the ground. Ashes
and empty clothes all that remained of him.

"What did you do to Timor?"

It was the Queen's voice. She asked not on how he had
departed—ashes and light was how Monères died—but at
what I had done to the filtering essence of him.

I turned eyes to her that I knew were aglow with the
vitality I had just taken in, and answered her. "I drank him
down. His light, his last essence."

Bewilderment and fear was in Mona SiGuri's eyes, and
in the eyes of the men about her. "What does that mean?"
she demanded.

"That he will not be demon dead. That he simply is no
more."

Sharp indrawn breaths sounded upon the dawning realization: no chance of afterlife in that other realm. Simply
no more. Something they had not known a demon could do
to them. A harsh judgment I had passed and knowingly carried out. And though the woman before me was not entirely
to blame—that was mine—she had precipitated things,
started events rolling that had led to this.

Mona SiGuri opened her mouth, her face twisted ugly
with fear, loathing, and most disturbing of all, determination. I knew that she opened her mouth to shout another
command to attack, to kill more of her men. And I could

not allow that. I circled my hand again and gently closed my fist. Mona SiGuri's cry, "Get—" was abruptly cut off.

She dropped to the ground, her hands gripping her throat as her men backed away from her, fearful that what was happening to her might spread to them. Her mouth opened and closed in a parody of speech but no further sound came. Just a trickle of blood. And then, a long immeasurable moment later, sounds of choking.

"What did you do?" Nico asked from the ground, his voice weak.

I knelt beside him. All that I saw in his eyes was the desire to know. No trembling fear, no abhorrence—the usual expressions one had when gazing into my demon beast face. And because he had asked it, I answered the question that all wondered. "I crushed her throat. Shut her up."

"Oh."

He bled still, a pool of redness spilling from his abdomen, darkening the earth. I pressed the back of my hand against the wound, putting pressure there to stop the bleeding, and looked around for assistance. A group of warriors stood indecisively ringed about their Queen. One moved forward to lift her from the ground. "Don't touch her," I snarled, and he leaped back away from her.

"You. Bring your healer here, quickly!" I snapped. The warrior's eyes, the one who had tried to help his Queen, met my flickering red ones, and he hastily left to do my bidding.

It was a stalemate for now, the guards fearing me too much to attack but unable to depart the battlefield because of their fallen Queen, whom I allowed none to touch.

A silent struggle drew my attention back to prey I had almost forgotten. My little black flower was fighting the mental bonds I had wrapped him in. Bonds that were weakening as my power waned. Because even though I had taken in energy, from many sources, I had expended much of it shifting into my demon beast form, and had wasted a great deal more in the hot spilling rage that had poured recklessly out of me.

"Ah, Talon. Thank you for reminding me." Rising from Nico's side, I went to the creature that should not have existed here, and saw, this close, the slight broadness of its shoulders, the wider hands, the subtle features upon its face proclaiming its gender—male.

The creature struggled, eyes wild, fighting to open his mouth, to break free. When he was unable to, he shrank down into his short self, cowering. The Queen grew agitated as well, shaking her head wildly as I approached Talon. Her hands lifted to point, to gesture. With a thought, I banded those irritating hands down by her side.

I turned my attention full upon what awaited me, and knelt by the trembling creature, lightly pushing his head to the side, stretching out his neck. He whimpered, his eyes wide and panicked, making piteous sounds of fright.

"Hush," I said. "One sip, I will be gentle," and bit down.

The taste of Talon's blood was not sweet but wild. Like something soaring through the wind, diving down from the sky. It shot through me and spread like white lightning, like Hell's own sweet warmth, punching me with a rush of power. Filling me with energy so splendidly abundant that some of it spilled out from me in momentary waste before I clamped down on it.

Drawing back, I licked the blood from my lips, and inclined my head to the dark creature. "A true Flower of Darkness. My thanks."

Lifting him into my arms, I carried him back and set him down beside Nico. Crouching beside my fallen warrior, I hooked my talons through the silver manacles still obscenely shackling his wrists and, with a tug, broke them apart and tossed them away. A flash of movement and the sound of rushing feet drew my attention back to the others. I watched as the healer, a dark-eyed brunette garbed in a maroon robe denoting her vocation, rushed toward the Queen. The warrior who had fetched her followed behind.

"No, Healer," I said, my voice gratingly harsh. "Here first."

The healer hesitated, looked down at her Queen. The

low growl trickling from my throat helped change her mind. She hastened toward us, and I retreated and let her minister to Nico.

Life was different from death in many ways, and the way we healed was one of them. We might dwell in heat, but the few demons that had the gift healed with a cool power. The cold-blooded Monères, however, healed with vibrating warmth.

I felt a slow steady trickle of energy flow from the healer's hands. Watched it slowly close Nico's belly wound, knitting torn flesh together, miraculously making it whole once more.

With that done, the healer rose to attend to her Queen.

"His arm," I said, stopping her. Frustrated, she sank back down, and though she was unhappy to be delayed, to have her triage so disordered by me, her hands were gentle as she settled them over Nico's grotesquely swollen and bruised arm.

She sent her power out, seeking and searching, sinking down beneath the skin to repair bone, to absorb the spilled blood and ease fluid out of the injured tissues back into the bloodstream.

As I watched her work, I attended to my own wounds. Calling forth my energy, an abundance of it now, I spilled it down my right hand to the forefinger, focusing it into the pointy tip of my talon until it glowed a dark amber red, like fire shining through honeyed glass. I ran it along my slashed wrist. Heat sizzled, and the stench of burned flesh filled the air, drawing all eyes to me. Not healing, but it stopped the leaking of my blood, burned closed the wound. I flowed power down into my left hand, and seared my other wrist.

Her task finished, the healer gazed at me, her eyes wide, her brow dampened with perspiration from her efforts.

"My thanks for your service, Healer. You may go to your Queen, but before you leave us, I would ask for your robe."

Without hesitation, the healer shrugged off the requested

piece of clothing. Wearing just her undergarments, she rose and, as quickly as her tired legs could take her, made her way to her Queen.

"Is the robe for me?" Nico asked. He sat up with a silly grin, as if the freedom from pain was a euphoric drug.

"No, for me. Later." His grin disappeared with my next question. "Who cut me?"

"Ezekiel did," Nico replied slowly, carefully. "But he did so on Mona SiGuri's order."

"And my blood. Did it all spill into the ground?"

"Yes, all of it."

"Then do not fear, I will not kill him. Not if he obeys me." In a deep booming voice, I called him forth. "Ezekiel, step forward."

All eyes swung to a man built like a big bull, with thick arms and barreled chest, his long brown hair secured back in a braid.

"Ah," I purred in deep, rumbling satisfaction. "The same warrior that whipped you."

"Also at his Queen's order," Nico said.

"So noted, although you are much more forgiving than I. Come to me, Ezekiel." My fangs flashed sharp and pointy. "Or I shall come to you."

The threat propelled him to me of his own shaky volition.

"Strip. Give Nico your clothes and daggers."

He did so hastily, tossing pants, shirt, boots, and weapons to his former captive, then turned to leave. I stopped him. "Not yet." My eyes must have flashed red again because he took a step back and would have run had I not froze him immobile. "Not until you repay my spilt blood with some of your own," I rumbled.

Grasping Ezekiel's long braid, I stretched out his neck, no longer gentle, no longer kind. I bit down viciously into his thick neck, plunged the claws of my left hand into his hip, and gulped fiercely, feeding from him without restraint, without care. Not giving him pleasure, oh no, but the other side of the coin. He writhed with agony, with lashing pain, as if his flesh was being ripped from him, piece by piece, with an invisible whip. And I fed on that too, drank it down along with the blood.

When I had drained him almost dry, when his blood had lessened to a mere trickle down my throat, when most of the energy had left his body, and his cries had turned weak and hoarse, I tossed him away. And my eyes locked with Mona SiGuri's.

She had been healed, could talk now, but did not open her mouth. Was too frightened to draw notice to herself. But my attention had found her anyway.

"Who brought Talon to you?" I asked.

The frightened Queen was readily forthcoming. "A demon called Horace," she said, not that it helped me much. It was a common name among both the Monère and demon dead.

"Describe him."

She did so, and that, too, was as generic as the name she had supplied: dark hair and eyes, of average height and build, no distinguishing marks.

"When?" I demanded. "When did he bring Talon to you?"

"Six and twenty years ago as an infant."

The information staggered me, made me reassess everything. "And he has been with you all this time?"

"I have kept him by my side all these years," she confirmed.

"When did you last see your demon?"

She hesitated for a moment, thinking. Impatiently, I took a menacing step toward her.

"Two full moons ago," she said hastily. "He comes here only once or twice a year."

"To drink Talon's blood?"

"Yes."

And she had known what his blood would do to me because it had done the same thing to the other demon. And she had allowed that blood rape to occur for over twenty-six years. What other things had she learned of our kind? I wondered, but in the aggressive state I was in, I dared not stay to find out.

"I will leave you now," I told her, "because if I question you anymore, I may kill you."

She stayed silent, her dark eyes brimming with relief.

"Other guardians will come to question you and your men. You will answer them truthfully or what I did to Timor and to Ezekiel will be as nothing to what they do to you. And the hurting will not stop, not even if we allow you to make the transition to demon dead. Do you understand?"

She nodded her head jerkily.

"Come," I said, extending a clawed hand to Nico. He wrapped his hand around my much larger one and pulled himself up. The borrowed clothes hung loosely upon him, but the boots seemed to fit well enough.

"You, too, Talon," I said, and released the bonds holding the black creature. "I'm taking you home."

The words surprised Talon. Stopped him when he would have fled. "Home?" he said, his voice a surprisingly light melodious sound. "Where is that?"

"Did you not guess yet?"

The creature shook his head.

"In another realm," I said. "In Hell."

NINE

WITH A PULSE of power—so much amazing power singing through me—I returned back to my demon self. Bones shifted and rearranged. Flesh grew smaller, and talons slid back in, moving beneath the skin. My massive height shrunk down until my torn clothes fit once more, although much looser. Airy rags now.

Donning the maroon robe—not for modesty's sake but so that I wouldn't attract undue attention on the highway—I swung into the car. Talon and Nico were already inside. I started the car under the hostile eyes of watching Monère, but none dared stop us. Nay, they were most eager for us to go, even though I was leaving with more than I had brought in. I marveled at how that had so unexpectedly come to be, and glanced at my black, unearthly young passenger. He was curled up, shivering, in the right backseat, farthest away from me. Nico sat in the passenger seat beside me.

"Buckle up," I said as we sped bumpily down the dirt road.

"Why?" asked Nico with the Monère's typical cavalier attitude toward safety.

"What?" Talon said simultaneously, perplexed over what I had asked him to do.

Impatience and anger flared hot within me at being questioned—partly my nature, but mostly from the excessive energy roaring through me, riding me. I clamped down tightly on it, on the urge to strike out, physically and with words.

"I meant put on your safety belt," I replied in as even a tone as I could manage as we wound down the mountainside, doing my best to appear calm and normal. "So that the police do not stop us. It is their human law. Nico will show you how to pull the strap across and secure it on the opposite side, Talon."

Nico twisted around to help Talon do as I requested, then secured his own safety belt.

"Have you never ridden in a car before, Talon?" I asked.

"No," Talon said softly, miserably, his arms curled tightly around himself, his body shaking with tremors.

"Are you cold?" My question came out harsher than I intended, making Talon flinch and shiver even more.

"I am always cold."

"Does it become dangerous for you?"

"In what way?"

"Do you ever begin to ghost?"

Bewilderment shone in those dark eyes. "What is that?"

"Your flesh thins, lightens. Becomes clear enough to see through."

"No." A brief pause, then he asked, "Will that happen to me now?"

"You have been here for over twenty-six years. Correct?"

"Yes. Since I was a babe."

"Then, no. If you have existed here that long, it will not happen now."

"She said that it would," Talon said softly, as if we would all know who *she* was. "That I would slowly fade into nothingness if I left this place."

"Who? Mona SiGuri?"

He nodded.

"She holds no control over your existence, nor does this place hold any special sway over your being. That miracle comes from your own power."

My words surprised him. "What do you mean, power? I am not strong." He gave a bitter laugh. "Far from it."

"You are a creature taken from another realm. You should not have existed in this one for more than a sennight, not without returning to Hell to replenish your energy."

"I have never left this mountain," he said. "You must be mistaken; I could not have come from Hell then."

"I am not mistaken. You are Floradëur. A Flower of Darkness."

"Floradëur. Is that what I am?" Talon said with a little catch in his voice. "Are there others like me?"

"There are many others like you down in Hell."

"Nico?" He looked askance at the only thing familiar to him now, his unspoken question hanging in the air: *Does she tell the truth?*

"All that she has promised, she has done so far," Nico said. "I believe her words hold truth, and that she acts with honor."

My turn to laugh bitterly. For anger to flare hotly again. "Honor? When I hunted you, captured you, hurt you, and returned you to that bitch Queen?"

"All that," Nico said, oddly cheerful. "And then you saved me. My own demon princess riding to the rescue."

I turned to him with angry startlement. But it softened into amusement at sight of that silly grin creasing the corners of his mouth. He'd been joking. He did not really know who I was.

"You acted foolishly, hurting yourself trying to protect me," I admonished. "You should have warned me of Timor's presence and let me take care of it."

"I didn't want to distract your attention away from the other two warriors you were battling."

"I could have handled three just as easily."

His cheeriness dimmed. "Ah, then I was indeed foolish in not warning you."

I shrugged. Amended brusquely, "You exercised your best judgment at the time. You did well."

"Did I?" he asked, that silly smile back on his face.

"Yeah, you did, with what limited knowledge you had. But I require better of you in the future. I shall expect you to protect yourself as well as me next time. It angered me that you were hurt, and an angry demon is not a good thing."

"No, it isn't," Nico agreed, the memory of what I had done to Timor reflected in his eyes. "I will do better next time. Thank you for letting me know what you expect of me as your guard. Or perhaps I am being presumptuous again. Perhaps you claimed me with some other role in mind." His voice grew caressingly softer, deeper.

The look I shot him was sharp and penetratingly deep.

"My, what a suspicious look you have on your face," Nico murmured with that cheerful, affable mood he'd been in ever since our escape.

"Are you feeling yourself?" I asked.

"Should I feel like anybody else?" he asked, smiling.

"Perhaps a better question to ask is: how do you feel?"

"Weak, tired, almost giddy with relief. But that is not what you are seeking. What do you wish to know, my lady?"

Not "milady," the proper address of respect. But "my lady." Two distinct words that Nico clearly savored, and I could not correct him. I had claimed him. But the obvious satisfaction he took in those words puzzled me. And worried me.

"Are you attracted to me?" I asked bluntly as we sped along the deserted country road. No other cars followed in pursuit, no birds winged overhead in the dark night sky. I detected no Monère presence other than the one sitting beside me.

"Yes," Nico said. "Very much so."

"Oh, no. You are demon struck." Worry and regret was bitter on my tongue. And anger at myself flashed hot and harsh within me. My eyes must have burned red, because the easy smile on Nico's lips completely disappeared.

"I should have given you pain instead of pleasure," I said. "I filled you too quickly, with too much in my hasty need. Now you burn for more of that same pleasure."

"More would be nice," Nico said with serious consideration. "But this time I would wish to give you pleasure as well as receive it."

"Give me pleasure, not just receive it," I repeated, vast relief pouring through me. "Then you are not demon struck as I feared."

"What is demon struck?"

"Becoming addicted to the pleasure we can give, obsessed with it. Willing to do anything to experience it once more. We cannot predict who it will afflict."

"Well I'd certainly like to experience it once more; it was wondrous, if a bit intense. But that desire is not the compulsive need you are describing," Nico said, then asked wistfully, "What is your name?"

"Lucinda."

Nico took a moment to absorb it, to relish it in his mind before asking, "My lady. What role would you have me play in your life?"

"I'm dead, darling. Or did you not notice?"

Some hot flare of emotion brightened his eyes for a moment, lightening the color to pewter gray. "In your existence then. What role did you have in mind for me when you claimed me?"

My eyes slid away from his. Turned back to fix on the road before me. "There is another warrior," I told him. "A rogue that may belong to me."

"Another rogue," he murmured. "And *may* belong? You have not claimed him?"

"Not yet."

Nico waited, but no further words were forthcoming. "And," he prompted. "Do you intend to claim him? Does he wish to be yours?"

"He said that he would wait for me as long as he could. But others hunt him—humans. He may have left already. If so, then your role as companion, Monère brother, and guard to him and his young Mixed Blood ward will not be necessary. If that is the case, then you can return to your human harem and reside in my territory under my protection for as long as you desire."

"In your territory, but not under your roof." He smiled ruefully. "So if this other rogue is not there waiting for us, you intend to toss me coldly back to the humans."

"The three attentive female arms you left behind did not seem cold. Indeed, not. Nor did you seem bereft among them, though I cannot conceive of any pleasure you might have received from them."

"I gave them pleasure, and I received pleasure in giving it to them. It felt good to touch, and to be held in turn, appreciated."

Sentiments I would not have understood a few days ago, but now I did.

"Very well, if that is your condition for keeping me," Nico continued with a mocking smile, "then let us hasten with all speed to this other rogue. That is our destination, is it not?"

"Yes, Massachusetts."

"Where is this Massachusetts?" Talon asked from the backseat.

"About three nights driving distance," Nico replied.

"I don't have three days to waste," I said. Leaning over, I retrieved a cell phone from the glove compartment.

"How many days do you have?" Nico asked, watching me power on the phone with a sharp press of nail.

"Only one day before I have to return to my realm."

"From what you said to Talon, it seemed as though you could stay in this realm for up to a week. A sennight."

"Normally. But my situation is not normal now. Not with Talon's blood singing in my veins."

"I don't understand. You obviously gained more power, more energy from drinking from him. It almost seems to spill from you now."

So much for thinking they wouldn't notice how revved up I was.

"Yeah, but it comes with a price. When the moon next rises, the effect will wear off. My energy will be almost fully depleted, and I will fall into a stupor that will last for an equal length of time as this energy boosts me now. I must be back in my realm before that happens."

"Or else what, you die?"

"You mean, die again," I said with dark humor. "But, yes, to your question. I will die, and this time it would be final."

"All right," Nico said, taking a breath. "So you return to your realm now, and come back when you have recovered."

"No time," I said. "We go there now."

"How do you propose to compress a three-day journey to less than one?" he asked.

"We fly."

"My other form does not have wings," Nico said regrettably.

"Neither does mine, as you saw. Metal wings," I said, delicately tapping out a number on the cell phone with the pointy tip of my nail. "We're going to catch a ride on a private jet."

T E N

WE ARGUED THE entire time it took to drive to the
small county airstrip. Or rather, Nico did.

Go now, he urged. Take Talon and return to Hell. He
would go fetch this Monère rogue.

No, I replied for the third time. Stefan might flee if
he sensed another warrior's presence, and I might never find
him again—my greatest fear and the reason for my urgency.
If I lost him now in this land full of millions of people, it
would be a miracle if our paths ever crossed again.

Nico tried another route. There were plenty of other
rogues, he cajoled. Him, for instance, and many others
like him who would be most grateful to serve me, to belong
to me.

Ignoring the total unlikelihood of that, I told him that it
was Stefan I wanted.

He spluttered and berated me. Even when I growled at
him in warning, he would not cease.

"He is not worth it." Nico glowered, his easy good humor having fled entirely, leaving a cantankerous bear in its
place. "He is not worth this risk to your life." At the droll

lift of my brow, he amended, "To your continued existence then."

"Oh, but he is."

No more words after that. He subsided into a brooding silence, watching me as I paced in burning impatience, in bristling energy, until a small private jet finally arrived and took us away.

On the plane, Talon was silent and withdrawn, a miserable shivering shadow sitting two rows behind us, as if he wanted to be a little distant from us, but not too far away.

Nico sat across from me, the foolish, fearless rogue, as I burned and bristled and thrummed, over-revved. Shrugging off his moodiness, and totally ignoring mine, he began pelting me with questions. Did I have a house in Arizona?

Yes.

How many bedrooms?

Four.

Would we live there?

Yes, if he survived this trip. Which he had a hell of a lot better chance of doing if he shut up and left me alone.

Springing up from the seat, unable to sit still a moment longer, I began to pace up and down the narrow aisle. My skin crawled with tension eager to be released. With a desire to run, to hunt, to spring in the air and bring down prey. My fingernails burned and tingled, as if they wanted to slide out and thicken into talons. Itched with the need to scrape across skin, to feel the pull and give of ripping flesh. My fangs emerged beyond my control, and saliva ran in a steady trickle down my throat. My beast wanted to come out, but I would not let it. I did not want Stefan to see me that way . . . if he waited for me, still.

My brisk steps became an almost swift run. Four bouncing paces, a powerful spinning turn. Four steps back. Spin and turn. Again and again, endlessly.

Energy . . . so much energy filled me up, wanting to be expunged in the most aggressive way. The air fairly crackled with the contained violence within me just waiting to be unleashed. Talon shrank himself against the wall, away from me. Thinned himself against it, trembling with fear. Which only made the tension in me worse.

The beast in me snapped and snarled and demanded to be loosened, to tear into the prey so quiveringly near. I subdued the impulse with an effort that made me tremble.

The beast in me howled. And burned to do something violent, something harsh. Something viciously, deliciously bloody.

"Talk to me, Nico," I said in a voice already gone deep. I heard the low, echoing timbre of my demon beast voice and knew I was in trouble.

"You told me before to shut up," he said mildly.

"Talk!"

"You'd rather fight, I think," Nico observed. "I'd be happy to oblige you, but your control is so thin, I'm not sure if I'd survive it."

"Then you are not as stupid as you look!" I snarled. Closing my eyes for a moment, I pulled myself back under control. "Sorry. That was not called for. You are far from stupid."

"A compliment. Be still my heart."

"You are foolishly brave, foolishly fearless. But not stupid."

"Ouch." The levity left Nico's eyes, and they turned frighteningly somber. "We are almost there. Fifteen more minutes." He'd gone to check with the pilot. "Can you hold on?"

I laughed, a brittle sound, far from pleasant. "Time is a funny thing. The closer you get to something, the longer and farther away it seems. And the harder it is to hold on." My control seemed to be slipping away from me, unraveling before my eyes.

"Would it help to take my blood?"

"Oh, Nico." My voice trembled. "It is blood I want, but not to drink it. Hush," I said, and did not know if I spoke to myself or to him.

I stopped suddenly. Held myself still . . . still. As if I

could quiet the monster within me by not moving. A moment of stillness, of peace, then a great shudder rippled over me, shook me, as if to say: *Enough. Move!*

But I was afraid to . . . So afraid of what I would do if I moved.

A hand touched me, cool, gliding across my warm skin. I felt the light press of a body behind me.

"Can you unleash your energy another way?" Nico asked. His voice was a sensual purr in my ear, his hand asking tacit permission as it skimmed down my arm in a light caress. Me granting it when I did not stop him.

"Sex." I shuddered against him, the animal part of me eager to spring upon that option . . . at anything. Anything at all. "You don't know what you are asking. In this state, it will be as dangerous as violence. I don't know if I will be able to separate the two."

"Do I have a better chance of surviving it?" Nico asked.

I made myself think, concentrate. Gave a jerky nod.

"All right. Then let's do it." He turned me around so that I faced him. He was not tall, only around five eight. But that was still six inches taller than me. I had to tilt my head back to look at him.

"Blood and pain is okay. Speaking of which, I'd better get rid of these." With a quick smile, he shed himself of his borrowed attire. Standing before me unclad, he said, "Okay, love. Let it rip."

I trembled. "Don't say that."

"I mean it." Intelligence and compassion flashed in those beautiful heather gray eyes. "Channel the aggression this way. Pain's okay." He smiled. "Especially if you throw in a little pleasure with it."

He brought my hands up to his chest. Leaned into it so that my sharp fingernails pierced his skin . . . and gasped. With the scent of blood, the sound that he made, my power roared out of me and slammed into him.

So much power. I barely had control of it. Was scarcely able to shape it so that it stroked him with a hard biting pleasure instead of a tearing one. It caressed Nico within and without, plucking the chords of sensation with more force than finesse.

He made a choking sound of pain, of pleasure, as ropes of power bound him and hung him suspended. Lifted him aloft into the air so that my nails raked down his chest, his belly—ah, the sweet release of tearing flesh—leaving behind ribbons of red blood and raw meat.

I fought desperately to control the force flowing from me. It was like a living thing. A thing that wanted to bite and claw and tear into him with mental as well as physical force, devouring his mind as well as his body. *Eat!* it demanded. And it did not care if it was pain or pleasure that it devoured.

I gave into some of its need. I lapped up the blood. Ran my nails in a cutting furrow down his hips, plunged the tips deep into his meaty bottom.

He cried out, arched into me in involuntary reflex, then held himself still.

"No. Struggle," I grated. "Fight me."

He gazed at me for a moment, breathing hard, then did as I asked. He twisted, he kicked. He bucked against the invisible bonds as I spilled more energy out, twining it about him, locking him still. Holding him secure until he called more of his power and broke loose for an instant, rolling in the air. I slapped more invisible ropes around him, and he called up yet more power, concentrating it all on just one spot—a clever trick. Focusing, focusing until that tiny focal point broke, unraveling my restraints so that he could twist and jerk and thrash once more. I threw energy around him, wrapping him again and again as he struggled and broke free, struggled and broke free through that one small point of weakness. He fought me as I had asked him to until his lungs heaved, and his skin grew damp and slick with perspiration and blood.

The urgency in me eased, and the beast in me rumbled with the pleasure of that small battle. Was happy with the helplessness of my victim, in subduing it. But it wanted more. More pain, more blood.

Give him pain, my beast whispered slyly. *Pain, so that he will not crave our touch, become addicted to it.* And for once, my other self was in agreement. *Yes, pain. Pain was good. The lesser of evils.*

I compromised and did as Nico asked—I mixed pleasure in with the pain. I lowered him down until his feet touched the ground, then licked up his body, lapping up his blood that was coppery sweet, with the taste of his sweat a salty tang beneath it. My tongue slid roughly over cut flesh, then into it, probing deep. And the little cries he made were like his taste, salty sweet with hurt and erotic pleasure. I licked up his chest, swirled my tongue around his nipple, bit down on it with pressure light, then not so light. He shuddered against me, his body tense. Groaning, crying, cursing, trying to move. But I held him still with a flex of will. Leaned back and tugged on that small captive bud. Released it when tension finally snapped it free from my grip. Laved that pert nipple, scraped raw and bleeding, unbearably sensitive now.

He cried out, "Lucinda!" as I took it back into my mouth. Worried the little soldier with teeth that had gone slightly sharp.

He began to glow with light.

"Let me touch you," he pleaded, struggling to lift arms I had banded to his sides.

I denied him.

He tried to slip from my bonds, throwing all his power into one spot, his right wrist. It broke free and I grabbed his hand, physically clamped it down. Lowered his body until my face was poised above his.

"No," I whispered, gazing into eyes gone a dark smoky gray, "I like you helpless," and covered his mouth, kissing him hard. His tender lip broke beneath the grinding force of my teeth. Blood spilled into my mouth like red wine, a teasing taste. But it wasn't blood so much as pain that I wanted to drink from him now. With a thought, I twined an invisible hand around the piece of flesh that rose up long and hard between his legs, circled the base of it. Stroked up that lovely shaft with phantom touches. At the same time, I probed the cut I'd made on his upper lip with the tip of my tongue, that tender flesh I had opened, and swallowed down his groans, his sweet moans of blissful torment.

Another invisible caress up and down. Then back up that thick full shaft. A secret phantom lick over the plum-like head as my nails dug deep into the back of his thighs, puncturing flesh. My sharpened teeth sank into his bottom lip, piercing flesh. And below, at the head of his shaft, I speared him with an invisible thrust. Entered him through that single weeping eye that cried out with tears of suffering delight.

Agonizing pleasure rippled through him, was released from him, as if all that digging and probing had unearthed a hidden well, and it spurted now in abundance with his cries. With his blood, semen, and tears.

ELEVEN

THEY ARRIVED IN Berkshire County Airport smelling of blood and sex. At least, Nico did. She was still untouched, unmoved.

His hands itched to touch her, truly touch her. Not just her cloth-covered shoulders and arms, but her bare skin. All that warm satin gold.

The only part of her that had touched Nico had been her sharp digging nails, and her soft luscious mouth so hard against his lips, punishingly hard. But for one sweet moment, they had softened against his . . . before she had bit down hard on his lower lip. Bit through it.

His punctured tissue throbbed; the bite on his neck where she had fed from him before ached. His buttocks and his thighs where she had punctured him deep with her nails just plain hurt. And his chest, belly, entire body was trailed with cuts and scrapes, adorned with ribbons of blood.

Rough sex, some might call it. They would have been wrong. It had not been rough at all, really. Nothing to what she could have done to him had she lost control.

She looked better now. Calm enough to return to her

seat, sit in it, and watch Nico with hooded eyes as he carefully dressed. Power vibrated from her still like a thrumming blanket. But it no longer rode her with edgy spurs. She had poured out enough of it onto him so that she no longer seemed a ticking bomb about to blow.

He had been the one to explode.

The remembered ecstasy was enough to make Nico close his eyes and pull in a deep breath. Sweet Goddess. The pleasure and the pain, twining as one.

She stirred, spoke. "You are free to go, if you wish. To leave me and go your own way. Perhaps it would be better if you did."

Ah. Guilt was prodding her. Nico was coming to know her better. She may look beautiful, cruel, and lush. Oh, so lush. Spilling with curves he wished to run his hands, his mouth, over. But her actions . . . they didn't match the outside packaging. Yes, she was lush. Yes, she was beautiful. She was even cruel and dangerous. But inside, at the core of her, she had a streak of goodness, this demon. Better than any of the queens he had served his long life. A guardian in truth.

"Better for whom?" Nico asked as he finished pulling on his boots. "Not for me, to forgo the protection and safe haven that you offer me. The opportunity to serve. Certainly not for you, before you know if you shall need me or not. Ah . . . I know what it is." He wagged his brows clownishly. "You are worried about your rogue lover seeing the passion marks you scored upon my body."

Unbelievably, she blushed. Then tried to cover it up. "Let's go," she snarled and brushed past him, out the door. Bemused by the unintentional accuracy of his jest, Nico trailed her down the steps onto the tarmac with Talon a silent shadow behind him. The small facility was quiet, the building almost deserted at this time of night. A taxi, called in by the pilot, sat waiting out in front. They slid in and Lucinda gave the driver, an older black man with a lilting Jamaican accent, the address.

"How long is the drive?" Nico asked.

"Not long. Ten minutes," Lucinda said as they pulled away from the curb. She seemed nervous. The energy had revved up a notch in her. She ran a hand through her hair, smoothing it, and fussed with her robe.

Nico grinned at her. She scowled back, stilling her actions. Noticing then the stares the driver kept shooting at them through the rearview mirror. She frowned and remained quiet until they pulled up before a tall apartment building.

The driver turned to face them, and Lucinda caught his eyes and bespelled him, held him to her will. "Why were you looking at us?"

"Because you be all cut up and battered, yet still beautiful. So different," he answered, eyes glazed. "Your skin warm like honey against the man's whiteness. And the young man . . . so black and odd-looking. He not like me. Not from Africa or India or any country I know."

They turned and looked at Talon, studied him. Tried to see him through a human's eyes. The inky skin, a true black darker than the driver's skin. The dark hair long and straight, not curly. Those large ebony eyes. The delicate elfin features on a head too big for a body so small and slender.

Nico said, "The driver is right. Talon looks nothing like him. In fact, doesn't look like any other human I've ever seen. He will draw unwanted curiosity and attention beyond what we already draw in our battered condition."

Talon's small hands reached out and grabbed Nico, revealing what the creature had taken great pains to conceal up until now—sharp, pointy nails like Lucinda's. Only black instead of ivory, and much smaller, like kitten's claws. A mockery of his name: Talon.

"Don't leave me," Talon begged, panic flaring in his eyes.

"We won't leave you, Talon," Nico said. "We just have to disguise you a little. A hat or something."

Lucinda went with the *or something*.

"Hold still," she said and smoothed a hand over Talon's

face. Not touching it but skimming just above the surface, leaving behind a faint shimmer of power in its wake. Where her hand passed, the skin lightened to a dark mocha instead of its former blackness, matching the taxi driver's skin color. Lucinda swept her hand down over Talon's neck and hands, and they lightened in color, also.

"What did you do to me?" Talon asked, frightened now in a different way as he felt the tingling energy left behind on his flesh.

"Lightened your skin until it matches the driver's. A thin coat of illusion. It will only last a few hours."

Finished with Talon, Lucinda passed her hand across Nico's face, disappearing the slash marks. She coated the burns on her wrists with illusion as well, and then slid out of the taxi, waiting until Nico and Talon had disembarked before turning back to the driver.

"You will wait here for us, and you will not remember anything unusual about us." With that command, she released him from her hold.

"We'll return in a few minutes," Lucinda informed the driver, who blinked up at her. "Keep the meter running."

The cabbie nodded. "No problem. I wait."

Lucinda turned and gazed up at the building.

"He's not here," Nico said, his voice flat and leaden like the sudden weight in his stomach.

"He is," Lucinda replied, walking into the building.

"I do not sense him," Nico said, frowning, following her.

"Because I am shielding us. He cannot sense us, we cannot sense him. But the slow heartbeat. You can hear it when I thin the shield. Listen."

Nico stretched his senses, searched for the sound and found it, faint but distinct among the many other beating hearts. Relief weakened his knees and lightened his head for a moment. Thank the Goddess. She still needed him.

The two of them took the stairs to the third floor, and waited impatiently for Talon, who huffed up the three flights almost human slow. One step at a time instead of the four or five steps they encompassed with each leap.

Lucinda stopped before the last door at the end of the hallway, and thinned the cone of silence shielding them once more.

"Stefan," she said softly, "I've returned."

TWELVE

Stefan's heart leaped and he wondered for a terrible instant if he had truly heard the words spoken, or if he were simply dreaming them in his heart-sore yearning. He moved swiftly to the door, sensed nothing beyond it, but that did not mean anything. He opened it, praying: *Goddess, please.* And found his prayer answered.

Lucinda stood there, tawny, golden, petite. Joy rose up within Stefan, then stilled as he became aware of the others behind her. A boy, slender and dark. And a man. A man with her bite mark upon his neck. A human, Stefan thought at first. Then whatever force had been surrounding them came down, and Stefan felt them. Not a human but a Monère warrior. And beneath the warrior's easy affable smile, beneath the cover of his clothes, he smelled of blood and passion . . . and of Lucinda. An emotion foreign and unpleasant welled up within him. It took Stefan a moment to realize what it was. Jealousy.

Unexpectedly, he felt Lucinda as well, an almost thrumming presence. But the dark-skinned boy, Stefan felt him not at all. He was a different creature like Lucinda, without heartbeat.

Like a magnetic needle pulled north, his gaze returned to Lucinda to drink her in. "My lady. Come in, please."

They entered the apartment, and Stefan shut the door.

Hearing their voices, Jonnie hobbled out from the bedroom. Catching sight of them, he stopped and stared, tensing at the sight of the other Monère warrior. "Stefan?" he said in quiet question.

"It's alright, Jonnie. Lucinda has returned," Stefan replied, and the boy's tenseness eased.

"You waited for me," Lucinda said, her eyes upon Stefan.

"As I said I would. Did you come back for us?"

"Yes," she said, and relief and joy soared up within Stefan.

"Who are the others?" he asked.

Her gaze dropped to the floor. "Nico, another warrior. And Talon."

"Are they yours?" Stefan asked.

Her eyes swept back up. "Nico is. Talon is someone lost, someone from my realm that I am returning home."

"And what am I to you?" Stefan asked, driven by that biting jealousy.

"What do you mean?"

"Do I belong to you?"

The smallest hesitation. "Yes, if you still desire it."

"I do."

"Then, yes. You are mine, too."

Stefan's eyes flared bright. He wanted to kiss her, pull her into his arms, feel the soft luxuriant press of her against him, but was constrained by the others present.

"It's a sweet reunion and all," Nico, the strange warrior drawled, amusement in his eyes. "And looking at him, I can see why you were so insistent upon returning here, milady. Yes, sirree, a real beauty. But we need to get moving. You've claimed him, he's accepted. All fine and dandy. I'll take him and Jonnie to your place. We'll be there waiting for you when you return."

"Return? From where?" Stefan demanded.

"From Hell," Nico replied, "where she needs to go before this energy high she's riding stops, and she crashes."

Stefan frowned. "Energy high . . . an appropriate description. Lucinda, why do you feel like this? Why can I sense you so vibrantly?"

Those dark liquid eyes skimmed away from his once more. "I can't explain right now, but Nico's correct. We have to go."

"We?" Nico said, his amusement slipping away.

"I'm flying back with you to my territory."

"Lucinda, no."

"I'm traveling back with you guys." She turned to Stefan and asked him, "Can you pack your clothes and quickly gather what you need?"

Walking to the hallway closet, Stefan took out two backpacks and a long carry bag. "What we need is in here. All else can be replaced. We have been ready to leave ever since you left us."

His eyes met and held Lucinda's. *I prayed that you would come back for me.*

And I did, her eyes conveyed silently back. *I returned for you.*

"Well, that was quickly enough," Nico said dryly. "My lady, I still—"

"Call me Lucinda." It was an order, not a request.

"Lucinda," Nico said. His eyes had lightened to diamond gray. "I swear upon my honor as a Monère warrior . . ." He broke off, his lips twisting. "Well, that can't be too reassuring. Sorry. I forgot for a moment that I am a rogue now, that I have no more honor to lose in another's eyes."

"You are no longer a rogue," Lucinda said. "You are one of my men now."

A rogue, Stefan thought, a poor cast-out soul like himself. And some of that stinging jealousy lessened.

Nico continued, his eyes fierce. "Lucinda, I swear upon all that I hold dear that I shall see these two safely to your territory."

"Nico," Lucinda said gently, "I would see you safe as well before I return to my realm." Leaving the blond warrior speechless for a moment.

Be generous, Stefan told himself, and he tried. But he could not help feeling envious of the easy way they interacted. And of the blatant statement she'd just made—that she cared for Nico, too.

Jonnie shuffled over to a chair and gingerly sat down, his movements slow and careful. To hide his feelings, and because it was something that needed to be done, Stefan set the bags down by the door and brought Jonnie's sneakers to him. He helped Jonnie ease into the shoes, and tied the laces for him. Jonnie flushed with embarrassment beneath the others' scrutiny but made no protest.

"The boy is injured?" the blond warrior asked, frowning.

"He was shot three days ago," Stefan said.

"As were you," Lucinda murmured.

"Is he able to travel?" Nico asked.

Stefan straightened. Met the other warrior's gaze. "He comes with us, even if I have to carry him the entire way."

"I can walk," Jonnie said quietly. "I just have to move slowly."

Nico crouched down before the boy. "Let me see your wound, Jonnie."

The young Mixed Blood glanced up at Stefan.

"I just need to see how badly you were hurt and how much you have healed," Nico said patiently.

At Stefan's slight nod, Jonnie lifted his shirt. There was a neat inch-long incision in front, another two-inch long incision in back.

"Were any organs damaged?" Nico asked.

"Luckily, no," Jonnie replied.

Nico thanked him and straightened, facing his other charge. "I need to see your wounds, too, Stefan."

"It has been three days," Stefan told the other warrior. "There is no need."

"There is every need," Nico returned. His voice was mild but his eyes took on a stubborn diamond-hard cast.

"I must know the condition of those I am to be responsible for."

Stefan's face became cold and shuttered, his voice a brittle warning. "You overstep yourself, warrior. You are not responsible for my care."

"On the contrary," Nico drawled, an inexplicable expression in his light-colored eyes. "That is the only reason I am here—for you and Jonnie. As companion, babysitter, and guard to you both."

"I don't need a babysitter," Jonnie said, his tone flavored with the same coolness that iced Stefan's voice.

Deliberately, Stefan reined in his rising temper. "Your protection of Jonnie would be appreciated," he said as civilly as he could manage. "But I can see to my own safety."

Nico shook his head. "Your reticence makes it even more necessary now for me to see your wound. You are wasting time, Stefan, when every second that passes endangers Lucinda's existence."

Stefan lasered him with a hard look. "What do you mean?"

"I mean that Lucinda could die—the final death—if this energy dissipates while she is still here on Earth. She must be back in her realm before that happens."

"Is that true?" Stefan asked Lucinda.

She nodded, one curt downward gesture.

"Then I must side with Nico. You must go now, my lady. We shall await you in your territory."

Lucinda shook her head. "In the Monères' eyes, you both are still outlaw rogues. I would see you to my province first. You'll be safe there. No one would dare enter without my permission first."

"So much for hoping that you would have more influence over her," Nico muttered, then snapped at Stefan. "Your wound, warrior. Quickly."

Jaw clenched tight, Stefan yanked up his shirt. Lucinda made a small sound of surprise.

Wounds still marred his body. Slowly healing wounds that would take another few days before they were completely healed. A week in total. A week to mend what should have mended in one day, two at the most.

"Why are you not fully healed?" Lucinda asked.

Stefan felt her vibrating presence draw near, and he burned with shame at having his weakness bared so obviously to her.

"It has been a long time since I have been in the company of a queen. I heal slower now."

"How long since you last Basked?" Nico asked, coming directly to the point.

Stefan damned the other warrior's perception.

"So long that I no longer remember what it feels like. Over twenty years," Stefan said. "And you?"

"Two months."

Two months to twenty years. Another reason to resent the other rogue. Because Nico was stronger than him in this way, a better protector. And for that reason—for Jonnie—Stefan swallowed down his antipathy. But the fear remained. Fear that Lucinda would no longer want him. She was beside him now, but he dared not look at her, dreading what he might see in her eyes.

"Not Basking for so long affects the speed with which you heal," Lucinda murmured with sudden comprehension, "as well as how quickly you age."

Stefan nodded. He kept his gaze averted, even when he felt her hand whisper lightly over his entry and exit wounds; stood frozen as she lifted her hand, shifted through his hair, and then stilled. And he knew what she had discovered—a white hair. Only two or three scattered among the blackness. But with time, a time that passed by more quickly than it used to, there would be more.

"How old are you?" Lucinda asked.

"I am a hundred and forty-five years old."

"White hair should not have appeared until you reached two hundred years of age," she said.

"The price for leaving my Queen. Without Basking, I age as humans do now. My twenty years spent here are as if sixty Monère years have passed instead, bringing my true biological age to two hundred and five. I am fast becoming an old man, with only ninety-five more Monère years to live."

A Monère's average life span was three hundred years. But that was for others, not for those who fled their queen.

"Which, in human terms, means only thirty more years left to serve you. Do you still want me?" Stefan asked, his face tight, expressionless.

Lucinda laid a gentle hand against his jaw, the light touch at odds with the coiled vibrancy he felt emanating from her. She turned his face down until his eyes met hers and he felt as if he were drowning in those rich chocolate depths. To his surprise, they were filled not with pity, but with a hard mocking light.

"At two hundred, you are a warrior in your prime. But even had you only one more year left, I would still want you." The mockery he glimpsed in her eyes deepened. "But since you bring up age, you should know mine. I've been demon dead over six hundred years."

Jonnie gasped.

Stefan felt a little shocked at the revelation himself.

She continued in that soft, languid drawl. "Is that too old for you, Stefan?"

"No." He answered without hesitation.

She smiled, stroked his jaw once more—so vibrant that touch—before lifting her hand and the feather-light graze of her nails away. "Then do not talk anymore of age. Let us be on our way."

THIRTEEN

AGE, WE DID not speak of anymore. But think of it, I
still did, as we walked down the corridor, silent but for
Jonnie's limping shuffle. Instead of heading for the stair-
well as I would normally have done, I walked to the elevator and pressed the button, waited for the slow mechanical
lift to ascend to our level. Talon was a silent shadow by my
side, a mocha-colored shadow now instead of jet black. The
boy, Jonnie, walked alone, grim, resolute, unaided, hobbling
slowly behind Stefan who carried both backpacks, one slung
over each shoulder, and the long bag in his left hand. Nico,
with both his hands free, brought up the rear.

Men and their pride, I tsked silently. I hadn't realized
it started so young. Such a heavy, awkward, and unnecessary burden they made it. I strode back to Jonnie, slid my
arm through his, and gave him the aid he would not have
accepted from the others. "Give an old lady a hand, will
you, darling. Perhaps your youth can prop up my decrepi-
tude."

Jonnie laughed then gasped. "Ouch. Laughing's not
good. Pulls on my stitches."

"Sorry," I murmured, discreetly supporting some of his weight.

Jonnie accepted the aid with a rueful smile. "You may be old," he said, "but you're far from decrepit."

"A most gallant defender." I smiled. He was sweet and refreshing. And had absolutely no fear of me, from the time he had opened his eyes and first seen me beside him in the hospital. But then, he'd had no knowledge of what I was. So young, I thought with a pang, feeling his youth, his reedy slenderness beside me. And he had nearly died. Life truly was not fair, oft taking the innocent, and leaving behind the wicked and undeserving, such as I.

The elevator pinged its arrival, and we all moved into the cramped confining space—one of the reasons why I hated these things so much. It left one feeling trapped, with little room to maneuver in a fight.

"When were you released from the hospital?" I asked as the doors closed, locking us in and starting its slow ponderous descent. Talk about old and decrepit. This elevator surely fit that description.

"They discharged me this morning."

I glanced up at Stefan, standing beside us. "You ventured out into the sun?"

Stefan nodded. "For a short time, to bring Jonnie back from the hospital. It did not bother me much."

The Monère were creatures of the night. The sun was their enemy; it burned their skin. Not right away. But an hour under its rays painted them with a visible redness. Four hours and the damage it rendered to a cold-blooded Monère were grotesque and life threatening. Stefan's skin was still perfect white, but it bothered me to think of him venturing out in the daylight, alone and vulnerable, no one to come to his aid should he need help. And he had been doing so for over twenty years.

"Stefan sometimes comes to my daytime games, even though I tell him not to," Jonnie said. "I play football."

"I enjoy watching you play," Stefan said. "And standing

beneath shade with hat, sunglasses, and thick cloth covering my skin, I hardly feel the sun's rays."

The last was a blatant lie. Old as I was, I still remembered the stinging bite of the sun across my skin. When the brightness of the sun touched you, it was as if fire ants were tearing off little bits of your flesh. You could withstand the rays for a time without visible damage, but the discomfort . . . that was always present.

Still, I did not contradict him as the elevator groaned and shuddered to a halt, and the doors finally opened once again.

The taxi was still waiting for us.

"Where are we going?" Stefan asked when I directed Jonnie toward the waiting cab.

"To the county airport."

"I know where that is," Stefan said. "I can drive us there."

That surprised me so much that I stopped and stared up at him. "You drive? A car?"

"Why does that surprise you?" Stefan asked, a smile brightening his beautiful face.

"Most Monères do not drive."

"I have lived among humans for some time. It is a skill I had to learn."

"You have a car?"

He nodded.

"We can only take it as far as the airport. You will have to leave it behind," I said, regretfully.

"That was my understanding. As I said, all other things can be replaced." Then he added, whisper soft, "All but you."

I blushed. I actually blushed. And marveled at the ability of this man to fluster me so. To make me feel things I had not felt for so long a time, if ever: vulnerable, nervous . . . shy.

Men did not usually treat me this way. I'd always been desirable, but not precious. They lusted after me. They did not treat me with gallantry and sincerity.

Nico spoke from behind, jerking our eyes apart. "Can we save this until later? Time, boys and girl. Time is ticking."

"Shove it, Nico." Slapping a twenty-dollar bill into his hand, I told him, "Pay the driver and send him on his way."

"Yes, ma'am."

My brow arched. "Ma'am?"

"I may not be able to drive a car . . . yet. But I can sure talk like a human," Nico said, and sauntered off to pay the driver.

The yellow cab sped off.

"No change?" I asked when Nico returned, empty handed.

"Change? I thought you meant to give the rest as tip?"

"Maybe two dollars as tip. Not ten dollars, the same amount as the fare," I said, shaking my head.

Another thing Monères usually didn't have much concept of—money. But why should they? They didn't use it. Power and sex were their usual currency.

"Another thing I'll have to learn about," Nico said ruefully. "Money."

"I'm surprised you haven't learned about it already. How did you manage to live while on the run? You seemed quite comfortable when I found you. Well cared for by your ladies. Or perhaps," I drawled, "I just answered my own question."

"They were my companions. You are my lady," Nico declared with that loopy smile once again on his face. "I had an arrangement with the owner of Smoky Jim's after I stopped a brawl the first night I was there. He provided me with a bed to sleep in and food to eat. In return I prevented his drunk and disorderly human patrons from fighting each other. A peacekeeper." He grinned. "An odd role for an outlaw rogue to play. But I distract myself. Time," he said, and made a shooing forward motion with his hands.

"The role of nanny also seems to come naturally to you," I observed dryly.

"There are many roles I would wish to play with you." He leered, wagging his brows outrageously. "But not now. Maybe when you return."

I rolled my eyes at Nico's silliness.

"My car is parked at the corner," Stefan said gruffly, pointing to a small SUV, a blue Ford Escape. A newer model, not more than one or two years old, I saw as I helped Jonnie into the front seat. Nico and Talon slid into the back, and I squeezed in next to them.

Stefan started the car and pulled onto the road, driving smoothly, with confidence. *Like the way he makes love*, the thought whispered in my mind. And my beast rose up within me, stirred restlessly, as the memory of those elegant white hands gripping me as firmly as he gripped the steering wheel now washed over me, heating me. *Not now*, I told it firmly. And not like this, when my beast was too much a part of me.

It snarled with displeasure. Raked me with its sharp claws, so that I shifted in my seat, bumped against Nico. He shivered slightly as my skin brushed against his. The beast liked him, too. He carried our scent, our marks upon his body, and smelled sweetly of hot blood and tender flesh. It wanted to play with him again, and stretched eagerly within me, pushing out.

No, I told it. *Not here. Not now.*

Yes, it urged. *Pain. Blood. Hungry!*

Never had the monster in me been so powerful, so dominant. So vibrant and strong, barely leashed under my control. Almost like a distinct and separate personality.

I glanced at the reason why I felt this way, so wild, so full of energy, so alive. Talon met my gaze. He looked at me with both fear and wary hope, huddled against the side of the door, with Nico between us.

I tried to imagine how it must be like for him, going away with people who were strangers to him, all but Nico. Leaving behind all that he had known, all that was, if not comfortable, then at least familiar. I tried to see him as a person, but my beast saw him only as food. Food and prey, stinking of fear.

My mouth watered and my teeth sharpened into elongated points at the remembered flavor of that one small taste of him . . . piquant, bursting with sweet and pungent flavor. Like a waterfall of life. Flower of Darkness. Flower of Life—another thing they were called, and why they were hunted. For the way they made us feel. Sweet Mother, how they made us feel. I'd never known.

Like a giant invisible paw, the power within me flared out toward Talon, reaching for him. *More*, it said with hungry greed. *Give me more. More blood. More power.*

I stopped it just before it reached him, barely, just barely, straining with the effort it cost me to hold those invisible reins. A taut leash pulled so tight, so real, it actually shifted me toward Talon, pushing me up against Nico. Trying to shift us both nearer.

My vision doubled and I suddenly saw with eyes that were separate from my own. Eyes that viewed Talon clearly, closely. So close to him. Not from the other side of the seat where I sat, but from inches away. Had I a heartbeat, it would have stuttered in fear.

"Mother of Darkness, what is that?" Nico whispered. But I could not answer him. I was too busy fighting myself.

Let me live! my beast demanded, straining, tugging, an invisible shimmering thing stretching out from me, trying to close those scant few inches separating it from Talon. And I knew what it thought, what it believed—that with one more drink, one more deep gulp of that bursting, flavorful blood, it would fully be. Not a part of me anymore, but a separate existing entity.

No! I cried out in my mind, yanking it back ruthlessly, with almost desperate mental effort. *Why are you fighting me? You have never opposed me like this before.*

Because we were oft in agreement before: survival, drinking blood. But now you hold me back. Blood! it demanded. *His blood.*

No! I answered.

Then his pleasure.

No! I shook my head, slowly, inexorably dragging it back into me.

His pain.

No!

It snarled, bared its sharp teeth at me, and jumped back into me with a reverberating force that shoved me back hard against the door.

"Why were you saying no?" Stefan asked, glancing back at me, making me realize that I had spoken aloud.

My body jerked and I gasped as punishing claws tore me up inside. "Stop the car."

"Why?"

"I can't stay. I have to leave you and go back to my realm now."

The car pulled to the side of the road.

Unseen claws slashed inside me again with roaring outrage, making me cry out in pain. A trickle of actual blood spilled out from the corner of my mouth. I wiped it away with a sort of stunned horror, swallowed the rest of the blood down, and sprang out of the car.

I tumbled to the ground, shockingly weak.

"What's wrong?" Stefan asked, coming around the car, reaching for me.

"No. Don't touch me!" I screamed, scuttling back away from him as the beast stopped raking me inside and turned its eager attention toward Stefan. *Food, sex, blood* it thought.

Stefan reached for me again.

"No," I said wildly, shaking my head. "Stay away."

It was Nico who stopped him. Nico who physically hauled Stefan several yards back away from me before Stefan furiously broke free of his hold.

"Easy, lover boy," Nico said. "Listen to her. Keep back. You'll only make it worse for her if you don't."

"What's wrong with her?" Stefan demanded.

"I believe she's having a difficult time controlling her beast. Am I right, Lucinda?"

"Oh, yeah." I half sobbed, half laughed.

"It wants you, it wants me," Nico said. "But it really wants Talon."

Moving slowly, painfully, like the old lady I truly was, I

crawled to my feet and stood listing in the wind, feeling as if I were teetering on an invisible precipice.

"Lucinda," Stefan said, drawing my attention. And the sight of him, hair raven black, skin white and tender, lips a lovely red like the blood that flowed within him, that beating call pounding so strongly in my ear . . . both parts of me wanted him, my beast and I.

I swayed toward him, almost took a step before jerking back, stumbling away. I lost my balance and fell to the ground again.

"Lucinda, why are you so weak when I can still feel the power emanating from you?" Stefan asked, his hazel eyes dark with distress.

"It's fighting me," I whispered. "And it's so frighteningly strong. Leave me now. Go to my province, you'll be safe there. I'll return in a few days when I am better. When I am more myself."

Worry tightened Stefan's voice. "Let us see you first to your portal, or at least closer to it. Is there even one in this area?"

I gathered myself, flung my senses out, searching. Felt a distant echo far, far away. Brushed up against a weaker sensation, closer, only miles distant. "Yes. There is something I can use, not too far."

I didn't try to search Talon out in the car, didn't want my beast to see him, to focus on him again. But I knew that he was listening, that he could hear me. "I can't take you with me now, Talon, I'm sorry. I'll return when I'm more in control of myself. I'll take you back home then."

"Yes, mistress," came Talon's soft reply. My beast turned its eyes in the direction of that melodious, disembodied voice. I yanked it back.

"Go," I said to Stefan, to Nico, my control thin and desperate. "If you wish to serve me, do as I bid and leave me now. I will be stronger when you leave. My beast will stop fighting me when you are no longer so temptingly near."

"My lady." From the corner of my eye, I saw Stefan bow

deep, his face bleak and unhappy. "We will wait for you in your home. Come back to us soon."

"I will," I said. "I will."

When the car pulled away and drove off, when their heartbeats grew fainter, distant, I got to my feet. I was not conflicted anymore. My prey had left. I smiled grimly as the other half of me clicked with snarling submissiveness back into place, my two halves whole once again.

I entered the woods that flowed along the road and headed east toward that faint spark I had felt. With that abundant, overflowing strength unified within me once more, I ran in the forest, swift and silent, a soundless blur of motion. I journeyed in solitude, alone and yet not alone, surrounded by life—animals foraging, hunting others, being hunted themselves, the natural cycle of life and of death. I passed by them undetected, disturbing little, what I had done for so many long years. Touching little. Touched little in turn. But now it had all changed, and my existence was richer, filled with more purpose and meaning. All the things that had seemed petty and trivial before, now called out to me. Life.

I wanted to live. To exist plentifully.

It had not mattered before. I had survived for so long, and time had seemed so endless and relentless. Alone, always alone. Numbed I was, but no longer. How ironic that now when I was beginning to tingle for life, I was faced with the prospect of final death.

I had not lied, exactly, but I had not told them the entire truth. You could not tell how long an energy boost like this lasted. It could go for several moonrises, or it could peter out in hours. I'd been gambling. I had wanted to see them safely back to my haven before I left them. But my beast had taken the choice away from me, knowingly or un-knowingly, I was not sure. It was a cunning thing, that side of me. Perhaps it had been aware of the risk I ran and had taken the choice from me. If so, it had only presented me with an even greater peril.

The faint spark grew stronger as I neared the site, an

old Indian burial ground. So old that no tombstones, no markers, no signs of life or of death existed. It was as if the land here had been untouched.

The pull in the ground said otherwise. Bones lay rotting beneath the rich fertile earth here. Blood left its lasting stain. And not just human blood, but traces of Monère blood mixed in with it. I was demon dead. And I was called by that which was dead. Called most strongly by the blood of what I had once been—Monère.

This had once been the burial ground for chiefs or shamans. More than one lay here. Half a dozen, at least, by the pull I felt. A few had made the transition to demon dead, leaving a faint bridge, a connection, behind. Not exactly a portal. Oh no, much less sure and secure a way than that. But it was a path home if one had enough strength and power to follow those tenuous threads. And if one were desperate enough, left no other choice.

I gave a harsh bark of laughter. It disturbed a few birds and they squawked indignantly away. *Get used to it,* I wanted to shout at them. *I am no longer going to skim over life, but actually try to live it now.* But I did not do anything so foolish, because I did not know yet if I had that option. And yelling something aloud like that was foolishly tempting fate. As if to say: *Nah nah nah. Come and get me.* Now, when I cared, it probably would. The irony of life.

The beast inside me balked for a moment, fighting me as I stepped atop those forgotten buried bones. *Madness*, it cried.

Our only choice, I insisted. And because it was, it relented.

I stretched out my hand, and didn't let my power flow so much as unspool toward that spark, building that faint bridge between the realms of life and death. A delicate process of growing that connection stronger, of channeling part of my abundant energy into it until a crack, a seam, was called forth—a hazy line that shimmered white, just barely visible.

I thought that the seam of Other I had called forth was

what I sensed. Too late I realized my mistake. Too late, after I felt something hit me in the back and splatter liquid wet across my cloak, soak into the cloth. The moment it touched my skin, it was as if an invisible cloud began to leisurely engulf me.

Oil of Fibara. A liquid that acted upon a demon much like silver did when placed against a Monère's skin. It shut off my senses slowly, bit by bit, relentlessly draining my strength, so that the shimmering seam I had called into view dimmed noticeably in brightness, much like what was happening to me. In a moment, it would be gone, and so would I. Not right away. But once that bridge was gone, I too would soon just fade away.

"I should have let you try it," said a voice behind me. A deep, familiar voice filled with amusement, disbelief, and sadness. It was the latter that had my stomach clenching as I whirled around too late, and found myself facing another demon. Black handcuffs dangled from his hand. "But I cannot risk even that small chance of you returning."

"Derek," I said, not in greeting but in acknowledgment of an opponent who had just struck me a fatal blow. I sounded calm, but inside my world tumbled because he had to be the demon who had stolen Talon to this realm.

He was not just a mere demon, but a former guardian who had betrayed his oath.

And he had just as good as killed me.

FOURTEEN

THE ATMOSPHERE IN the car was far from happy. In
fact, the farther they drove, the grimmer the air felt.

"I'm going back," Stefan said. He braked and made a
U-turn on the empty road, glaring at Nico through the
rearview mirror as if expecting him to protest.

"I won't argue with that," Nico said mildly. "It's a good
idea." But his agreement did not seem to make Stefan any
happier.

"I won't go after her," Stefan said, casting another grim
look his way. The old warrior's face was set in harsh lines,
yet still he managed to look exquisite, like a dark dour angel. "I just want to ensure that Lucinda is on her way. Not
lying there, weak and helpless."

But Nico was no longer concentrating on the words.
Because in Stefan's eyes smoldered not just unhappy frustration, but a tinge of something darker and most unexpected. Something that took Nico completely by surprise.
Jealousy. The ridiculousness of it washed deliciously over
Nico for a moment before he leaned forward and put the
old chap out of his misery.

"There is no reason to resent me," Nico said. "You have her heart."

Their eyes met in the mirror.

"She seems to care for you, as well," Stefan said.

"Felt sorry for me, is more the case," Nico said with a twisting smile. "Our Lucinda is far more compassionate than she would have others know."

Another searing look from Stefan at Nico's unknowing slip of tongue—*our Lucinda*. A possessive term he had unconsciously used. Nico sighed, and set about soothing ruffled feathers once more. "Do not fear. She is more yours than mine. I concede that readily."

"Why are you trying to be nice to me?" Stefan demanded.

"Because everything she has done, including claiming me, she has done for you. You have her heart, you stupid rogue."

"You said that before. And yet her bite mark is on you and on Talon. Why did she feed from the both of you when she refused to feed on me?"

So that was the cause of his jealousy. A little smile danced along Nico's lips at the role he found himself playing. He had never had to be the perceptive one before. "After you were wounded?"

Stefan nodded.

"And had lost a lot of blood?"

Stefan nodded again.

"Then the reason for her refusing the bounty of your blood was simply the lack of it at that time," Nico said with simple deduction.

"Why are you smiling?" Stefan asked, a dangerous glint in his eyes, his fingers wound tightly around the steering wheel. Obviously Nico wasn't doing too good a job of soothing and reassuring him.

"Because I should be the one jealous, not you. Wake up," Nico snapped. "She's halfway in love with you, if not flat-out all the way head over heels wading in the syrupy, sticky emotion by now."

Stefan looked shaken. "Do you think so?"

"Yes," Nico said, his turn to look unhappy. "She came back for you at great risk to herself. To claim you."

"She claimed you, too."

Stubborn ass. "To free me from my Queen. Then she was more than willing to toss me back out again. She offered me my 'freedom,' if that's what you call it, to roam the world on my own, or to reside in the safety of her province but not in her home. She gave me the option of protection without really belonging to her. Talon can verify the truth of that."

"Is that true, Talon?" Stefan asked.

"Yes," came the creature's soft reply.

"If you had not been here waiting for her, she would have cut me loose because she would have had no need for me then. My presence, my purpose, is solely to serve as brother companion and fellow guard to you and the boy."

"How do you know?"

"Because she told me!"

That took Stefan aback. "She did?"

"Yes. Why is that so hard to believe?" *Jackass. Idiot.* The words were not said, but they hung in the air.

Stefan's jaw clenched. "She is at ease around you, but stiff and uncomfortable around me."

Nico sighed. *Unbelievable,* he thought. "You have been around humans much longer than I. Do you not know that when a woman acts like that, it means she is attracted to you?"

"I think Stefan has a hard time applying such human behavior to Lucinda," Jonnie said from the passenger seat, startling Nico. He'd almost forgotten he was there, so quiet had the lad been.

"Why?" Nico asked. "Because she is demon dead?"

Jonnie nodded. "And before then, Monère."

"And not just Monère, but a queen," Stefan said quietly.

Nico whistled. "A queen . . ."

"And Monère Queens do not act shy and awkward around their men," Stefan said.

"How do they act?" Jonnie asked.

"Certainly not shy," Nico said dryly. "Arrogant, assured, entitled. But . . . and an important *but* here . . . Lucinda is no longer a Monère Queen. Has not been so for a very long time. And my impression is that she has been alone for most of that time. I doubt if she has ever claimed anyone before, not since becoming demon dead." Nico let Stefan chew over that for a moment. "I am no threat to you. I am not even close to becoming one."

"What do you mean?"

So many questions the other warrior had. "You are comely, fair of face, with a wondrous beauty that others would die for. I am not even handsome. Granted, I have my own charm." Nico smiled, thinking fondly of his lovely human companions and the flattering boost they had given his ego. "But looks-wise, you and I are in completely different classes—the reason why I was with Mona SiGuri and lasted with her so long. That is a Queen who only surrounds herself with people less attractive than herself. You . . ." Nico smiled with sardonic sharpness. "You, with your breathtaking loveliness, would not have lasted in her court for even a fortnight before she killed you."

"Looks may not matter with a demon," Stefan said. "Perhaps only power does, and you and I are both of equal power."

Mentally, Nico threw up his hands. "I give up. Nothing I say or do is going to convince you. Is it? Okay, I concede defeat. You don't have to like me. We don't have to be bosom buddies. You just have to tolerate me and let me do my job."

"How long were you among the humans?" Stefan asked.

"Just over a month's time."

"You picked up quickly their way of speaking."

"From watching lots of TV and from spending all my time with them. A delightful people."

"Some of them," Stefan agreed.

"The women certainly were." Nico grinned.

"You were with human women?" Jonnie said with surprise. "Stefan was never attracted to any of them."

"Ah, so that's what it is," Nico said, suddenly enlightened. "You have been over twenty years out of practice. Don't worry, old chap. It'll come quickly back to you. Like picking up a sword again." He slapped Stefan on the shoulder with good cheer. Stefan, on the other hand, looked like he wanted to gnash his teeth. Or maybe rip off Nico's hand.

"We're here," Stefan said. The car slowed, pulled to a bumpy halt along the side of the road, and they got out.

"I think this is where we left her," Stefan said, walking to a patch of flattened grass and kneeling beside it. "I smell the faint scent of her blood here, where it dripped from her mouth."

"Well, she's obviously not here," Nico said with relief. "She should be fine."

"No," said a quiet voice behind them. "She's not."

Stefan spun around, raven hair flying, to find Talon crouched beside him. He had gotten soft living among the humans, used to their easy detection. It unsettled Stefan greatly to have this creature be able to glide right up to him like that, without his awareness—no sound, no heartbeat, no presence. And so odd looking, the dark creature was, not just disproportionately short as if his growth had been stunted, but something even more than that. Something with the eyes. They were odd, different.

"What do you mean?" Stefan asked. "What do you sense that I do not?"

"Another demon was here. *He* was here." The shivering increased, shaking Talon's body almost violently.

"He?" Stefan said, not so much a question as a demand.

"He means the demon that brought him to this realm," Nico said, his voice sober, almost hushed. "That continued to drink his blood. The demon that called himself Horace, though I doubt that was his real name."

"Then Lucinda is in danger," Stefan said.

"Yes," said Nico, all his amicability falling away, leaving a hardened warrior in its place, eyes cold and resolute.

A fellow brother with the same goal—the need to protect their lady.

"How the Darkness did he find her?" Stefan asked.

"Mona SiGuri must have warned him. And he must have tracked us here, followed us somehow."

"We have to help her," Stefan said.

They sent their senses flaring out. Picked up nothing but the scent of those few drops of her blood that had wet the ground.

"Anything?" Stefan asked.

Nico looked uncharacteristically grim. "No. You?"

Stefan shook his head.

As one, their eyes turned to fix upon Talon.

"Can you track her, Talon?" Nico asked.

"No," Talon answered, "but I can sense *him*. He headed that way." He pointed east.

Stefan loped back to the car and returned with sword in hand, and a gun holstered at his side.

"A gun? How human," Nico said. The Monère warrior in him wanted to sneer, but the sensible rogue that he'd been forced to become was envious of the efficient little weapon. All he had were his daggers.

"And practical. Let's go," Stefan said sharply. But Talon stayed crouched on the ground, unmoving but for the wild tremors that shook him. He looked a delicate thing, frozen by fear. Panic flared his eyes round, and only then did Stefan realize what was odd about those almond eyes. There were no whites. Just the blackness of his pupils, and the same continuity of color extending to his irises and beyond. A sea of ebony darkness.

Nico knelt beside Talon, gently clasped a slim shoulder. "Talon, I know you are scared of the demon, but if we do not help Lucinda, he will kill her. And then he will kill us, the only other witnesses, the only ones who know you exist, and take you back as a captive, putting you back under Mona SiGuri's care once more." Although *care* was perhaps too kind a word. "Our only chance . . . *your* only chance is if you lead us to them now, before it is too late. Lucinda is our only hope."

"And if we are too late?" Talon asked. "If he has killed her already?"

"Then we are all doomed."

Talon looked up. Met Nico's eyes. "That's what I always liked about you, Nico. You tell the truth, no matter how unpleasant it is." Oddly adult words, coming from so young a voice and face.

The shaking eased, disappeared, and the slight creature stood, his eerie eyes going distant as he sensed with that part of him what the others could not sense. "This way," Talon said, and loped off into the woods, Nico right behind him.

"Stay in the car. Lock the doors," Stefan told Jonnie, this young man he had raised like his own son. "If we don't return in an hour, drive away. Don't go to the airport, they may be waiting for us there. Just leave this place and keep driving. Promise me."

Eyes somber, Jonnie gave his word.

Stefan took off after the other two, trailing after Nico's heartbeat.

FIFTEEN

D EREK WAS ONE of the older guardians. One that had served as such for over two centuries before he had retired coincidentally enough a little over two decades ago. A formidable guardian I had respected, if not entirely liked. But now I realized he had simply been serving himself more than others.

"I'm sorry," Derek said. Real regret shone in his eyes. "I always liked you."

"Funny," I drawled. "I was just thinking the opposite. I never liked you."

He smiled, looking the way a hero should look, tall, with noble brow and wise deep-set eyes the color and clarity of the Caribbean Sea when the sun shone brilliantly down into its depths. A handsome facade covering a treacherous spirit.

Derek's eyes drifted over me. "I used to look up to you, almost worship you when I first became a guardian. All of us did. The beautiful huntress, the golden princess. You were a legend among us, lasting so long."

"But no longer," I said. "You just saw to that."

He dipped his head in acknowledgment. "You should not have taken what was mine."

"You know as well as I that a Floradëur belongs to no one it does not willingly choose."

"An old law that is as archaic and outdated as the High Lord."

"You have broken some of our most sacred edicts by bringing Talon here among the Monère. Broken a few more by keeping him against his will and taking his blood as you have so done."

"But that is the whole point . . . as I have so done. And will continue to do for a long, long time to come. Long after you will have gone. You cannot begin to imagine what I will do with the power he gives me." He smiled handsomely, evilly. The smile widened as he tilted his head slightly, as if he heard something. "Unbelievable. They come to me like a bird to hand, saving me the trouble of going after them."

My muffled senses picked up then what Derek had already discerned. Two slow heartbeats.

"Your men that you claimed as your own." Derek shook his head. "The utter gall of royalty, taking things for themselves then telling other demons all the things they cannot have."

"The difference that you cannot seem to grasp, Derek, is that I gave them a choice. They are willing. Talon is not."

"Willing or not, I will take and hold what you claimed but cannot keep. Talon. Not your men. Their existence I will have to extinguish, unfortunately. But do not worry." He smiled with chilling coolness. "You will join them in the great Darkness soon enough."

I struck then, gathering the remnants of my quickly waning strength, using up the last reserves of that buoyant energy boosted by Talon's blood, unleashing my beast, brutally pulling upon that final reservoir of power. In a blink of time, with a ruthless willing, I gathered that strength, gathered it all, and let it fly from me like an invisible hand of power. One narrow shaft of brilliant force that vibrated the air, sang through it, and struck Derek across the neck with a blow as sure and true as if I had physically leaped the distance and hit him. His spine snapped with an audible crack, and both of us dropped to the ground. Me like a puppet with its strings suddenly severed, and that was how I felt—completely without power, without strength. He, with both hands clutching his head, trying to hold it steady atop his broken neck.

"Bitch," he gasped and then laughed maniacally. "You always were a crazy, unpredictable demon bitch. Thought you'd try for the bridge. Not for me."

"Run," I said, looking up at him as I lay there on the ground, utterly helpless, unable to move, the sound of my men running swiftly toward us, the beating of their hearts loud in my ear. "Run before my men arrive and finish what I started."

He staggered to his feet, clutching his lolling head. "I will be the one to finish things, demon bitch. I will have all the time in Hell to come back and finish things. You only just delayed their deaths. I'll be back, rest assured of that. May you rot in Darkness and never find peace." With that last hurling curse, he ran awkwardly away, his head wobbling grotesquely back and forth over its loosened base as he fled into the woods.

Moments later my men spilled into the small clearing, led surprisingly by Talon. The slender creature moved with the quiet grace and quickness of a natural child of that other realm. A realm that I would not see again. Funny, now that I knew I'd never go back, that was when I actually missed it. Such contrarian creatures we were.

Those wholly black eyes gazed for a second where Derek had fled, then turned and fixed unerringly to where I lay on the ground, a splash of maroon and gold against the leaf-strewn forest ground. I knew that he had found me not by sight but by feel—that awareness of Other, of like and yet not alike that creatures from Hell sensed in one another. Different than what we felt from a Monère. But faint . . . how faint it must be to him now. Faint because I knew I was starting to wane, beginning to grow insubstantial. Beginning to ghost. But at the sight of Talon, at the visual reminder of this poor misplaced creature from Hell, I rallied. Tried to fight what was slowly taking me over, breaking me apart, dissolving me.

Him, perhaps, we could still see home. And the men behind them . . . my men. My duty to them rested heavily upon me, making me strive to try and speak, to open my mouth and push out words, even though the oil's smothering blanket covered me completely now, so that everything seemed muted, dimmed. My demon senses, my demon strength, were completely cut off, leaving just primitive basic ability behind. So that even though I still saw, still heard, could still sense through touch, compared to the way my senses had soared before, it was as if I were blind and deaf and amputated, with only stumps left behind. A feeling of claustrophobia made me gasp in air. A silly thing to do when I didn't need to breathe. I was dead. And now I was dying once more. Had, in fact, willingly chosen that course.

I'd used the final remnants of my strength to strike a disabling blow to Derek instead of making a desperate attempt for the fading bridge with the last of my power. For what reason? It was hard to remember now.

Memory was jostled when Stefan and Nico spilt to the ground beside me, their faces grim with anguish and fear.

A shiver rippled my skin. One and then another, a continuous nonstop flow of coldness as it settled its icy fingers into me.

"Lucinda! You're shaking," Stefan said, lifting me onto his lap, cradling me. "Foolish woman," he said, tears shining his eyes. "You should have tried to save yourself. Not us."

It was surprisingly hard for me to speak. "You heard."

"Yes."

"Lucinda, are you hurt?" Nico ran his hands carefully over me, finding no blood, just the wetness on my back.

Ah, yes. My men. My dark and beautiful Stefan, so lovely that even now, racked by shudders, it moved something in me just to gaze upon him. And rugged, fair Nico whose careless facade hid a shrewd intelligence, a kind heart, and a stubbornness that put a donkey to shame. I still had a duty to them.

I opened my mouth. Spoke. Although the words that came out were really more of a whisper. "Go to . . . High Council."

And faint though my voice was, I knew they heard me because Stefan's porcelain white face blanched even paler. High Council. Words that struck fear into a rogue's heart. I almost smiled but didn't have the strength for it. The few threads of fading power I clung to were fast slipping from my grasp. I pushed more words out of me before the strands unraveled completely. Important words. Essential words.

"Tell . . . Queen Mother . . . you are mine. My brother will protect you . . . and see to Talon."

"Your brother?" Nico said.

The almost convulsive shaking was easing, lessening. And in its place seeped coldness so pervasive, so deep, it almost seemed to freeze my thoughts, my words.

"Lucinda, what's wrong?" Stefan demanded, hugging me tightly to him, running his hands up and down my arms as if to warm me. It was a measure of how low my temperature had dropped that his cool skin felt warm against me now.

"She's ghosting," Talon said, his face closed, inscrutable, completely still. His shivering disappeared as mine grew more violent.

What was it that I needed to say? . . . Words . . . Oh yes. Just a few more. I pushed them out. "Brother . . . Halcyon."

"Your brother is Prince Halcyon?" It was Nico's turn to whiten, for his voice to grow faint. "The High Prince of Hell?"

One last shaking shudder, and the shivering stopped completely. Somehow I was able to smile. "Yes."

The shocked look on their faces squeezed more words out of me. "Don't worry . . . nice. Tell him . . . Derek . . . demon who brought Talon here." Then the last of my energy slipped from my grasp, and I felt myself drifting away and did not fight it.

"Lucinda." The look in Stefan's eyes wrenched something deep inside me, kept me holding on a moment longer.

"Don't leave me," he whispered, his voice raw and terrible.

I made an enormous effort. Lifted my hand and touched his dear face one last time. His skin . . . I was barely able to feel it. And my hand was faint, transparent. I could see through it.

One more word. "Sorry." And with that touch, that one last feel of him, I closed my eyes and dropped my hand. Released my will and let it slip free.

SIXTEEN

TALON HAD BEEN afraid all his life. He'd lived it, existed with it. Even in his dreams, he could not escape it for it followed him, surrounded him even there. Others had taunted his stunted growth by saying that fear had beaten him down. And they were right. He was a coward. Since a child, all that motivated Talon was avoidance of his Queen's anger. And that of the demon that visited him every season or two to drink his blood. Who beat Talon until he drank the demon's noxious blood in turn. Who tried each and every time to force Talon to bond with him. The demon that Talon was both drawn to and repelled by.

At one time, Talon had thought the demon his father. Even with their skin color so unalike, the demon was the only one similar to him with no betraying sound beating within him, moving his body. Only with the demon had Talon felt that almost thrilling, tingling awareness, a presence unlike any other. Like a burn that did not hurt. But now Talon knew it not to be true, not to be unique. He had felt that same tingling rush and awareness with this female demon. The same attractive–repulsive push–pull toward and away from her. And it was even stronger than it had been with the other demon, Derek. The demon's true name that he had heard Lucinda whisper.

She had been different from Derek. And she had fascinated Talon from the very first glimpse, the very first feel of her. Small. Almost as small as he. With a body that burst forth with an abundance of ripe peaks and tantalizing valleys. Skin golden rather than the dark brown of the other demon's skin, with hair so vibrant—a striking, metallic gold color bouncing, moving, a constant teasing sway that framed that beautiful, cruel face. She was the warm color of the sun but instead of heat that burned you, she exuded a cool cynical sexuality, a dark knowingness in her eyes, in the mocking curve of those full lush lips.

But it was her oddly attractive power, the feel of it brushing up against him, raising every single hair on his body, that scared Talon the most. Because it called so strongly to him.

Then she had captured him and taken his blood. His fear had flooded back, almost drowning him in its intensity. Yet she had been gentle in the taking. Had drank only a small amount. She had not gorged herself as Derek always did, drinking so much blood from him that it had left him weak and drained for weeks afterward. He'd always thought that was the way it worked: that the drinker would gain strength while the donor lost it. Another fallacy laid bare.

In the car, when her power had stretched out invisibly toward him, an unseen part within him had wanted to rise up and go to her in turn, to meet that power, twine about it, become one with it.

Talon had thought he was going mad, drawn so much to her when she was so obvious a danger. But now she was dying, and all hopes of going home lay dying with her.

Her last thoughts, her last words, had been for her men . . . and for him. Sending them all into the care of her brother, this Prince Halcyon. A demon whose name struck terror in the two rogues' hearts. A demon he did not know, much less trust. But her . . . Lucinda. Talon said her name for the very first time in his mind. Lucinda. It rang like a bell within him. *I want her,* something inside him cried. *Her, not anyone else.*

And as he watched her fade, watched her grow lighter and lighter in texture, color, and substance, going away from him, dying . . . everything inside him rebelled. Fear died away, the shivering disappeared, and a stillness and rock-solid resolve came together within him. *No*, he screamed in his mind's vastness. Then said it aloud. "No."

Like a sleepwalker awakening, Talon found himself crouched down by her side, reaching for her, pushing Nico aside to kneel beside her.

"Give her to me," Talon said, and the dark warrior, Stefan, glanced at him with tears of sorrow and despair wetting his eyes. A man as beautiful and as striking as she. Ivory paleness to her golden darkness. They were like the sun and the moon, had they arms and legs and breaking hearts. He was a fitting consort to her. Not someone like him—small, stunted, weak, with skin an ugly blackness. But tall and beautiful and fair of skin though he might be, this Monère warrior could not save her. And something . . . something inside of Talon cried out that he could. He could, if he dared.

"Give her to me," Talon repeated. Demanded. "Quickly, before it is too late."

Hope flared in those tear-sheened eyes. Without a word, the warrior passed her into his arms, and Talon felt her for the very first time. Barely. The soft press of her flesh against his arms, the light weight of her resting over his thighs. She had seemed so big before, vibrating with so much power. But now she lay tiny in his arms. So small and light that he could have picked her up and carried her had he needed to.

"Can you save her, bring her back?" Stefan asked.

"I shall try." With his sharp teeth, Talon cut his wrist, brought it down to her mouth, and smeared the dripping blood across her lips. Her eyes fluttered, the lids translucent.

"Drink," Talon urged, finding himself saying something he would never ever have imagined himself saying to a demon. Saying something that he meant and yearned for with all his heart. "Drink my blood."

He felt her lips brush weakly across his blood-slicked wrist, felt her lips open wider. He pressed his wound eagerly against her mouth. "Drink and live," he murmured. Willed.

Her throat moved, a tiny bob up and down.

"She swallowed," Nico said.

She swallowed again and all of them watched, waited, and prayed. Watched as her body grew denser.

"She's coming back," Stefan whispered and took her hand, wrapped it in his. "I feel her more."

Talon felt her, too. Not just physically, but with that other sense. That awareness that was always there between them. An awareness that had almost faded into nothingness. It returned now, but weakly. So weak to what it had been.

Her lips moved more strongly against his wrist, and she drank down more of his blood, not just the liquid that flowed freely into her mouth from his cut, but drawing it out of his veins faster with her own suction and pull.

She drank and grew more solid, heavier in his arms. She drank and came slowly back into awareness.

Open your eyes. See me, Talon willed. Her lids fluttered once, twice, then lifted and she looked up at him.

"Talon." She pushed his wrist away with sluggish movement. "What are you doing?"

"I'm bringing you back."

"No good," she muttered. "Oil of Fibara . . . blocks my power. Energy boost gone . . . crashing . . . Tired, so tired." Her lids fluttered closed. As soon as they did, Talon felt the awareness between them dim, lessen, felt her presence begin to fade away. Her skin grew more translucent, and she began to lighten again.

"No," Talon cried and shook her awake. "Keep your eyes open."

Her lashes lifted up, heavy, like the slow sweep of a fan.

"Drink more of his blood," Nico urged.

A sad, sweet smile touched her lips. "Won't help . . . not with oil."

"This?" Stefan asked, touching the wet substance on her back.

"Yes." A small breath of sound.

Stefan tore open her cloak, stripped it gently from her, along with her tattered shirt, and wiped the oily substance carefully from her skin as Talon shifted her up against him for easier access.

"No good. In my skin already," Lucinda said, her voice thick and muffled with her face pressed against Talon's stomach.

Stefan tore off his own shirt, gently slid her arms into the sleeves, and drew the garment around her. Talon lowered her back down, and Stefan buttoned up the shirt, covering her once more.

"Her skin is so cold," Stefan murmured, his brows knitting together.

"Lucinda, how long does the oil's effect last?" Nico asked.

She turned her sleepy eyes to him with effort. "Hours."

"You just have to stay awake then, until the effect wears off, sweetheart," Nico said.

A wry, twisting smile. "Sweetheart?" she whispered.

"Only right I call you sweetheart. You called me darling before," Nico said, his voice light but his eyes tender. Darkened with the worry that haunted them all. They were losing her.

Her voice grew fainter, until it was the barest wisp of sound. "Not one of your . . . human harem." Her dark cinnamon lashes fluttered down, as if the weight of them was too heavy for her to bear up any longer. "So tired . . ."

Open your eyes! It was a screamed mental command. A strong urging of will blasted out from Talon.

Her eyes blinked open, like a sleeper rudely shaken awake. She looked up at Talon. "Let me go . . . leave here."

"No," a soft reply echoed internally by a much harsher one. *No!*

A couple more blinks and then her lashes drifted down again in that fanning sweep, like a floating feather inevitably pulled down by gravity. And Talon knew she spoke true, that she could not last that long. That his will could not sustain her. Not without a greater bond. A bond he knew and yet did not know how to create.

Talon took the next step. He lifted up her forearm—so light, so delicate, such a fragile thing—and sank his sharp teeth into her skin. Blood, sharp and acrid, almost stinging, filled his mouth, and he swallowed it down. And with that blood bond, Talon knew more of her thoughts, her feelings. Instead of repelling him as it had with Derek, it drew him closer. He knew now that she had chosen to save their lives when she could have tried to save hers instead. And he knew that his choice—her—was the right one.

Lucinda's eyes flew open. She gasped in pain, in shock. "What are you doing?"

"I'm binding us."

"You cannot drink her blood," Stefan said, his voice tense. "She said that you would die if you took her blood."

"I am demon kin, of that other realm. I have taken their blood before and it does not hurt me," Talon said. And then with that part of himself that he had always held so tightly closed before—that yearning, attracted part of himself . . . He didn't just loosen it, let it go where it wanted—he thrust it sharply into her. He felt that part of him enter into her and found that flicker of power, the element of her that had reached out once to him. He twined around her beast, so weak now, barely there.

Merge with me, that other demon Derek had demanded, time and time again. But no matter how terribly he had hurt Talon, punished him, beaten him until bones had broken and flesh had split open, Talon had held that part of himself back. No longer.

"No . . ." Lucinda moaned, shaking her head, mentally trying to push him away. Too weak to do so. "No . . . you will die when I die."

"Then we go together." His face was utterly tranquil,

peacefully calm. How wonderful it felt not to be afraid. With that inner serenity, Talon wrapped himself around the fading power within her that was her beast. With a blissful shudder, he sank into it. Became a part of it. Merged wholly with it.

A kaleidoscope of colors, of powers, of feelings and emotions, tastes and sounds. Echoes of a heartbeat. The fertile earth, the vibrant wind. The sun, moon, and stars. An explosion of feeling, a shaking within as if the realms themselves moved.

And then the emptiness and totality of darkest night.

SEVENTEEN

THEY WERE AS still as death. Even when they carried them on that long trek back to the car, the two of them together, their bodies touching, they did not move. But the ghosting had stopped . . . as long as they were touching. All it took was that one time when Stefan had lifted Lucinda up into his arms, only to find her quickly growing lighter in weight and density, so startling fast. And not only her, but Talon, too. Both of them fading almost completely in the brief moment it had taken to lower Lucinda back to the ground. Back to Talon. The moment they had touched again, black skin to gold, they solidified once more.

The illusion of dark mocha skin that Lucinda had coated Talon with before had been stripped completely from him the moment he tipped over and sprawled limp and unconscious on top of Lucinda, leaving him a creature of darkness, of blackest night once again. But the darkness could fade, too. And black skin could ghost as easily as fairer skin of gold.

They did not make the same mistake twice.

"I'll carry them both," Stefan had declared. And he'd done so while Nico stood guard with Stefan's sword in his hand, the thin handcuffs at his waistbelt. Charcoal black handcuffs that Nico had found lying on the ground, almost lost among the leaves. The demon alloy felt oddly warm against Nico's skin as they made their way slowly back to the car, as if it still retained heat from that other realm.

They were so still. Oddly still.

Without their consciousness animating them, Nico became fully aware of their complete lack of sound and movement. Living creatures were noisy things, never silent. Within them, always, even in sleep, was the rush of blood traversing vessels and the pumping of that blood, the swish of air moving in and out. Not so with these beings from Hell. And yet, even now with that silence, that eerie stillness, Nico did not truly think of them as dead. Just different from living things.

Jonnie was waiting for them in the car, and the relief on the young man's face when he glimpsed them was echoed in Stefan's. Such a close bond between those two, Nico noted with a pang of envy. He wondered briefly what it would feel like to have a son, then shook his head at his own whimsy. He would likely never know. Few Monère ever did.

"What happened?" Jonnie asked as they lowered Lucinda and Talon onto the backseat, Talon's light body sprawled on top of Lucinda. Nico scrunched in beside them, keeping the two of them touching, together, while Stefan pulled on a clean shirt he took out of his backpack. Dressed once more, he slid into the driver's seat.

"Lucinda started to ghost," Stefan said as he pulled onto the road, driving fast. "Talon bound himself to her somehow. As long as they touch, he keeps them from completely waning."

"Why is Talon so dark?" Jonnie asked.

"That is his true color," Nico explained. "What you saw before was just a thin coat of illusion to help him blend in more naturally among the humans."

"Is Talon a demon, too, Stefan?"

"I don't know, Jonnie. I thought at first that he was, but he called himself demon kin."

"I don't think even Talon knows what he is," Nico said sadly. "A demon brought him as a babe to Mona SiGuri and she has kept him in secrecy all this time. His existence here in this realm surprised Lucinda greatly. She called him a Floradëur, a Flower of Darkness. Their blood seems to greatly enhance a demon's powers."

"Derek," Stefan said. "She named the demon Derek. Is he the same demon who stole Talon here to this realm?"

"If it were a different demon, it would surprise me greatly," Nico said. "Demons are not that common. Quite rare, in fact. I doubt Mona SiGuri dealt with more than one demon. And she had to be the one who warned him, sent him after us."

"I'd like to kill her," Stefan said flatly. And though Nico felt that way himself, it was a jarring shock hearing it said aloud. To hear put into words one of their greatest taboos—killing a queen. A sacred lady of light.

"I think that's what the good Queen had in mind herself," Nico said. "To kill us. To get rid of all the witnesses, recover Talon, and then all would be as it was. The demon's goal, as well. He tried to stop the greatest threat to him first—Lucinda. He will come after her again when he has recovered. And then us."

"Lucinda injured him. Badly enough to send him running," Stefan said, then asked that next all-important question. "How quickly can demons heal?"

With a light finger, Nico traced the burn wounds along Lucinda's wrist. The illusion had fallen away from them the same moment Talon's illusion had dropped. "They cut her wrists to drain her blood. She burned her own flesh to stop the bleeding. It has not healed in any discernible way that I can detect."

A light muttered imprecation as Stefan turned and caught sight of the charred flesh Nico traced. With an angry tightening of lips, Stefan turned back once more to face the empty road they sped along.

"I don't know how fast they heal. But based on Lucinda's wounds, my guess is not at all in this realm," Nico said. So much they did not know. But what they did know was enough to shake his world. In a low voice that reflected the stunned awe he felt, he murmured, "She said her brother was Prince Halcyon."

"Prince Halcyon?" Jonnie asked, craning his head over the front seat to peer down at Nico. "Who is that?"

Nico gave a sharp bark of mirthless laughter. "Just the High Prince of Hell. The ruler of that other realm. Someone that every Monère knows and fears." He caught the flash of Stefan's eyes in the mirror. "Does Jonnie even know about it, that other realm where some of us go after we die?"

"I told him after we met Lucinda," Stefan said. "I did not tell him much before of the Monèrian world I left behind."

"Wise, perhaps. Perhaps even wiser to keep it that way and part company here and now. Not only him but you as well," Nico said to Stefan. "A demon hunts us. He will come after Lucinda first. You may have a chance to escape."

"And run where, pray tell?" Stefan asked. "No, I will stay with Lucinda."

"And I will stay with Stefan," Jonnie said.

"Then so be it. We all go to High Court." Stefan watched with amusement as Nico paled at those two frightening words. Smiling grimly, Stefan turned his attention back to the road. "And we seek out the Queen Mother and Lucinda's brother, Prince Halcyon." Two names that represented the highest powers among their people. Names that struck both fear and reverence among the Monère, and sheer terror in any rogue's heart.

"I'd almost rather take my chances with the demon," Nico muttered.

In truth, so would Stefan, had it been only he. But it was not. "It was our lady's last order that we go there."

"Our lady." Nico sighed the words, savored them, though frank amusement tinged his next words. "So you've decided to share her with me, old man."

"I decided nothing," Stefan said. "Lucinda made that choice. I can only accept it."

"And with such grace," Nico said dryly.

"Does that make her a princess?" Jonnie asked Stefan.

"What?"

"You said her brother was a prince, a ruler. Does that make Lucinda a princess?"

It was a stunning realization, echoed in the brief look Stefan shared with Nico.

"Yes," Stefan answered. "That makes her a princess."

"Our Princess," Nico amended. "For as long as she continues to exist." And they would do their best to see that she did.

There was no sign of Mona SiGuri's men at the airport, and the small jet lifted from the ground without mishap. The pilot was an older man, a human who eyed Lucinda and Talon's unconscious bodies with obvious concern but asked no questions. All he had said when Stefan told him of their destination was, "I know the coordinates," and disappeared into the cockpit.

They laid Lucinda down in the narrow aisle with Talon's small dark body lying atop hers. They were almost the same size, funny to realize that. Lucinda had seemed so much bigger, her presence so powerful it had made her seem a foot taller than Talon, rather than the mere inch that separated them in height. And tiny thing though she was, Talon was even smaller, light and slender where Lucinda was lush and full.

They were still. Totally unmoving. Nico knew because he watched them closely. They both did, Stefan and he. They sat on the floor, Stefan on one side of the aisle, Nico on the other.

Then movement came and surprised them all. Blood

scented the air. Flowed bright and scarlet, trickling down between black and gold skin. Nico cursed and rolled Talon's body half off of Lucinda, so they could see their bellies. Dark rivulets of blood ran from a gashing wound in Talon's right side. Talon's blood, not Lucinda's.

Talon's eyes flew open, and the black void of his eyes stared up at Nico with panic and desperation in their depths.

"Nico, help me," Talon cried, reaching for him. Nico grasped the black outstretched hand.

The moment their skins touched, he pulled Nico in.

EIGHTEEN

T HE PLANE, THE seats, the narrow aisle, the bright
lights all disappeared, and Nico found himself in twilit
darkness. In air hotter than he had ever felt or breathed in
before. Motion came at him, striking at him, stopping just
before it hit him, slicing open fabric but not skin. A clawed
hand with nails long, sharp and deadly, hovered there, trembling above his white skin. A startled gasp drew Nico's
eyes up.

Lucinda stood before him.

Crouched behind him, he felt Talon, the creature's small,
sharp nails digging through the fabric of his pants.

"Nico. What are you doing here?" Lucinda asked, a
shocked look on her face.

"Talon brought me here."

"No!" she cried and stumbled back, so weak that her
legs collapsed and she sank to the ground. Anger and sorrow swirled in those dark bittersweet eyes.

"Take him back," she commanded fiercely, looking at
Talon, her voice, her will, still strong though her body was
not. "And go yourself. Leave me."

Talon shook his head. Crawled cautiously to where she sat sprawled on the ground. "No, mistress. I will not leave you. We are halfway bound already, can you not feel it?"

"No. It isn't complete. You still have a chance if you go now."

Talon shook his head.

She lunged for him, her movement rough and jerky. Struck at him and missed, those lethal claws plunging into the ground as he darted away.

Nico didn't know what this was, dream or reality. All he knew was that she fought Talon, and that Talon was trying to save her. The weight of the demon cuffs flared warm against Nico's waist, reminding him of their presence. Without hesitation, Nico grabbed them and snapped them around Lucinda's wrist. A quick twist, wresting her arms behind her back, and he secured both her hands together. Only her weakness allowed Nico to do so. Only her weakness kept her from breaking free of the restraints.

"What are you doing?" she snarled, thrashing beneath him.

"Trying to save you," Nico snapped back, pinning her to the ground. Weak though she was, it still took effort to restrain her.

"You cannot do that: save me."

"But Talon can."

"He cannot. He is not strong enough. All he will do is die when I die."

"He is strong enough to keep you from ghosting, you foolish woman. Stop being so selfish!"

The bitter accusation surprised Lucinda enough to stop struggling. She looked up at Nico with bruised eyes. He steeled his heart against them, sensing that softness would not win this fight.

"How can you say that?" she whispered.

"I say only the truth. If you die as you seek to do, you leave us alone and unprotected."

"My brother . . . Halcyon will take care of you."

"Someone who does not know us or care for us."

"Halcyon is honorable. Good. Far better than me. He will protect you and avenge my death."

"He will likely kill us himself when we bring him news of your death. When we come to him with no proof and only wild claims."

Lucinda shook her head. "He is not like that. He will give you fair hearing. And there is Talon. Talon is your proof."

"Talon will likely die with you," Nico said harshly. "And gone will be our proof."

Silence and her quiet despair painted the barren landscape an even duskier hue, as if reflecting her emotions.

"Why do you fight to die when you should fight to live?" Nico asked roughly. He could not understand that. "Why?"

Nothing but that agonizing silence.

"Why?" He demanded again, shaking her in his frustration. "Tell me why."

A tear overflowed, trailed slowly down her cheek. "I am evil. I do not deserve to exist or be happy." Her voice was a bleak and desolate sound.

"You are not evil. Who called you that?"

Her answer stunned him. "My mother. Because I'm a bastard. She named another as my father instead of the High Lord. Then she killed herself, leaving me behind."

"And you believed her?"

"Her blood runs in my veins. She was beautiful and cruel. Some called her evil." Lucinda laughed. "And I am her daughter."

"Halcyon has her blood also, does he not?"

"Yes, but he is more the High Lord's son. The spitting image of him in looks and personality, as I am the mirror reflection of my mother."

Nico released her arms, smoothed her hair roughly away from her face, and cupped her cheeks in the palms of his hands. "Would your mother have claimed two rogues as her own? Would she have risked her life for theirs?"

Lucinda answered quietly, "No."

"Then you are less your mother's daughter than you think. However much you may resemble her in looks, your actions are different. Do not pattern them after her in this last and final act, in seeking your death."

Her eyes hardened, glinted dangerously up at him, and her words came out chillingly cold. "Do not think that you know me by my actions of these past few hours. Believe me, that is not how I usually act. I am not usually so nice."

Nico laughed with genuine amusement. "Nice is not how I would have described you. But neither would I call you evil. I'd use the words that you applied to your brother: fair and honorable."

The air quivered for a moment in silence, in denial.

"Dying is the easy way out," Nico said. "I know, I tried to take that route also, but you would not let me. Now it's payback time." He gripped her face gently, urgently. "Stop being a coward and fight to live. Or take us with you now, Talon and I. We are not leaving you."

A moment passed as they gazed at each other. A brief weighing and measuring of will and resolve before she asked mildly, "Do you plan on removing these handcuffs?"

"Yes," Nico said slowly, "I do."

"Then I would be careful with your words, with who you call coward," she said with soft silky menace.

"That's my girl." With a smile, Nico rolled off her and pulled her to her feet. "Do not think to chase us off," he warned as he removed the restraints. Then spoke the words that he knew would hold her most effectively to the right course. "Or the next person Talon pulls in will be your precious Stefan."

"I hate you," she said without looking at him, rubbing her freed wrists.

"I know, darling," Nico said easily. "Now what do you need to do to complete the binding?"

"I don't know." She stood there swaying weakly with an uncharacteristic uncertainty on her face that almost broke his heart.

"Talon?" Nico murmured.

"She has to stop resisting," Talon said in that pure melodious voice of his as he came silently to Nico's side.

Nico looked askance at Lucinda.

"I'm not resisting anymore."

"She's not resisting anymore," Nico repeated back to Talon. "Now what?"

A look of uncertainty passed across that dark face. A look this time that did not break Nico's heart so much as scare it shitless.

"I don't know," Talon said, those eerie black eyes unfocused, gazing inwardly. "It's there. Do you not feel it?"

The moment he spoke of it, Nico became aware of it. The hush. The quiet weight of expectancy hovering in the hot air, like something alive, something eager. But something faint. Like power waiting to ignite, but too weak to do so. Like hovering storm clouds, too scant, too few to bring about the promise of rain.

"I am too weak," Lucinda said, her voice emptied of emotion, but her eyes . . . they swam with regret. "I used up what little power I had trying to drive Talon away." She gazed at the dark creature. "Send Nico back," she said softly. "Return him, and go back with him."

"I don't know how," Talon said in a small, subdued voice.

"How did you find him, bring him here?" she asked.

"I just thought of help, when you were chasing me, and Nico was suddenly there. He touched me and we returned here." Talon turned that too-large face up to Nico. "I'm sorry," he said.

Nico patted the slender shoulder. "Nothing to be sorry about, Talon. The solution is simple. We just need to get Lucinda back up to strength again."

Their eyes turned back to both their problem and their solution.

"Can you drink more of Talon's blood?" Nico asked.

Rage, frustration, fatigue, and sorrow swam in those chocolate brown eyes. Too tired to stand any longer, she sank down to the ground. Nodded. "Yes, I can try."

Talon glided to her, a small wary creature approaching a more dangerous predator. When he stood before her, he lifted his shirt, baring the wound in his side that she had ripped with her claws. A deep furrowing gash.

"You still bleed," she murmured. "Why did you not heal yourself?"

"I do not know how to."

"You are Floradëur. You take your power from nature itself. Healing is one of your gifts."

Talon shook his dark head. "I have no gifts, I have no power, and I heal slowly."

"That you heal at all here is miracle already." So saying, Lucinda leaned forward and put her mouth against the open wound. Her throat, smooth and golden, moved gently against the blackness of his skin as she drank from his wound. She swallowed twice, then drew back and just sat there and waited.

The air thickened a little. Grew denser, but nothing else happened.

"The oil of Fibara blocks the potency of his blood from me," she said. "It is not enough."

"Blood is not the only way you can gain power," said Nico.

Her eyes were a sudden swirl of emotions he could not read. "You are correct. I can also feed from other's ecstasy. But I do not have the mental strength to bring you to your peaks."

"We have to orgasm for you to feed?"

She nodded.

"We're men," Nico said with a grin. "And you are a woman, lush and beautiful. You do not have to use your demon wiles to bring us to orgasm. We could do it the basic old-fashioned way."

"I will not have sex with Talon," Lucinda said.

Silence reigned after her harsh, abrupt statement. Talon turned, would have stepped away in hurt silence had she not stopped him with a hand on his slender arm.

"I understand, mistress," Talon said, his face averted. "My ugliness disturbs you."

A finger, with nail carefully lifted away from the tender

vulnerable skin, gently turned his face to hers. "You are
far from ugly, Talon."

"I am stunted and distorted, a creature of blackness."

"You are Floradëur, a beautiful Flower of Darkness.
But you are young and you are virgin. Am I not correct?"

He did not deny it.

"I am centuries too old for you," Lucinda said, "and I
will not be your first. That you should save for someone
special."

"I understand," Talon said quietly and slipped away.

Lucinda wondered at the truth of his words. Did he really understand? She doubted it.

Another voice reached out. Stroked her in that still,
twilight darkness that she had unconsciously painted like
her home realm. A voice that was deep, low, and husky.

"What about me?" Nico asked, his face unusually somber, all teasing gone as he closed the distance between
them.

"I am not a virgin," he said softly. "Will you have sex
with me?"

NINETEEN

IT WAS THE yearning in that blunt, rugged face that moved me most. The need, the naked wanting. Or maybe it was just him—stubborn, sweet, and gallant Nico. First foe, hunted prey, and now friend. When had that happened?

He had such a grand heart, and he held his own life too cheaply. Was so willing to give it up in service to me. He did not value his own life as I valued it. Did not utter a single word of complaint, of accusation that it might end here and now because of me. Because of my stupidity and fear.

My intentions had been good. But you know what humans say about good intentions: that it paved the way to Hell. I laughed softly inside. Here's hoping. But still . . . I'd rather he'd had the chance to live life fully first.

Regrets . . . so many of them. And the noble warrior before me now—valiant and chivalrous, like a knight of old— was one of the biggest of them. A treasure thrown away by a Queen too blind to see his worth.

I had tried to save his life, only to end up being the

cause of his death. Now he knelt beside me and asked of me the one thing I could still give him.

His question hung in the air between us. *Will you have sex with me?*

"Yes," I said as somber as he, "if that is what you want."

Nico let out a ragged breath. Laughed. A joyous sound that brought a smile to my lips.

"Oh, yes. I want." Then he turned noble on me again. "But you don't really have to. Just . . . touching me with your hand or your mouth should be enough to have me coming," he said with a wry, deprecating grin.

I reached out and laid my hand against that broad cheek, that strong jaw. "I would give you pleasure, if I can. But I do not know if that will be possible without my demon wiles, as you call them." I had not known how much I had come to rely upon those powers.

"I'm a man, Princess. All I have to do is be inside of you, and that will give me pleasure."

I closed my eyes at the image his words invoked, his strong body moving over me. In and out of me. The first tendrils of arousal stirred. But still the doubt remained.

"Perhaps we should do as you suggested. You seemed to enjoy the feel of my mouth—"

"Believe me, I enjoyed it most sincerely and will again," Nico said with a smile that was very male. "But if you are giving me the choice, then I would very much like to know what it feels like to be sheathed inside you. That is my greatest desire. To know you in the most intimate way a man can know a woman."

"How can I not grant a warrior's last wish?" Sadness tinged my smile. "As you desire. I only hope that I do not disappoint you. I am weak and without power."

"That's what this is all about, Princess. To get you more power." He grinned again with easy lightness. But his eyes gleamed with eagerness, a smoky gray hue, dark and intense. "Just lie down," he said huskily, easing me back, "and let me do all the work."

I did as he said, but could not help frowning and fretting. "It feels odd to do so. To let you do all the work."

He laughed, his gray eyes dancing as his hands undid the buttons of my shirt. "Enjoy the novelty. As I shall, too."

He eased down my pants then crouched over me, parting my shirt with an almost reverent flourish, his gaze sweeping with slow quiet savor over my naked breasts, down my unveiled body, before lifting his eyes back to mine. He sighed and smiled sweetly. "Thank you, Lucinda. Just letting me see you like this . . . it brings me great pleasure."

His words pleased me more than any lavish praise would have. And the subtle tension that had unknowingly gripped me relaxed away. "It is just a body." A tool. One I had used to tease and entice with, but rarely used this way, in physical coupling.

"Oh, no." Nico's long lashes swept down and his lips lowered to my neck. "It is not just a body," he murmured and placed a soft kiss in the dipping hollow where my shoulder curved into my throat, to where my pulse would have beat, had I one. "It is your body." Another kiss, a soft caress of lips whispering over my collar bone. "And it is like you. Lush, generous. Spilling over with generosity."

"I am not generous."

"Yes, yes, I know." He sprinkled more kisses down the arch of my collarbone. "You are not nice. You are not generous." He trailed a teasing finger round and round the fullness of my left breast before finally cupping it in his hand and squeezing it lightly, sending a pleasant jolt arrowing down inside me. "But your body is. Oh yes, your body is."

He brought his mouth to hover there, just above my nipple, plumped up by his cupping hand, his breath blowing softly across the tip. Waiting until it peaked into a pouty, pointy hardness. "Sweet," he said, smiling, and covered it with his mouth.

Warm wetness.

A flick of his tongue, a rough rasp over the nipple, and

my body suddenly zinged with sensation. I gasped, arched up, pushing more of me into that mouth, surprised that I could feel this way. That he could make me feel this way. I had agreed to sleep with Nico more for the debt I owed him than for lust of his body. There had not been any before. Lust for his body, that is. But now there was.

He crooned, the trill of his vibration tripping sharply through me, and began sucking on me. My hands lifted and reached for him, my nails scraping lightly across the shirt covering his back. "Your shirt," I muttered, twisting beneath that sucking mouth. "Take off your shirt."

He lifted up, stretching my nipple taut before releasing it with a wet *pop*, a tight pulling sensation that spilled a startled moan from my lips.

"No," he said, eyes dark and knowing, filled with something I had not seen in them before . . . arrogant assurance. No, that wasn't quite right. Confidence. Filled with confidence.

"I'm not done enjoying you yet," he said, capturing my hands, pinning them above my head. And the look in his eyes, the dominance in his words, his crouched position over me, the real physical weakness that held me now . . . No one had ever dominated me like this before. Unbelievably, I found myself liking it, excited by it. So much so that another moan almost slipped free from my throat. So much so that the air grew thick with the scent of my liquid arousal, so that he knew without touching me that my body had softened, prepared itself for him. His nostrils flared wide, drinking in the muskiness of my aroma, his eyes darkening with the knowledge of what he had stirred to life. And the hot smoldering passion I glimpsed in those stormy gray eyes stirred me even more. A look that—Darkness help me—with my hands pinned above me, made me feel even more helpless.

My body reacted beyond my control, my expectation, almost as if a stranger suddenly inhabited my body. Fear, excitement, and loss of control swirled like an unsettling wind within me.

"Nico . . ."

"Hush." Staring into my eyes, in a voice gone velvet dark, he said, "Open your legs for me, darling." A gentle command. But a command, nonetheless.

Had I a heart that beat, it would have been pounding by now. I licked my lips nervously. "Nico—"

"Do it." He compelled me with his blazing eyes, the tautness of his body poised over mine, in the hard shackling strength of his hands about my wrists. *Yield to me,* those passion-smoked eyes demanded with a frightening will. That was his real strength, that unbreakable will.

With a trembling sigh, I submitted. Opened my legs until they came up against his spread knees. He released my wrists, and I started to lower them down.

"No, keep your hands like that above your head."

I froze. "It makes me feel vulnerable," I said plaintively.

"I know." His voice was a deep husky caress, his eyes a knowing echo of his words as he brought my hands back up so that I lay stretched out beneath him, arms up and legs spread wide. "I want you to feel that way."

I swallowed, closed my eyes against the knowing glimmer in his. But that made it worse, made me feel even more vulnerable, and brought my other senses sharply into play so that I heard him, sensed movement, felt him shift between my legs. Cloth rustled and I opened my eyes to see those agile fingers slipping buttons free. His shirt slid off in a slow, gentle tease, falling to the ground. But my eyes were not on the shirt. They were on his magnificent chest, his bulging biceps. At the obvious strength carved out there on his flesh in swelling muscles and rippling sinew.

"You've seen me naked before," Nico said, a little smile playing on his lips. Masculine, knowing.

"Yes, but that was different. Before I was looking at you as food."

"And now?"

"Now I am seeing you as a lover."

He stilled, his hands frozen upon the first button of his pants, but only for the barest instant. They resumed their nimble movements, pushing, releasing. Slowly revealing more of himself to me. He stood, pushed down his pants, and stepped out of them.

I stared at him—fully aroused, fully male, fully warrior—and found him beautiful. All of him. His need, his desire, his strong and stubborn will, his ability to laugh at himself and others. And the loveliness of his form. Shoulders broad, chest wide and deep, arms strong and powerful, sloping down to neat hips, taut muscled thighs. My gaze lingered there, where he was most male. That part of him that would enter me. Appreciating now what I had not appreciated before when I had been more intent upon his blood. He was built like his height, his stout stature. Of average length, but wider, much thicker around. One and a half times wider than that of other men.

"Oh." My eyes rounded with surprise as I stared at his potent package.

He lowered down to me. "I hope that's a good 'oh,'" Nico said as I felt the warmth and hard thickness of him brush against my thigh.

I swallowed, laughed nervously. "Yes . . . I think it is."

"Tell me you're not a virgin." Mock horror was upon on his face, making me laugh again.

"Far from it. I've had many lovers before. But that was long ago, hundreds of years ago."

"Before your mother declared you a bastard."

An accurate surmise. "Yes. Life, and even afterlife, had been joyous before then. Not afterward."

Braced on one elbow, he played his hand lightly over me. A featherlight touch here and there, roaming at random will. "Then let me reacquaint you with pleasure."

I wriggled a little beneath that teasing hand. "I thought this was all about your pleasure, not mine."

"Don't you know," he said softly. "Your pleasure is my pleasure."

"You said that all it took to bring you pleasure was to be inside of me." Emptiness stirred my legs wider, inviting him to fill it with that delicious breadth. Need built suddenly. A desperate need to be stretched by him.

"I lied," he whispered. "Hush, darling. Let me learn you."

And he did. With ruthless thoroughness, with patient fact gathering. He learned the exquisite sensitivity of my neck, just behind my ears. That touching me just so along the ribs elicited a giggling ticklishness. That tugging on my nipple with lips and teeth brought forth a sweet sigh. That a bite, here and there, rougher and darker, brought forth cries of need, of desire. A wanting of more.

"No blood," I said, writhing in the pleasure he was making me feel with his hands, his teeth, his mouth racing over me, plunging my secrets. "All other things you may do, but you cannot taste my blood."

"I won't," Nico promised, and delved in for more treasures, more secrets, more desire. He found what few of my lovers had found, what I myself had not entirely known because none of my lovers before had dared do to me what he did to me. That I enjoyed a little pain. Not just giving it, because I could drink it down, but actually experiencing it myself. He found that sweet, licking nibbles combined with an almost bruising grip upon my breasts brought forth the sweetest moans. I enjoyed it a little rough, he discovered, and he enjoyed giving it to me. I enjoyed being dominated a little, so he dominated me. Commanded me. Made me do things I did not want to do.

"Cup your breasts. Lift them up to me."

I did. So carefully, so dangerously, feeling my sharp nails brush my own skin.

"Squeeze your nipples, darling. Show me how you like to be touched."

I did that, too, to his approving murmur. And it wasn't the actions themselves that stirred me so, but that dark voice of his telling me to do them.

I touched, I squeezed, I caressed. I obeyed him. And inside of me I cried, yearned to be filled.

"Nico," I murmured, and he kissed me. Drew my lower lip into his mouth and nipped me, hard enough to hurt, hard enough to please, my soft humming sigh his sweet reward.

"Put your arms back over your head, darling. Yes, like that. Lovely," he crooned, as my breasts stretched and lifted up to him as if begging for his attention, and they were. They were.

That position, leaving me so open, so vulnerable, so displayed, and those particular words, the look in his eyes as he said them. . . . Oh, that really did it for me. Wetting me so much that actual runnels of arousal trickled down my thighs and perfumed the air. I bit back a moan and he punished me with a light slap on the rear, startling me, using enough force to leave my skin red and stinging.

"No," he said, eyes glinting. "Let me hear you. I want to hear what I make you feel." His eyes caught and held mine, and his voice lowered until it was whisper soft. "Do you like me telling you what to do?"

Goddess help me.

I swallowed, confessed in a small voice, "Yes." No point trying to lie. My body would not let me. He knew. Oh yes, he knew. The knowledge was there in his storm gray eyes.

"Tell me what you want most."

And what should have been easy was suddenly made hard, because he had asked it of me. Demanded it of me.

"I want you inside of me."

Nico smiled, pushed away from me, and sat back on his knees. With hands that gripped my thighs hard enough to bruise, he pulled me to him, lifted my hips up, and plunged his tongue into me, bringing me screaming at the sudden, unexpected shock and pleasure of it, making me jerk in his hands. The roughness of his stubble abraded my dewy nether lips as he stabbed deeply into me, swirled around, pulled out.

A deep slide in again.

He pushed that agile tongue in and out of me for a few hard strokes, then retreated and ran the flat of his tongue along my outer lips, making me shudder wildly. Making me jerk and cry as he ran his tongue up and found my hidden pearl, the swollen nub of me, the nexus of my pleasure. He hummed, swirled his tongue around the tiny button, laving it with the flat rough surface, suddenly stabbing it, flicking it with the tip of his tongue, making my body dance and jerk with tiny little spasms, with moans and groans and heaving shudders as he played with me that way, drawing me higher, winding me tighter, but leaving me hanging there, always, at the edge.

"Please, Nico."

"I am." He rubbed his chin, his bristly stubble, lightly, exquisitely over my tender, swollen nub. A scrape, a brush. Almost, almost too much, skirting that line between. "I am pleasing you," he rumbled, warm breath striking me. "You said you wanted me inside of you. I complied."

"Not like that," I moaned, jerking like a puppet pulled by invisible strings. Strings of pleasure that danced with that sweet edge of pain.

He shoved two fingers into me, and the sudden and abrupt way he did it made me groan, arch up into him, pushing me more against his mouth, rubbing me harder against that coarse stubble for one blissful moment that almost was enough to take me over the edge.

Then he drew back. Away. "Like that?" he asked.

"No." I wanted to whimper with frustration, but growled instead. "No. Your fingers are nice . . ." He rewarded me with a deep push in, a leisurely slide out with those two aforementioned fingers, drawing forth another moan. "But it's your big cock that I want inside of me."

"Ah." Nico lowered my hips back to the ground, his fingers reluctantly sliding out of me. "For that, you have to say the magick word."

"What word?" I asked, feeling a bit desperate.

"Darling. You have to call me darling."

I lifted my eyes to his and said the word. "Darling." And saw what I had seen before pass once more through his eyes. Watched as his pupils ran wide and black, expanding to the very rim. I said it again, softer, huskier, and watched his skin ripple and shiver, as if the words had stroked him in a tactile caress, though it had not; my voice was as empty of power as I was. But I was discovering that I was not as devoid of influence as I had thought. Just that one word was enough to pull the light from him, to ignite that soft glow within him.

"You like it when I call you darling. Why?" I asked.

Nico shuddered and dropped back down on top of me, positioning the blunt end of himself at my gate. "No one's ever called me darling before," he whispered, and began pushing his way into me.

"Darling," I said again, and his body gave a hard involuntary surge forward into me, making my lids half close at the wonderful, stretching feel of him entering me like that.

He groaned and shivered, with pleasure, with restraint, the muscles of his arms and back and thighs knotted tight. "Easy," he murmured to me, to himself as he became a shimmering creature of light blanketing me. "That's enough."

"No," I said, and smiled up into his eyes. "It's not enough. Not yet . . . *darling*."

Nico shuddered and heaved into me. Another delicious fat inch more.

"Don't, Lucinda," he choked, his tense muscles vibrating above me. "No more. I don't want to hurt you."

"You won't hurt me. Or maybe you will, just a little. Maybe I want you to." And I whispered the word once more into his ear. His body jerked deeper, then stilled, trembling all over. I shook, too, with excitement, with near bliss. With stretching, stretching pleasure.

"You fill me so sweetly," I crooned, undulating my body beneath him, tempting him, urging him forward. "More," I said. "Deeper," I whispered. "Harder," I breathed.

He shook above me, trembling like a leaf blown by a ruthless wind, his eyes dark and wild. "No, Lucinda."

"Yes, Nico." I said the word again. "Darling." Stroked him with it. "You are my darling."

"Am I?" His voice was incredibly harsh as he looked down at me with eyes that were lost, almost hazed blind, though I should have been the one blinded. Dazzled by the brilliant light he shone with now.

"Yes," I said. "You are."

That tenuous hold over his control broke, as I needed it to break. With a cry, he plunged himself into me the rest of the blissful way, stuffing me full, cramming me tight. He heaved himself into me, thrust himself in and out as he glowed above me, within me. As I cried and sighed beneath him and urged him on in that wild ride.

The tight friction eased as my wet juice coated him and anointed him, and then he was sliding in and out rapidly, desperately, with hard grunting force, pounding into me, taking me, giving himself to me, wildly, desperately, freely. A beautiful glowing thing above me.

"Lucinda!" My name was a moan, a plea, a demand upon his lips. He shifted above me, angling himself so that his thick root rubbed against where I needed him most, and surged into me once, twice more. It was as he shafted not only himself into me but his light. Making me shudder and cry. Making me tighten around him. Tight, tight, so tight. Pushing me over, making me fall. Splintering me in a shattering release that convulsed my body in splendid rapture and drew him deeper still into me. I held him there for a deep blissful moment, mine, fully mine, as I came apart. As I milked him with my powerful contractions, squeezing him to his own release. Feeling him spurt hot and sweet within me. Feeling him burst within and without me, over me and above me, showering me with a rainbow of energy, of power, of light.

I drank it all down.

Renewed by his pleasure, by his light, my power stretched out and flexed gloriously . . . and sensed another watching from the deep shadows, a part of it. Talon. And it sensed not only his presence—that odd, cold-burning feel of him—but his need. The fullness, the aching of his groin.

I knew that he required but the barest touch, the lightest stroke. And I gave it to him. I touched Talon with an invisible hand, squeezed him tight for one hard moment. And spilled him over, too. His cries and his release filled the air. Filled me. With power and with something else. Something that entered me and hovered, once inside, for an infinitesimal moment. Then it sank down, settled into place, fitting in seamlessly, smoothly, with an almost audible click, blending, merging, not only with me, but with the other person still within me. Nico. Melding us—all three of us—into one.

Nico's eyes rounded with surprise. And then as I watched, they rolled back in his head, his body growing limp and heavy above me.

"No," I cried and our world shifted. The dusky twilight left us and we were back in the plane. I was lying in the narrow aisle on the floor, with not just one man on top of me but two. Talon's weight shifted off me, light and quick, leaving Nico's heavier weight half-sprawled over me, still and unmoving. A sense of motion had me turning my head to the left, and I encountered Stefan's blue green hazel eyes. Behind him, I saw Jonnie's light brown curls.

"Lucinda," Stefan said, "are you all right?"

"Yes, but Nico isn't." Gently, I lifted Nico up and eased out from beneath him, laying him flat on the floor in my place.

With just that small movement, Nico stirred. His lids fluttered up. He saw me hovering over him, saw me awake and well, and smiled. Then a ripple moved over his flesh as if his skin was water and a rock had been thrown in, breaking the calm surface. The smile fell away. His eyes widened. A moment of hushed stillness. Then he began to convulse.

TWENTY

I N THAT CALM bliss of nothingness, Nico was born
again. A distant rushing sound filled his ears, vaguely
familiar. If he reached for it, he would know what it was.
But why reach for it when it was so calm, so comfortable
here? Peaceful like he had never felt before.

He frowned.

What had he felt before? Nico wondered curiously, a
part of him reaching out for that memory. Then it all came
back to him . . . sadness. Not tall enough, not handsome
enough. Never the one most beloved, although some queens
had appreciated his skill in bed, his adaptability, his enjoy-
ment of what they most enjoyed. But they had tired quickly
of him once the novelty had worn off, and he had been
passed down as he had grown older and his power stronger
to queens less and less desirable until he had come under
Mona SiGuri's rule. Became just another one of her less
beautiful people, existing in her rustic mountain court, lasting there for over a decade. Longer than he had expected.

Nico thought he was back there, up on the mountain, for
one moment before his eyes fluttered open, because he

ached all over. A whole body soreness and twinging pain
that usually came from severe punishment.

Then he opened his eyes and saw a beautiful face hovering above him. A golden, sultry angel.

"Lucinda," he murmured. "Am I still dreaming?" Because if he was, he did not want to wake up just yet. He did
not want to return to Mona SiGuri. To that harsh, barren
reality of tantrums and flogging, of punishment and petty
jealousy.

"No," said someone to his left. Nico turned his head
slowly, achingly, and saw Stefan, who, oddly enough, was
holding down his arm. From the periphery of his vision,
Nico glimpsed the solid blackness of Talon down by his
feet, holding those two leaden limbs down. And he not only
saw him but sensed him somehow.

"Why are you restraining me?" Nico asked, then realized where they were—in a small jet, flying high in the air,
cutting through it. That was the rushing noise that filled
his ears. And suddenly, he remembered it all. Everything
that had passed.

"Not dream. Reality," Nico mumbled. "And far sweeter
than any of my dreams ever could be."

"Then your reality must have really sucked," Jonnie said,
his youthful face peering down at him from over a seat.

"It did."

"You were convulsing," Lucinda said, her voice oddly
strained. "So badly that I thought you were going to break
apart."

"Was I? Is that why I feel so sore?"

"Do you remember what happened?" she asked.

Nico remembered a lot of things. But most searingly, he
remembered being inside Lucinda, stroking in and out of
her as she lay stretched beneath him like a golden offering.
He remembered that wave of power . . . of something that
had filled her, entered her, then entered him, too. Passing
up through her body into his. An unsettling weight that had
filled him with crushing heaviness, smothering him like
death.

His eyes narrowed. "Yeah, I remember."

"We bonded, Talon and I. And . . . I think you bonded with us."

Her words surprised, no, shocked him. Because he could feel the truth of her words . . . a tugging, invisible line spooling out between the three of them.

"That is not possible," Nico said. "Is it?" Because he was alive, and they were, well . . . not alive. More than just different realms separated them. Life itself did.

A ripple flowed over his skin, or rather under it. Like how the ground trembled a split second before an earthquake. Nico's eyes widened. "Oh shit," he muttered, as one of his lovely human ladies liked to say, when that heaviness stirred within him again. Something foreign, unsettling. Something Nico felt his body reject and prepare to rid itself of.

That something flowed within him again and his body tensed, rippled, knotted up unbearably tight as if iron flowed over his muscles and molded them crampingly taut in an unrelenting grip. Hands held down his arms, his legs, and a giant heaving convulsion shook him. Then another, and another. And this time he was awake and aware.

Nico felt as if his body would break apart. As if *he* would break apart. And all that anchored him, kept him from flying up and shattering apart into a million brittle pieces were those hands holding him down. A shuddering paroxysm took him over, shook him like a rag doll for a long, breathless time. And then it stopped and something worse started.

Heat built within him, seared him. Flashed up within him with bursting light, opening his mouth in a soundless scream. But the agony he felt was too vivid to express in mere sound. He started to glow, and it was not light that was pulled out from pleasure or taken in from Basking. No. The lunar glow gushed from him as if something were chasing it out . . . or trying to take it over. That light, that pure iridescent light that was him, that was Monère, changed. Darkened, hazed, and became red. Red like spilling blood.

"Mother of Darkness," Lucinda gasped softly, and Nico realized that what he was seeing was true, that his vision had not hazed from the searing, wrenching pain that roped him tight. That, indeed, he glowed with a color that no child of the moon ever possessed.

Had Nico been able to think, to breathe, he would have been afraid. But there was no room to be afraid, not when pain and cramping ache and heat was your entire world, and that world was on fire, blazing within you, and all you could do was try to not go up in flames with it.

He thought he had felt pain before. That it had become almost like a familiar, comforting friend in these last few years as he had grown stronger and Mona SiGuri had grown crueler, punishing him more, dancing that line, closer and closer each time, to killing him. What he felt now made all the punishing pain he had experienced under her hand pale like a petty lantern before the sun.

Now this was true pain. Unbearable, knotting, aching agony. Unescapable. And that's all you wanted to do—escape. Even if the only way to do so was through death.

But it was a merciless heat. It licked you alive, did not consume you. Just filled you. Spilled from you. And all you wanted to do was scream, and you could not even do that. No breath, no power of motion. Just a silent, frozen rictus of unbearable, sundering torment that felt as if it were tearing you up into little shreds, flaying you alive, with no end in sight to the suffering.

"Sweet Mother, his skin is hot. He's burning up," Stefan said, looking at Lucinda with fear in his eyes. Heat was the one thing that Monères could not withstand. They were cold-blooded creatures, children of the night, and heat, the sun, destroyed them. "We have to cool him down."

Lucinda did not answer. In fact, she did not move. Her skin was a color Stefan would not have believed possible for her—an almost ashen paleness beneath the tawny brown surface. Her body was held with that same rigid immobility that gripped Nico, and an echo of that silent agony screamed from her eyes.

A quick glance at Talon showed that the same pain echoed in his black eyes. That the same rigidity locked his body tight and unmoving.

"Goddess help us," Stefan muttered. "They're all caught up in the same suffering."

He released Nico's arm, scrambled across that bloodred blaze of light that streamed out from the warrior, and pried Lucinda's hands free from their tight grip around Nico's wrist. He pushed her back away from Nico, shoving her between a row of seats until her body was no longer in contact with the Monère warrior she had bonded with.

Lucinda gasped, her body loosened, and she fell back limply against the wall. "So much pain," she whispered.

"Jonnie, get Talon away from him," Stefan barked and heard movement behind him as Jonnie struggled to do as he said.

"I still feel it," Lucinda said, her body rippling with tremors, "echoes of his pain." She crawled out between the seats until she could see the two others who shared her bond. Talon rested limply, his body trembling like hers, propped against the edge of a seat, Jonnie round-eyed beside him. Nico, though, was still caught in that frozen silent rictus, with Hell's own moonlight shining darkly from him.

"Why is his light red like that?" Stefan asked.

"Our third moon shines that color in Hell," Lucinda said, and some of the appalled astonishment she was feeling was reflected in her voice, her eyes.

"Why does it shine within him?"

"Because I carry a small flicker of that light within me when I call forth heat. Now it is within him, too."

"It will kill him unless you do something."

"What? What can I do?" Her dark brown eyes churned even darker until they became almost black.

It was Talon who made the next suggestion.

"Suck part of his essence down into you as you did with the other warrior."

Hearing his high tenor voice, so bell-tinkling sweet and

melodious, suggesting something so vile, so evil, made Lucinda flinch.

"Not all of him," Talon said, as if he'd caught the echo of her thoughts, or felt them. "Just enough to cool him down. To take away some of that heat."

What he suggested . . .

"No," Lucinda said, shaking her head.

"Not to kill him. To save him," Talon said. "And if you do kill him . . ." His voice grew hushed. "I think he would prefer that rather than continuing in this agony."

But it was not that easy now.

"If he dies," Lucinda said. "If I kill him, we may all die."

"If the heat continues to consume him, he will die shortly anyway . . . and perhaps take you two with him," Stefan said. He cupped her cheek, turned her face to look at him. "Is there a chance that this can work?"

"Yes," Lucinda whispered, and gave this man who held her heart the full ugly truth. "But what I do . . . what you are asking me to do may take away not just this life, but his afterlife." She shook her head. "He may still have a chance at afterlife. I don't want to take that from him."

"He's crying," Talon said, pulling their attention back to Nico. It was hard to look down at the fallen warrior, to see such obvious suffering etched so deep and frozen upon that face. Even more unsettling to look full upon that eerie crimson glow that poured out of him.

Stefan would not have seen it had Talon not called their attention to it. A drop of liquid fell from the corners of Nico's eyes, tracking slow twin paths down his face. It was not clear and transparent as human and Monère tears were. It was colored red. And the faint, unmistakable scent wafting from it confirmed what it was. Mother Moon help him . . . Nico was crying tears of blood. As demons were rumored to do.

As they watched, Nico's lips moved slightly. Moved again with great trembling effort.

He whispered one word. *"Please."*

"Oh, Nico." Lucinda's voice broke upon the utterance of his name.

Stefan looked up to see matching streaks of redness tracking down Lucinda's face, confirming true what the old legends whispered of.

Lucinda bowed her head. Then with bleak resolve did as Nico had begged her to do. She opened her mouth, opened her power, and began to breathe him in. She pulled that eerie light into her. Literally drank it down. It swirled tight and thin, a funnel of unearthly light pulled from Nico, down her mouth, into her skin, the darkly tanned flesh absorbing it all.

She drank down Nico's essence, his heat, his light. And yet still that terrible tension gripped his body, did not let go. She drank even more with deep even breathing, in rhyme with his heartbeat, with her eyes closed as if asleep, as if lost in a dream. Finally, he muted.

When the light spilling from Nico was dimmed, when his power felt faint and his presence even fainter, she stopped. The light hovered before her mouth, licked over her lips like a knowing, living entity seeking a way into her. When it found no ingress, it returned from whence it came, reluctantly seeping back into Nico.

When the last of the crimson glow faded into him, that muscle-clenching tension finally released its hold over him.

Nico took in a great shuddering breath. Weak, so weak. Where that searing roping rigidity had gripped him before, now a sweet, almost floating lassitude lifted him up, pulling him from the heaviness of his body.

"He's ghosting," Nico heard Stefan say, and dimly realized they were talking about him.

Is that what's happening to me? Nico wondered, and found it not so bad a thing. A relief, almost, after that terrible unrelenting anguish.

Then hands touched him, nails sank into him sharply at his wrist, another piercing bite at his ankles. Blood spilled from him and pain sang through him, chasing away some of that floating lethargy, pulling him back. Pain and something else . . . a twin pulse of power, a pulling from two ends.

Nico hovered there in that hazy floating state he was half in and half out of, and realized it was Lucinda and Talon who held him back.

Let me go, he thought. *It doesn't hurt anymore.*

The answering echoes of two thoughts, of two entwined wills, came back to him. *No. If you go, you take us with you. Stay with us.*

But though they bound him, partly held him, Nico knew that he could still float free. And take them with him.

If you die, we go with you, those twin wills whispered.

It was the word *die* that jarred Nico, shook him free a bit more from that floating lassitude. Die. Such an ugly word for such a beautiful feeling, that cessation of pain. For himself, perhaps, he might wish it, but not for the other two. Not for Lucinda or for Talon. With regret, with a deep mental sigh, Nico stopped fighting them, and let them pull him back into the heavy weariness of his body.

Back into pain.

TWENTY-ONE

NICO GASPED IN air, his heart beating once more, and I wanted to cry. In happiness, in sadness, in relief. All of it.

He shivered uncontrollably, his body trembling, ours trembling along with his. Talon fallen across Nico's feet. I splayed across Nico's chest, my nails dug into his wrist, slick with his blood. With a quickness that was more kind than slowness would have been, I pulled my nails out from his pierced flesh. And conscious, so conscious of Stefan's gaze upon me, I licked those puncture wounds clean until blood no longer flowed from Nico's wrist. Then I licked my own nails spotless as I pressed my body against Nico's. Pressed down on him, and within, held him to us with the force of my will.

"I'm here," Nico muttered, his voice weak and faint. "Not going anywhere."

I wondered if he commented on my physical hold or on my tight mental grasp upon him. Below, Talon clung to Nico's legs, daintily licking his own nails clean.

Blood bonded us—Nico's blood—and more. I felt in

Talon's mind a fierce determination to keep Nico with us. *Mine*, his mind whispered, then amended, *ours*, as I hastily withdrew my mental probe, something I had unknowingly done. I curled up around Nico, shivering almost as much as he.

Sweet Hades. What had we done? To ourselves and to poor Nico?

"His skin's cool," Stefan said with frank relief as he pressed his hand to Nico's face and neck. An almost paternal touch he must have learned from caring for Jonnie, his young Mixed Blood ward. "He should be better," Stefan said frowning. "Why is he shivering?"

"Perhaps," I said, my own teeth starting to chatter. "Perhaps his body temperature needs to be warmer now." Warmer like a demon or a Floradëur.

Stefan's cool hand brushed my cheek softly, and I almost closed my eyes in relief . . . that he touched me voluntarily, willingly. That he did not shun me because of fear or disgust after he'd seen what I was capable of doing. Then his words broke the illusion. "You're cool, too. Cooler than you should be."

He'd only been checking my temperature.

"I think all three of us are cooler than we should be," I replied, my voice even, as if I were not crying inside. "It took great effort to bring Nico back." And to continue to anchor him to us.

"Your mind," Nico chattered, the edges of his teeth clicking together. "No need . . . to hold me so tightly."

"There is every need. I took too much of you, your living essence." And the essence of that Other. "What remains is too fragile."

"Darling," Nico said. He may have been shivering, but a very male, very roguish smile curved his lips. "You took . . . just enough of me," he said, sexual innuendo heavily coating those words.

"Jonnie," Stefan said abruptly. "Bring me all the blankets you can find."

When he had done so, Stefan sent the Mixed Blood up

front to the cockpit to sit with the pilot. "To give them some privacy," Stefan told the boy.

I watched as Jonnie moved with slow caution down the aisle, reminding me once more of the Mixed Blood's recent injuries. "Is Jonnie all right?"

Stefan nodded. "His stitches are holding, and he is not bleeding." With that same cool efficiency with which he had assessed our temperatures, he began unbuttoning my shirt.

"What are you doing?" I asked, shaking from cold, trembling from weakness, my body playing a variation of the same theme over and over again: shake, shake, tremble, shudder. And repeat.

"You're weak," Stefan said, "and weakening yourself even more by continuing to exert mental energy. Am I correct?"

My silence confirmed his guess.

"Bare skin," Stefan said calmly, stripping the shirt efficiently from me. "You need more skin-to-skin contact with each other. The bond between you should be strengthened with that physical connection, and you can all share body heat."

He lifted me from Nico briefly to peel off the Monère's shirt, and then lowered me back onto Nico's naked torso. The moment our bare skins touched, the shivering eased. A second later, I felt Talon's bare chest spoon against my back. I stiffened but did not protest. Because the moment we all touched—not just Talon and I touching Nico, but Talon and I touching each other as well—the shaking subsided almost completely. Blankets covered us, and our bodies, initially cool, quickly heated beneath the covers with shared warmth.

Stefan was right. Touching made the bonds stronger, and I expended less energy holding Nico mentally. Didn't need to. With physical touch between us all, it was as if all the bridges were suddenly connected, and the circuit running between us built up energy instead of consuming it. The flicker of Nico's life force strengthened into a small and steady flame, and I relaxed my hold on him. He maintained his vitality on his own.

I blinked once, twice, with sleepy languor. Lethargy assailed me, and I let it seep into me.

With warmth behind me and beneath me, with Nico's reassuring heartbeat reverberating in my ear, and the gentle rising and falling rhythm of his chest rocking us all, I fell asleep.

TWENTY-TWO

WHEN THE PLANE started to descend, the whine of the engines, and the scream of the air changing its pitch awoke me. I was enveloped in men, beneath and behind me. But it was the man who didn't touch me at all that drew my eyes, my heart. Stefan sat on the floor less than a foot away, his long length folded up tight between two seats, his head resting on bent knees. If I reached out my hand, I could touch him. But I didn't.

He was sleeping, the long sweep of his lashes looking both dark and delicately soft. Something you wanted to run your fingertips over just to feel the faint, tickling brush of it against your skin. His hair fell forward in silky straightness about his face, a wash of inky darkness. A lovely contrast against the alabaster white of his skin, the ruby redness of his mouth, the velvet softness of those lips. As beautiful as a man could be. But it was his inner beauty that drew me most. His goodness, his self-sacrifice, his care for a boy that was not his own. Even his extraordinary forbearing with the humans who had hunted him, with the man who had shot both Jonnie and him. A man that I would have killed.

The darkness in me was drawn to that goodness. Wanted to wrap it around me so that I could be as good, as pure, as kind. And a tiny part of me was like that. But an even greater part of me was not. Odd that it was this smallest part of me that yearned most for him . . . and felt most constrained by him.

It was Stefan's presence that had almost made me refuse to draw Nico's essence into me. I had not wanted Stefan to know of this one most ugly thing I could do.

Even more than wanting to hide that other side of me from him, my demon beast, this was the one thing I had never wanted Stefan to see. But he had, and I wondered now what he thought of me. What I would see in his eyes?

I made no sound or movement. Only my gaze touched Stefan, but he felt it somehow. Those long, sooty lashes lifted, and his eyes met mine. I concentrated on the little things instead of the confusion I felt inside. Surface details like the color of his eyes fresh from sleep, neither blue nor green but a magickal color caught in between.

It was he who reached out to touch me. A gentle brush of fingers against my cheek, a tender reassuring caress that squeezed my heart painfully. That could not be mistaken for anything as mundane or impersonal as checking the temperature of my skin, though he noted that, too.

"You're warmer," he whispered, the barest sound. "How do you feel?"

"Better. How long did we sleep?"

"Several hours."

I tried to slip out gently from between my two sleeping men, but my movements awakened them both.

Nico blinked his eyes open as I seized a couple of blankets, wrapped them around me, and sat up. Were it just the two of them, Nico and Stefan, I would not have minded my nakedness. Perhaps would have even flaunted it, but it was not just them. Talon's small hand, which had wrapped around my waist in sleep, slipped limply down to my hip as I sat up. I felt his fingers suddenly tense as he roused from slumber. That small hand retreated, leaving me free, and I stood and stepped away from them, retrieved my clothes where they had been draped over a seat. Turning my back, I dropped the blankets and dressed, listening to my men rustle and stir behind me. I had no need to ask how they felt, I could feel it. They were like me, rested, somewhat recharged, as much as we could in this realm. The greater healing and replenishing would only occur when I returned to Hell. My thoughts thus distracted, I did not see what my men saw when I turned around.

"Your wounds are healed," Nico said. With his thick chest white and bare amidst the blue sea of blankets that overflowed the aisle, he looked like a pale lustrous pearl. Talon, dark beside him, like an exotic black pearl found in China's deepest seas.

"What?" I said with surprise.

"Your wounds are healed," Nico repeated.

I looked down at my wrists. The ugly burnt flesh I expected to see was not there. In its place was flawless healed skin. It so shocked me that I ran my fingertips over the smooth skin, not believing what my eyes beheld until my touch confirmed it. I had healed.

"How can that be?" I whispered.

"Why are you so surprised?" Nico asked.

"Because I cannot heal here, not in this realm."

"You just did."

"Yes." My gaze flew to my men, looked at them with new and different eyes. "Your wounds are gone as well."

They glanced down at themselves. Nico murmured, "Well that was a little fast." But Talon looked as astounded as I.

"Do you normally heal this fast, Talon?"

"No, mistress. It usually takes me weeks."

"Your wounds were unchanged two hours ago," Stefan said, perched sideways on a seat, "and now they have disappeared. Even Monères don't heal that fast. Do you heal that quickly down in your realm?"

I shook my head. "It would have taken me two days, not two hours, for those burn wounds to repair. This came from our binding." Then, even more specifically. "This came from Talon."

"Me?" Talon said with surprise.

I nodded. "Floradëurs are known to heal quickly."

"But I don't."

"In Hell you do. That is one of your gifts."

"There is so much I do not know of my kind," Talon murmured.

"You will know more, soon enough," I promised him. "But first we go to High Court."

Excitement and fear shone in those pure black eyes. Talon had home to look forward to afterward. But in Stefan and Nico, I sensed only fear.

"The Queen Mother. High Court," Nico muttered. "Why go to all that effort to save me if you were just going to toss me to the Council?"

My eyes touched upon both Nico and Stefan. "Do not worry, you are no longer rogues. We will be welcome there. Well," I drawled, compelled to be truthful, "at least by some. Not all. But no harm will come to you there."

We descended down through layers of clouds, landing softly on a narrow airstrip surrounded by wild forest. We deplaned and watched from the lighted tarmac as the jet propelled itself quickly airborne again. Robert, the pilot, had been quite relieved to see me conscious once more.

"The pilot asked no questions," Stefan said, standing beside me.

"He has been with me for many years. And he took me—us—to where I had instructed him to go were I ever wounded."

Just leave me there and fly away had been my mandate.

In this quiet pocket of time before the others descended upon us, I took the opportunity to give my men some important instructions as well. "Speak of our binding to no one else."

"Why?" asked Jonnie.

"While it gives us strength, it also entails weakness that our enemies might seek to exploit if they knew of it."

"What weakness?" Jonnie asked.

"That if you kill one, you might kill all of us."

"Oh. I guess that is a pretty big weakness," he said.

"We will not say anything to others," Stefan said. "Will you tell your brother?"

I nodded. "And the High Lord; they will have to know. The only one in this realm who I will inform will be the Queen Mother."

"Why tell her? Would she not be the last person you would want aware of our secret?" Nico asked.

"She is the one person here that I trust most to keep it."

None of them asked why, though I knew they wanted to. I was glad they did not, because it was a question I could not have answered.

"So do we just wait here?" Nico asked, restless.

"Yes, they are aware that someone landed and will come seeking us shortly. Better that we be here, waiting, than approach them unknown from the forest. That might make them nervous."

They proved to be nervous enough as it was. On the tail of my words, two vans sped onto the private airstrip, halting abruptly and spilling out a dozen Monère guards armed to the hilt with swords and daggers and a few discreet guns tucked here and there.

A tall dark-haired man, powerfully built, with a sweeping mustache, the kind that curled up at the ends, stepped out of the third vehicle, a green sedan. He nodded to us cordially, but his eyes looked over our little group with sharp assessment, noting our few weapons—daggers only, the sword and gun once more in the long carry bag. His look swept over my men, lingering curiously on Talon.

He approached with a smile, bowed with courtly flourish, and took my hand in his, kissing the back of it. One of the few men I allowed to do so. "Princess Lucinda," he greeted in a husky baritone. "We are surprised but most pleased to see you here again."

"Captain Gilbert," I said, sliding my hand gently free from his. "My apologies for not being able to notify you ahead of time of our arrival. These are . . ." I made the barest pause before adding, "my men." And introduced them to him.

"Is Mona SiGuri, or any of her men, here?" I asked.

"No, Princess."

"Good. If she should arrive, I would ask that I be notified at once, and that she not be allowed near any of my people."

"It shall be as you wish," Captain Gilbert said, nodding.

But I was not yet finished with my requests. "And if there are, perchance, any other demons that you might see—my brother and the High Lord excepted—I would ask that the same orders apply to them."

Captain Gilbert's eyebrows raised so high that they disappeared beneath the sweep of his dark hair. "Believe me, Lucinda," he said, my remark startling him out of his distant formality for a moment, "if another demon appears, you will be the first one we will come running to."

Accompanied by the guards, we drove sedately into a compound nestled deep in the wilds of Minnesota along the northern border abutting Canada, where the air was brisk and clean, and human neighbors nonexistent.

Seated between Nico and me, Talon shivered. Only a small ripple of skin, but Nico sensed it and turned so that his knees brushed Talon's. His two hands reached out, engulfing our smaller ones, connecting us, black skin, white skin, and gold.

"Cold?" I asked Talon, though his skin felt warm. Nico's skin was actually the coolest among us, though not cold exactly. It was neither cold nor heated, but a temperature in between.

"No, mistress." *Just nervous*, said his eyes.

"Call me Lucinda," I said. *We are bonded, after all, you and I and Nico.*

"Yes, mistress," Talon said, his eyes lowering to the floor, contradicting my order. I let it go with an inner shrug as we pulled up before the grand manor house, an old stately building that towered three stories above us.

Tradition. Even the Monère had it. And standing, waiting in welcome for us, was one of those traditions—the steward of the great house, an impeccably groomed man the same height as Nico but slenderer, with flashes of white sprinkled among the blackness of his hair, proclaiming the seniority of his age.

He bowed in deep welcome. "Princess Lucinda. You honor us with your presence."

I gave him one of my rare smiles, a smile with nothing but warmth. "Mathias," I murmured and reached up to give him a kiss upon the cheek that flustered the little man. A pleased blush pinkened that dignified face.

"As proper as ever, keeping the rest of us in line by the example you lead," I teased and introduced the others to him. "My men," I said, finding it less awkward to say those words aloud the second time around.

The steward bowed again in welcome. "Gentlemen. Princess. Please do not hesitate to let us know how we can be of service to you during your stay."

"I will not be staying long, Mathias."

Mathias continued as if I had not spoken. "Perhaps you might find it easier to take a suite in the Great House, Princess."

I smiled at the predictability of the little steward, a game of sorts that had started many years ago and continued on between us during my infrequent visits: the briefness of my rare visits, and his urging for a longer, lengthier stay.

"Thank you, but no. I will stay in my brother's lodgings, as usual. And in there, only briefly."

"Is there anything you might need, milady?"

Here we veered from my usual habit—which would have been to decline his kind offer. "Yes," I said, surprising him. "Please send a healer to my brother's residence; one of my men has need of her skills. And if you could possibly find some fresh clothing for Nico and Talon, I would much appreciate that."

"It shall be brought to you shortly, Princess." Mathias

bowed again, and quietly gave instructions to two hovering footmen, sending them running off in different directions.

Captain Gilbert, who had been standing quietly throughout the exchange, took my hand once more in his. "Princess Lucinda, I will inform the Queen Mother that you wish an audience with her." His dark eyes gleamed up at me as he bent over my hand once more. "I will see you shortly," he said, a question neatly couched as a statement.

He waited for my soft answer, "Yes," before releasing my hand. Then strode off briskly across the courtyard toward Council Hall, where the Queen Mother presided. Three of his men followed behind him; the rest dispersed to their various posts.

At Mathias's instructions, a young footman picked up our belongings, the two backpacks and long carry bag, and trotted off in the opposite direction toward the small, private residences flanking the Great House. We followed behind at a more leisurely pace, moving as fast as Jonnie's slow and careful walk.

"Do you think the healer will be able to help Jonnie?" Stefan asked in a quiet voice too low for the Mixed Blood to hear.

"I don't know," I replied, equally soft. "There are scarce few Mixed Bloods among the Monère, even less than I have encountered during my travels. Perhaps the healer will have a better idea; we had two Mixed Bloods residing here at High Court not long ago."

"Are they here still?"

"No, they departed to the south territory of Louisiana, in the service of Mona Lisa, our first Mixed Blood Queen."

This surprised Stefan enough to make him stop walking; I halted as well. "A Mixed Blood Queen," he said, stunned by the concept. As we all had been.

"Three-quarters of Mona Lisa'a blood is Monère, only a fourth of her is human. Our Mother Moon blessed her with our strength and gifts, and with the ability to draw down its rays. To Bask."

"I would very much like to have Jonnie meet this new Queen one day, and the two Mixed Bloods who serve her."

"Perhaps one day he will." The mention of the future turned my thoughts inward, and we traveled the rest of the way in thoughtful silence.

The house where my brother resided during his frequent visits to High Court was nestled farthest back from the Great House, apart from the other small residences, with the thick woods but a dozen yards away. I stepped into the small abode and breathed in Halcyon's familiar scent; not only his physical scent but his psychic one—the lingering traces of his power that were detectable only to another demon dead. Good thing, because my men—how quickly I had come to think of them as such—were unsettled enough as it was. They stood unmoving at the threshold.

"Come in," I urged. With a distinct swallow, Stefan and Nico entered. Jonnie and Talon followed cautiously behind, peering with awe at the comfortable but simply furnished nest that was like any other human house in all things but one. The closed decorative shutters outside were simply that—decorative. There were no windows inside.

The footman, a young Monère with light sandy hair, emerged from the adjacent room. "I put your bags in the bedroom, Princess," he said, a rosy blush darkening his cheeks, his eyes darting fascinated gazes at me before flitting shyly away.

"That's fine," I said and murmured my thanks. Throat bobbing nervously, the young Monère darted away.

"Have a seat, make yourselves comfortable." I waved my hand toward the settee and wing chair by the far wall. "I'm going to clean up." And so saying, I walked into the bedroom.

The shower felt like a luxury, hot water beating against my skin, washing away the grime of dirt, sweat, and blood . . . and the stink of fear and desperation. By the time my hair was lathered and washed and skin cleansed, only sad regrets lingered like a faint bitter aftertaste.

The threat of Mona SiGuri could be neutralized, or

controlled at least. But the other demon, Derek . . . For as long as he was still in existence and loose, he would be an ever-present danger, hovering in the background, always ready to strike. If not at me directly, then at my men. Thinking and worrying about that brought me to a solution that solved so many things. A solution I would not have sought, or even thought of, had not the presence of the other demon compelled me to it. Perhaps I should thank him for that before I killed him.

Nah. On second thought, probably best just to kill the demon bastard.

I toweled myself dry and raided my brother's closet. Many clothes but few colors. Typical Halcyon. I selected a few garments and slipped into them. His white silk shirt strained tight across my bosom, and the sleeves hung long beyond my fingertips. His black pants fit just as badly, stretching across the flare of my hips, the fullness of my bottom, but gaping loose at the stomach and going inches beyond my feet. The latter was taken care of with a belt. The other problems, the too long sleeves and pant legs I rolled up.

I stepped back out into the small living room, toweling dry my hair, to find them still standing there by the door, unmoved from where I had left them. A pile of clothing was stacked neatly in a chair.

"Oh, good. They brought you clean clothes. Go ahead and use the shower. Extra towels are in the linen closet by the bathroom."

They just stared at me in silence, stunned looks on their faces.

"What?" I asked.

"You look . . ." Stefan's voice trailed off.

"I know," I said, tossing the wet towel onto a side table. "Quite ragged. My brother, as you can see, is taller and slimmer than I."

"Far from ragged," Stefan murmured, his eyes warm and appreciative. "You look lovely. Stunningly so, in fact, in your brother's colors." White shirt and black pants, Halcyon's preference. Just as mine was a maroon or a deep wine red top paired with black leather pants.

I dismissed the compliment, feeling sloppy in the ill-fitting clothes. "Have you met my brother?"

"No, I have never had that privilege. But all know of him." Stefan's eyes fell to the sleeves that chose at that moment to loosen and roll down. If the pants did so during an awkward time, I might trip or worse, be thrown off balance accidentally and stab someone next to me with my dagger-sharp nails. A potential hazard I could not afford. Regretfully, I slashed off the extra lengths with an easy slicing of nails, butchering my brother's quality apparel.

Stefan gazed at the ragged edges of my pants and sleeves. "You need to stitch those up."

"I don't sew," I said, waving my fingers, long nails flashing. "Handy for slicing and dicing, but not for domestic chores."

"Allow me then." Stefan retrieved a small sewing kit from his backpack. Leading me to the settee, he knelt and began to hem up my right sleeve with neat little stitches.

"You sew," I said, surprised.

"And I am handy at many domestic chores." He grinned, looking so boyish for a moment. Until the light caught and reflected the few silver strands scattered like white tinsel among the silky darkness of his hair. Those signs of his age, of his life, racing quickly by, sobered me.

The others still dithered at the doorway, as if they couldn't decide who should shower next. I decided for them. "Nico, why don't you use the bathroom facilities next?"

He hesitated. "Lucinda. I don't think that's a good idea. The High Prince—"

"Would want you to be clean before meeting the Queen Mother."

The stalwart warrior gulped. "We are to go before the Queen Mother?"

"Yes."

"Couldn't you just go?" Nico asked plaintively.

"I'm afraid not," I said, my tone gentle but firm. "She will want to meet you."

He swallowed, looked shaken.

"She will want to meet all of you," I added for good measure, and watched the rest of them blanch.

"Go on, Nico." I waved him toward the bedroom. "Shower quickly so the others will have enough time to clean up also."

Reluctantly, Nico did as I bade, advancing timidly into Halcyon's bedroom, almost making me smile. Almost, but not quite. Not with what gleamed white and vivid before my eyes.

My hand—the free one—reached out and lightly stroked the few silver strands decorating the raven darkness bent before me.

"Does it bother you?" Stefan asked without looking up. "My white hair?"

"No," I replied. But I lied. It did bother me, this evidence of the years of life irretrievably lost to him, wasted so unnecessarily. A part of me wanted to know the name of the Queen, the last one who had finally compelled Stefan onto the path of outcast rogue, stealing those years from him by forcing him to leave the sanctuary of her shared light. A part of me whispered it would be better not to know, in case I ever met her. So I did not carve my nails down her face, tearing flesh from bone if I knew who she was.

I could not do anything about those years Stefan had already lost, but the rest . . . that I could do something about.

A piece of paper resting by the pile of clothes caught my eye. I picked it up and read it. A handwritten note from Mathias. The efficient steward had remembered something I had forgotten—the feeding of my men.

Bring them down to the dining hall in a short while, he wrote. *I will have some light repast prepared for them.*

Perhaps our bloodied and dirt-stained clothes, our paucity of baggage, had clued the efficient steward in to our hasty flight here. Or perhaps Mathias had simply known that a demon would not have thought of something she did not partake in herself here—food.

I glanced around the room I sat in. One other thing this place lacked was a kitchen. No need for it when all demons required was hot blood directly from the source of provision.

Silly to have forgotten something so necessary to the well-being of my men. Emphasizing how ill equipped I was to see to their proper care.

Would I have thought of their need for food when I had gone to slack my own hunger? Perhaps. I would never know now.

Nico emerged from the bedroom garbed in clean borrowed clothes. Jonnie went next into the bedroom as Stefan finished hemming my sleeves and bent down to my pant legs, lifting and putting first my right foot, then my left on his bent knee. I watched the nimble play of his fingers wielding the needle deftly and dexterously like a little sword. Admired the neat, even stitches he placed. Admired even more his comfortable matter-of-factness in doing what was traditionally women's work. And felt touched by the pleased smile that kicked up a corner of his mouth, the obvious satisfaction he took in doing this small thing for me.

"Much better," Stefan murmured when he was finally done, and rose to his feet. Pulled me to mine. Taking my hand in his as if it were the most natural thing to do, without thought, without fear or worry that my nails would tear his skin. So much trust in that simple gesture.

I murmured my thanks. For one sweet moment I let my hand linger in his. Then I slipped free of his gentle grasp. Made myself walk slowly to the door so that I could tell myself: *See, I'm not running from that lopsided smile*.

Eyes looking out the door, one foot over the threshold, I paused. "When everyone has cleaned up, and when the healer has finished, return to the Great House. Mathias, the steward, will have some food ready for you. I'll meet you there," I told them.

Slipping outside, I closed the door gently behind me.

Twenty-three

T HE PLEASURE STEFAN had felt in caring for his lady
drained away with her withdrawal. With her leaving.

Stefan watched Lucinda go quickly down the stone walk-
way, heading in the direction of the manor house. No sound
betrayed her movements or told of where she headed. He'd
had to open the door after she left and peer after her like a
lovesick swain, which he was. A jealous lovesick swain. One
that burned to know where she went.

The spray of the shower from the other room filled his
ears, and the sense of another's presence brushed his awareness as Nico came to stand beside him in the open doorway.

"They let us keep our weapons," Stefan said to the other
man. "And set no guard to watch us, even though the captain had to know, or at least suspect, what you and I are—
rogues." The thrum of their power, stronger than any of the
guards that had milled about them, as strong as the captain
himself, would have betrayed them, if nothing else.

"We are no longer rogues," Nico said mildly. "We are
Princess Lucinda's men, and they are treating us as such."

She disappeared around the bend. Was no longer visible to Stefan's sight or to any of his other senses.

"She does not know how she looks in her brother's clothes," Stefan murmured.

With her wet hair slicked back from her face, those gilded locks darkened almost to bronze, she had been a study of contrasts and colors. The ivory silk had brought out the loveliness of her warm, tawny skin. The hair, that striking golden mane that danced and flowed about her face when it was dry, had been dark and subdued, allowing one's eyes to appreciate what it could not before—the striking beauty of those dark chocolate eyes, the exquisite arch of high cheek-bones, the straight patrician nose, the delicate line of her jaw, the flare of her brows like dark wings painted across her aristocratic brow. Female beauty in its purest aesthetic form . . . until your gaze fell upon the ripeness of those exotic lips, the flare of her hips, the womanly roundness of her buttocks, the lush swelling of her breasts pushing against the tight constraint of her shirt with her nipples faithfully outlined in exquisite detail.

The obviously masculine attire, the bigness of it, the inward cinching of a man's belt tight across her waist . . . they only served to showcase the wonderfully feminine body beneath it; Goddess, woman, soft and spilling, warm and generous, lush and full, abundant. A body a man could sink into with bliss, and lose himself forever in.

Even the nails, which she was ever so conscious of. Those lethal nails that had sliced across the too-long sleeves and the thicker fabric of her pant legs with almost frightening ease . . . even that had only added to the dangerous allure of her potent sexuality. An innate quality that exuded from her always, drawing men to her like moths pulled to a flickering flame.

"No," Nico agreed, "she does not know how she looks. How she appeals, dressed as she is."

"Where do you think she goes?"

Stefan's seemingly idle voice fooled Nico not for a second. "Where *you* think she goes. To feed."

"From who?"

"Oh, probably the big and willing Captain Gilbert, who practically ate her up with his eyes." Dryness prickled Nico's words like a scratchy blanket.

Stefan straightened from the doorframe. Took a step out the door.

"Where are you going?" Nico asked.

"After her." Stefan turned steely eyes to his fellow warrior. The man who had first been saved by Lucinda, then in turn had saved her, bonded with her. And Stefan could no longer bear any resentment against the other rogue; it had faded beneath the gratitude of having Lucinda still here with them. But gratitude stretched only so far.

"Let her see to her needs," Nico said quietly to his new brother in arms. And though his words were reasonable—wise, even—his eyes shone with the same malcontent that Stefan felt. But unhappy though he may be, he was willing to let their lady slack her thirst on another. A willingness Stefan did not share.

"I can see to her needs," Stefan said.

"She does not want you to."

"Only because she still thinks me weak and recovering from my wounds."

"Which you are," Nico said.

"My blood volume, though, is adequate."

"And the healer?"

"Should she arrive while I am gone, see what she can do for Jonnie. If she cannot await my return, then so be it." With those words, Stefan strode down the path after his lady love, his Princess. After his thirsty, wayward demon who had wandered off to sink those lovely sharp fangs into another.

TWENTY-FOUR

I HEADED IN the direction of the stables. Toward that solitary heartbeat that awaited me. But it was the heartbeat that trailed after me that caused me to veer off my chosen path and blend into the nearby forest, woodland that grew abundant and rampant and untamed about the small pocket of civilization carved out among the wild. An appropriate metaphor for what High Court stood for. The one voice of reason and restraint, of rules and protocol. The only thing checking what would otherwise be the unlimited rule of the queens. Individual fiefdoms though they ruled, even queens had to bend their stiff knees and even stiffer wills to the High Council. For the Council had the one thing that all, even the most arrogant of queens, were afraid of—Halcyon, the High Prince of Hell. Ruler of a place they themselves might one day find themselves inhabiting. And before him, so long ago that many had forgotten, had been his father, Blaec. The High Lord of Hell.

Through the cover of leaves and branches I saw Stefan round the path, lithe and graceful, walking swiftly. Somehow I had known it would be he.

Lost amidst the dappling moonlight and autumn red leaves—the silence of my body—I watched him stop and pause. Felt him send out his power in a silent seeking wave, searching for me. And wondered if I should leave it as nature had intended: naught for him to find.

He called out my name, as if he knew that I watched him, hidden, unheard, unfelt.

"Lucinda." Just my name, breathed like a soft prayer. And I found myself unable to resist. Found it impossible not to answer that call. That mix of question, plea, and demand all tumbled together in the low timbre of his voice.

"Here," I whispered.

With that one word, that one sound, he turned and came unerringly toward me, finding me.

"Where do you go?" Stefan asked. Nothing in his voice but gentle question. But in his eyes . . . oh, his eyes . . . they betrayed him as his body did, with the hastened rhythm of his heart, the more forceful drumming beat. His eyes were a stormy mixture of thunder and sea, of lightning spilling down from the sky and striking the depths of the ocean. A flashing, thunderous turmoil were those eyes.

"Captain Gilbert awaits me," I said.

A silence, a heartbeat.

"I am here now," Stefan said quietly and reasonably, like a patient husband who had chased down an errant wife and was willing to forgive her. An image that would have brought a smile to my lips had it not panged me so.

"No," I said. A gentle rejection.

"Yes," he returned, the singular word spoken with deceptive mildness.

Perhaps it was the shock of it—the blatant opposition to my will—but it amused me and saddened me. Because it was what made Stefan—and Nico, also, that stubborn intractable rogue—so special to me. No others would dare talk to me so, without fear, with such sure presumption to their right to me. A right that I had granted them but had to withdraw now for their sake. Because I had come to realize that they were not really mine to claim. In a short while, if events unfolded as I hoped they would, I would give them to another far better equipped to provide them with what they needed—security, protection, constancy. Life-giving light.

And part of this . . . all of it . . . shaded my voice when I replied. A yearning for one more time; a last time to claim him as mine. "Very well. I will send the captain away. Wait for me here."

I left him amidst the windblown leaves with their vibrant splash of color silvered under the hovering moon above, and made my way silently behind the stables.

Captain Gilbert glanced at me with rueful eyes.

"You heard," I said.

"Yes."

"I'm sorry."

"Not as much as I, Princess," the big man said, regretfully. "I half suspected from your constraint, but still I hoped." He pushed away from the barn wall and approached me. Put a gentle, cupping hand around my neck. "I will always be here if you should ever have need." With a last brush of his thumb across my nape, he took his leave.

I pondered his words long after he had left. Examined the truth in them as I went soundlessly to where Stefan awaited me. He *would* always be here, Captain Gilbert, if patterns of the past held true for the future. The beauty of serving here at High Court, and why all Monère who were past their first century of life vied for positions here. Younger men thought of it as something they would strive for, afterward. After the first flush of their youth and virginity was romped away in their queen's bed. After that same queen, once eager and ardent and affectionate, grew tired of them, or perhaps frightened of their growing power, and turned them from their arms and bodies. Then and only then did they cast their eyes toward High Court and yearn to serve the most ultimate of ladies—the Queen Mother. Not for a chance in her bed—she did not take lovers, at least not any that were known. No, they wanted to serve her because her powers were far greater than any other queens, and in equal measure, her tolerance higher for her men and their warrior power. No warrior had ever grown too strong for her, not even her Warrior Lord.

Serve her well and faithfully, which in turn meant serving the Court, and a warrior's position here was secure for the rest of his days. Men who would have otherwise been rogues, found a rare berth of safety here among their highest ruler. A lucky few.

I pondered the other part of Captain Gilbert's words that had struck me true. My constraint. How aptly put, and how different I must seem to him from my previous visit. That had been the real me. The me I would remind Stefan of once more. Deliberately I cast off those invisible ties binding me . . . the uncharacteristic hesitance, the fear, the constraint. I shed them, let them slide from me. Let my body relax, so that I swayed gently with each gliding step I took closer toward him—my drink, my meal, my living fount of blood.

The arrogance, the cynicism, the utterly ruthless sexuality that was my greatest power and weapon unwound and flowed from me, seeped out from my pores, coating me truer than real skin.

He wished me to drink from him, and I would. I would take blood from him as I would from any other man, giving back pleasure in even exchange. I would let him see me as I truly was. And perhaps then, he would not mind so very much when I passed him to another.

SHE CAME TO Stefan in silence. In the whisper of the night. An ethereal, glistening being. Shimmers of dusky brown and golden hues. A tawny goddess toppled down from the heavens, come to walk among man. Not an angel. No, far from that. For she moved with a lethal grace and dangerous beauty. With the promise of darkness rather than of light gleaming from her eyes. She came to him with lazy menace, with a liquid swaying grace, loose and free. Unrestrained.

A good word the captain had used . . . constraint. And Stefan damned him for knowing Lucinda that well. Better than he. For Stefan had never seen her like this. Like a cup not just full but overflowing. Brimming with dark passion and the promise of even darker delights.

Where she had been beautiful before, now she was breath-takingly sultry. Where she had stopped the heart, now she pounded it with a fierce primal rhythm, with a primitive beat, with a rolling hunger and blatant sexuality unleashed. Until the one gazing upon her felt the keenest of ache, and the desperate desire to satisfy that ache. To impale himself on the sharpness of her fangs, to feel his life blood flowing into her mouth. To experience the sharp dagger point of her nails sinking through his skin like sweet, painful bliss. Owning and possessing. Feeding and being fed.

Her eyes flashed dark and knowing, and a wanton smile teased and tantalized. Unsubtle delights were promised by those lips, not red but flushed dark mauve like vintage wine aged to perfection. Something that would satisfy the palette with a taste of the exotic and sublime. Something that would leave you thirsting and dying to taste her one more time long after she had left you, this ephemeral crea-ture of passion unbridled, of lust unreined.

Stefan knew that it was otherwise. That she was more than the overflowing lushness of her body, of the breasts almost spilling from her shirt, of the fullness of her hips, and the tantalizing dip of that tiny waist that called for a man's hands to try and span it. As if by holding her there, locked and secure, he could truly possess her.

No man could ever hope to possess her, a voice inside his head whispered. Stefan brushed it away like a buzzing gnat. Not own, not possess. But belong to—yes! . . . if she gave herself to you.

"Lucinda," he said as she took him by the hand and led him deeper into the woods. When they came to a grassy meadow at the base of a knoll, he felt a shimmer of energy and sensed something encircle them, enclose them.

"What did you do?" Stefan asked.

"Ringed us in a shield of silence." She released his hand and turned to face him, so small in stature but large in something else. Not presence, exactly. Nor was it a queen's aphidy. No, what oozed from her pores, filled the air with her essence, was something even more potent—a raw and untamed sexuality that promised to unmoor and unhinge one's very soul.

He pondered her words for a moment over the pounding of his heart, giving it a moment to calm—giving *himself* a moment to calm. "No one can hear us?"

She shook her head, eyes dark and slumberous with mystery and allure, answering with a siren's dangerous smile that scraped his nerve endings like a cat's sharp, playful swipe.

"You could scream and beg and plead," she whispered, "and no one would hear you but me."

The concept of an invisible barrier of sound encircling them in complete and utter silence, in total privacy from acute Monère senses, was both tantalizing and frightening.

"Why are you doing this? Being like this?" Stefan asked.

Her eyes drifted down his neck, landing with an almost palpable caress upon where his pulse bounded in accelerated rhythm. She smiled, flashing the tips of her fangs.

"You wanted to be my food. This is how I treat my food," she purred and stepped closer until her ripe breasts almost grazed his chest. Had she taken a breath, she would have touched him. But she did not take a breath. She did not breathe. And never was Stefan more aware of her total stillness, of her complete and utter difference from himself than now, when her silence was juxtaposed against his noise. So aware of his beatings of life, the constant pulsation, and her lack of it.

Then she touched him. Not with her hands or nails or mouth. But with an invisible caress. With phantom hands that floated over that beating pulse that she gazed upon so hungrily. She touched him with a soft and feathery stroke that pulled a sound from his lips of surprise and of pleasure.

He bent down, his lips hovering over hers, his breath puffing softly across her lips.

"You don't need to do this," Stefan said, "to seduce me. I am already yours." Because that was what she was doing: seducing him, with an alarming ease that raised the tiny hairs of his body up on end. Phantom hands stroked across his face, rifled through his hair, drew him even closer so that her mouth touched his.

"But that is what I do," she murmured against his lips. "Seduce." The word hissed sibilantly into his mouth. Arrowed down into him with a sudden dart of sensation that made him gasp. "I seduce you for a taste of your blood."

Her voice licked across his skin, an incredible sensation, like the silky brush of fur against naked flesh, making goose bumps rise up all over his body . . . and something else down below. Then it was not her voice that touched him but her actual hands. A physical touch upon his swollen thickness, a touch far sweeter than the brush of any phantom hand could be. Feather-lightly she touched him, and he broke from the sweetness of her lips so he could watch her hand trace over him, outlining his dimensions. So he could watch and feel the scrape of those dangerous nails over the head of him.

The sight and sensation was almost too much, making Stefan close his eyes, shudder and tremble against her, his breath stumbling and catching in his throat.

"Lucinda." Her name was both a plea for mercy and a cry not to stop. He yearned for her, needed her, lusted after her . . . and was unsettled by her, by what she was telling him, showing him. That these wild emotions, these knee-weakening surges of pleasure were what she gave to all who let her drink of their blood.

"You don't need to do this, my lady," Stefan said, dropping to his knees, baring his neck to her, a silent pale offering before her.

"Oh, but I do." She stroked with her hand just above his skin, along the ivory sweep of his throat stretched out before her as if his power, his male essence, was something tangible she could feel. "For it is not just blood I feed upon, you see." She bent down, deliberately breathing deeply, taking in his scent, smelling his blood. "I also feed on your release . . . and your light. I take that, too, into me, and for a brief moment, it makes me feel almost alive again."

"All that you need, all that you would have of me is yours." Soft words, a quiet pledge of devotion still that brought not pleasure but a sting of tears to Lucinda's eyes as she hovered over his tantalizing pulse.

He did not fear her yet. Not as he should.

She wrapped him suddenly tight in chains invisible, in bonds unbreakable. She felt him tremble beneath her phantom hands as she ran them down the swell of his chest, swept them over his wide shoulders, his muscled arms, both strong and weak and immobile beneath her mental touch.

"You do not know all that I need, all that I could take from you," Lucinda said, her eyes suddenly flashing fierce. Her voice became dark and cutting, something that flayed the skin instead of caressing it. "What can please, can also hurt."

Stefan could not help his involuntary flinch or the sudden speeding of his heart as he knelt frozen before her, utterly helpless beneath her power.

"I can feed from pain and suffering, too," she whispered, each word lancing his skin like a scorpion's sting, a throbbing tender ache for a moment before easing to just a tiny pain. "I do not have to coax the moon's light from you in pleasure. I can rip it from you in painful ecstasy. Although the ecstasy would be more on my part, not yours."

"Why are you doing this, Lucinda?" Every part of him was frozen but for his voice and his eyes. They looked at her with pleading, with confusion, with hurt. "Why do you want me to fear you?"

"Because you should," she said, walking slowly around him in unnerving silence, softly flaying him with her words, each syllable a tiny pinching sting. "Because I am demon dead, and you are alive and living and something we feed upon: your blood, your pleasure, or your tears; your light that we no longer carry in us." She laid the sharp point of a nail on the back of his shoulder, ran it in a dangerous scraping tease across to the opposite shoulder. Sank it through cloth to prick his skin, feel it quiver beneath her needle-sharp touch.

"Because if you understood the thirst that we carry with us always, not just to feed upon your blood, but to bathe in it, to wallow in it . . . then you would only just begin to comprehend the danger you foolishly dance with each moment you are with me. You do not truly know what the demon dead are capable of. And your ignorance does not make you safe." She circled to the front of him in a silent slithering undulation, knelt before him and ran her sharp nails in a fabric-piercing dance across his chest, a lethal prickling tease.

"So I will show you a little of what I can do. I shall give you a small taste of me, as I take a small taste of you." A demon oath. Traditional words taught to them to speak during an exchange. A reminder. Not to the supplicant who yielded his life-giving blood, but to the demon that drank it. A reminder to take only a little, so that they did not inadvertently kill their donor. An oath more applicable to a fragile human blood yielder, but oft said when drinking from a Monère contributor, as well, for their richer blood, their more potent power, was a heady temptation.

Deliberately, Lucinda grazed the tip of her fangs over that smooth, unblemished neck. Over that vibrant, pounding pulse.

His body tensed against his will.

She scraped his skin again, a sharp-gentle caress, and he shivered. Would have leaned into her had he been able to, but her bonds held him still, so he was unable to move either toward or away from her.

With a sudden lunging strike, she bit him with a force that reverberated like a blow throughout his body. A sharp hard burst of pain, a moment of inherent fear, and his primal survival instinct kicked in, too late, gripping him as she drank the first mouthful of his blood.

Then his need to struggle, to escape, subsided. And in place of panic, a sweet lassitude drifted over Stefan, through him, took him over. An easing of the limbs, a relaxing of the will. The fear faded and pleasure took its place, seeping in like a potent drug. Aided by invisible phantom touches along his skin, and deeper caresses within him, as if she had reached down, deep inside, and plucked the chord of desire, twanging it through him.

With the second gulp of hot blood, it changed. The chord of desire was plucked again, this time not so gently. With a deliberate jarring force, so that pleasure vibrated more strongly through him. The invisible bonds holding him eased as if she knew she no longer had to hold him; that the pleasure singing through him like a hot fierce song would keep him bound to her more forcibly than chains ever could.

His body arched against her like a bow pulled back, drawn taut, and she accommodated his body's natural response with but the barest incremental adjustment of her own body. With an ease and knowledge that could have only come from experiencing a thousand countless other such reactions.

With the third swallow of his blood, Lucinda ramped up the sensation like a screw suddenly turned tight. She gathered desire and pleasure like an invisible force and shoved it down Stefan. Rammed it inside him like a sharp, piercing arrow.

A storm of bliss broke inside him.

His light shot from him, illuminating Stefan with blinding brilliance. His desire crested like a wave smashed against the shore, and he fractured, splintered, came apart in her arms, heaving and shuddering against her as she pressed her weight against him from above, his sex pulsing and ejaculating down below. In a haze of lassitude and floating release, he felt her teeth disengage. Felt her mouth leave him. Felt her arms lower him down to the ground where he lay as helpless now, utterly relaxed, as he had been arched up against her, drawn tight with desire.

Even drifting in the lethargy of passion ignited and released, Stefan was aware of how quickly and effortlessly she
had built up that pleasure and spilled him over into release.
Of how easily she had called forth his light and his climax
from him . . . with an almost impersonal detachment.

Even caught up as he was in the post-climactic languor,
a part of Stefan was outraged. Not because it had been de-
tached and impersonal, but because she had tried to make
it seem so.

Some of what he was feeling must have shown in his
eyes, because hers fell away from his.

He sat up with a great concentrated effort. "It will not
work," he said.

"What will not work?"

"Whatever you were trying to do, to show me, tell me.
That I am just one of the thousands of men you have fed
upon before, the thousands of men you will feed upon in
the future. *That* won't work." His hand reached out and
touched her face with rough tenderness. "I know you care
for me."

Lucinda flinched, the tiniest movement beneath his hand,
before she withdrew from his touch. "Have you not learned
yet?"

"What?"

"That you cannot trust a demon, much less their emotions."

TWENTY-FIVE

THE LESSON DELIVERED, I dissolved the sound barrier I had erected around us.

A voice pierced the air. My name "Lucinda!" called loudly with urgency. Jonnie's voice.

And then Talon's cry. Softer, weaker, but just as desperate, joining the youth's. "Princess! We need you quickly."

I felt it then, what I had not felt with the sound barrier around us. The pull of the other two caught in our bond, one of them weak and strained, the other alarmingly faint.

"Nico." His name was a soft prayer on my lips as I leaped toward the lodging where I had thought them safe—in Halcyon's private abode, in the protection of High Court. Of all possible places on Earth, I had thought they would be safe here.

I crashed through the door, and the sight that met me was not the battle I had envisioned. No others were in the room but those I cared for. Nico lay collapsed on the floor, a pale transparent shimmer of himself, his eyes dazed and unaware. Ghosting.

Talon lay a tangle of utter blackness beside him, shivering, arms and legs wrapped around the fading Monère, trying to keep him from fading more with his physical touch, with the bond they shared. Jonnie knelt beside them.

"We couldn't feel you," Talon cried, his black eyes wide and panicked. "You were just suddenly gone."

I realized then that the barrier I had erected had not only blocked out sound, it had cut off my link with the other two. A crucial mistake, almost fatal.

I dropped to the ground and wrapped my arms around them. So cold. How cold they both were! Especially Nico. Gone beyond the point of shivering anymore.

With my touch, with all three of us in contact, the connection flowed strong and undiluted between us, and the power I had freshly harnessed from my recent feeding poured from me into Nico and Talon. Talon's shivering subsided, and Nico's shivering started up as their temperatures quickly warmed.

"Oh," Talon breathed. "That feels wonderful."

"For you, maybe," Nico muttered, teeth chattering. "I feel . . . like I'm going to break apart . . . from all this damn shaking."

We wrapped ourselves around him. Jonnie left the room, returned with blankets, and piled them on top of us.

A sound, a movement, drew my eyes to the door.

Stefan stepped inside and shut the door quietly behind him, my fresh bite mark loud and glaring against the whiteness of his neck. The scent of passion spent and seed spilled permeated the air, making the wet stain on the front of his pants almost redundant.

"What happened?" Stefan asked.

I shook my head, the only part of me not covered by the layers of blanket. "Later." I dared not waste energy erecting a shield of privacy around us now, afraid that it might take away from the power flowing into Nico. "Don't worry. We're okay now," I said, reassuring him. Reassuring all of us.

Stefan went into the bedroom. A moment later, the sound of running water drifted to my ear, almost drowning out the footsteps coming up our path. But the heartbeat that floated—sang—in my ears, and the approaching presence tingled my senses. A Monère. And not a warrior, but a woman. How could I tell? Perhaps the lightness of her footsteps . . . women walked differently than men. And she felt like a woman somehow to my senses. It could only be the healer.

The three of us huddled here like this, weak and shivering, was not something I wished her to see and whisper of to the other Monères. The sight might not have been so remarkable had it been just Talon and I, a demon and a strange creature, black as night, entwined together on the floor beneath a pile of blankets. That could have been explained away. But not the Monère sandwiched between us. Heat was not something cold-blooded Monères normally needed. It was something they avoided, actually. Too much of it could kill them, and the thick pile of blankets covering us definitely counted as too much.

I burrowed my way out of the cocoon of covers. Reaching down, I scooped up everything into my arms—the two men, the nest of blankets—and brought them into the bedroom, laying them on the bed.

"Shut the door behind us, Jonnie," I said, and caught the brief glimpse of surprise in the Mixed Blood's eyes before he closed the door. I crawled beneath the covers, connecting the three of us together once more, and thought of how it must look in Jonnie's human eyes . . . a small woman carrying two men, one much larger than her, with apparent ease.

Stefan came out of the shower, dressed in clean clothes.

"The healer is here," I said, my gaze skittering away from his. A polite knock sounded on the front door.

Stefan nodded and closed the bedroom door behind him as he stepped out into the other room. "Let me get it, Jonnie," I heard Stefan say.

Nico's body temp had warmed enough so that he stopped shivering. He relaxed against me now in warmth. The crisis over, tiredness rolled over me, and my lids grew heavy.

"Wake me up after she leaves," I murmured and let sleep cradle me briefly in its comforting embrace.

THE SOUND OF the front door closing woke me up. I found myself in a tangle of bodies and limbs. Nico's sleepy eyes blinked drowsily open inches away from my face. My left leg and arm were thrown over the stocky Monère, and my breasts nestled against the warm, muscled swells of his arm and chest. His hands were wrapped around my waist, and Talon's arm and leg thrown over mine, with Nico sandwiched between us.

My movement, as I tried to untangle myself, roused Talon as well. Not that I could see him; I saw only the black darkness of his hair tucked up against Nico, across from me. But the sudden tension in the slender limbs that had been relaxed a moment before, and their discreet withdrawal from me, let me know that he was awake.

Heat radiated from Talon, and Nico was that odd temperature of in between. He no longer had the coolness of a Monère, but neither was he as hot as the demon dead.

I shoved off the blankets and crawled out, leaving Nico still drowsing lazily on the bed.

"How do you feel?" I asked.

"Comfy," Nico said with a sleepy smile.

The sweetness and ease of that smile told me he had not realized yet the significance of what had occurred. What it meant for him and his chances of survival. Of ours as well, Talon and I.

"Talon?" I said to the dark shadow half-hidden behind Nico.

"I am well, mistress."

"Lucinda. Call me Lucinda."

A brief hesitation before he softly repeated my name. "Lucinda," he said.

I wondered if Talon had grasped the situation, but I couldn't see his face and read his expression.

The door opened and Stefan entered, Jonnie behind him. The Mixed Blood moved slowly, but less gingerly.

"Was the healer able to do anything for you, Jonnie?" I asked.

"Not much actual healing, but she took away almost all the discomfort. Which is a wonderful thing," Jonnie said, grinning.

Stefan questioned me with his eyes. *What happened?*

I motioned Stefan and Jonnie closer to the bed. When they were near enough to the others, I enclosed us all in a cone of silence and spoke.

"I've thrown a temporary shielding around us, a sound barrier. No one can hear what we say, but neither can we hear anything from outside. The barrier apparently severed my bond with the other two when I erected it before when feeding."

"Which is when Nico began to ghost," Stefan observed. And in his eyes, I saw that he understood the complexity of the situation.

"Yes."

The unease in Nico's eyes showed he was beginning to realize some of the complications as well.

"You are their power source," Stefan said.

"Nico's most definitely. I'm not sure about Talon. He may simply have drained himself by trying to sustain Nico. He was certainly the less affected of the two."

"We have to know for certain," Stefan said.

"How do we do that?" Nico asked cautiously.

"Talon," I said, turning to the Floradëur. "Would you be kind enough to walk to the door?"

Obediently, Talon slid out of bed and walked across the room. The encircling energy field rippled slightly as he passed through it.

Is this far enough? he asked when he stood by the door.
Only Talon wasn't speaking words that we could hear. His
lips moved but no sound reached our ears. Only by reading
his lips did I know what he said.

"Yes, that's fine," I replied, nodding. And watched as
startlement crossed Talon's dark face. He knew it was a
sound barrier, but the knowledge hadn't really sunk in until
that moment, when he found the sound of my voice blocked
from him.

We watched him.

A full minute passed by in ticking silence before I gestured Talon to return. He stepped back into the cone of silence with a little ripple.

"Now you, Nico," I said.

"Somehow, I know I'm not going to like this," Nico said
grimly as he left the comfortable refuge of the bed and
moved toward where Talon had stood. He never made it
that far.

As soon as he stepped outside the barrier, he began to
falter. One step, two, and then he could walk no farther. He
turned, and with eyes that were both fierce and despairing,
his body began to teeter as if drunk. Abruptly, he dropped
to his knees.

I dissolved the barrier and went to him.

"Not good," Nico said, shaking. My hands grasped his,
and energy flowed between us with the contact. Talon joined
us, laying his hands on top of ours, adding his energy.

"No," I replied. "It's not good."

"It's easy enough to prevent it from happening again,"
Jonnie said. "Just don't cut yourself off from Nico anymore."

"Lucinda will have to when she returns to her realm,"
Stefan explained. "Which is something she will have to do
very soon."

"How soon, Lucinda?" Nico asked.

"As soon as we see the Queen Mother," I replied.

"Oh. That soon," Nico said softly.

"So Nico just goes with her," Jonnie said.

A sudden awkward silence fell.

"Yes, he shall have to go with me," I said grimly, eyes mournful, my throat bitter with apologies I made myself swallow down.

"So why is that so bad?" Jonnie asked, discerning from my expression that it was.

My words tolled out like death bells. "Because no Monère has ever survived the trip down to Hell."

TWENTY-SIX

WHILE THE MEN ate in the dining hall, I wandered
down the west corridor of the manor house. The corridor of time, as I privately dubbed it, where portraits hung of
our great leaders and dignitaries down through history. One
painting was of a slim, elegant man with dark hair, silvered
across the temples. He stood out, not just because he was one
of the few males in that gallery, but because of the color of
his skin: a warm bronze that contrasted sharply with all the
other's whiteness. That and his dagger-sharp nails.

The High Lord. Once upon a time, my father.

I gazed upon that portrait, lost in a study of the past
until I felt a presence join me. No sound other than what all
living bodies betrayed. Can you tell one heartbeat, one
pattern of breathing apart from the rest? I did not know.
All I knew was that I was certain that it was Stefan standing beside me. That scent, uniquely his, teased my nostrils,
and I inhaled in a tiny bit of it, took him into me with
secret pleasure and sadness.

Would I one day look upon a picture of Stefan and say
to myself: *Once upon a time, he had been mine, too.*

"Your father?"

At his quiet question, I turned to stare up at him. He was studying the portrait much as I had, seemingly casual, but his essence—the essence that I could feel—vibrated with a terse tenseness. An unhappiness.

Because it was the easiest answer, and because all the Monère had long ears—one of the disadvantages of being among them: no privacy—I nodded. The High Lord *had* been my father once. In life, and, for a brief time, in death.

"If you lightened his skin to burnished gold, and took away the silver in his hair, you would have a picture of my brother, Halcyon," I murmured, our words constrained by where we were and the secrets we held.

Had we been able to talk freely, would we have conversed about my impending death, and that of Talon's and Nico's? Or would we have spoken of how I had cavalierly treated Stefan as a living, walking blood donor, one of countless many?

More questions I could not answer.

The frustration of bottled-up words glittered like bright green shards in Stefan's eyes.

Perhaps it was just as well those words could not be spoken. But the one thing I could say, in this last opportunity to speak to him alone, I did.

I lifted a hand and let the pads of my fingers brush his jaw. He was freshly shaven, the smoothness of his white skin so soft. We think of men as hard, but that is not correct. Their skin could be as soft, as delicate as a woman's in some places; even more so in other places. I reached up farther and stroked the silky strands of his hair, my sharp nails hidden in the thick raven darkness so that my hand appeared for a moment like any other hand, ordinary.

"I'm sorry," I whispered.

His hand lifted up to cover mine in a gesture both tender and quiet, to press it firmly against his cheek. "Don't be," he said, ready forgiveness in his eyes, in his words. "I'm not."

I wanted to cry at the sweetness of this man. And rail at the goodness in him, even as it drew me.

"Just say that you will come back to me."

And like before, I could not do that. "I cannot promise that."

His eyes darkened.

He thought that I withheld the promise because I did not know if I would survive the trip to Hell . . . or more accurately, if Nico would survive the trip, therefore Talon and I along with him.

"Promise me that you'll try."

But I couldn't do that, either. Because if I did continue on in my long existence, I was determined not to return to High Court for the next one hundred years, until which time Stefan would have passed and gone. If he was not mine, it would be kinder to us both if we never saw each other again.

Remember me, I wanted to say, but held back the words. For likely he would, and it would not be with fondness or affection, no matter how good my intentions were.

Then the others came, and the moment was broken.

The past could never be recaptured, I had learned. You could only go forward. And so I did. Grimly. Leading my little party of men, a group that was far from merry, to see what that tricksy fickle creature fate had in store for us.

TWENTY-SEVEN

T HEY WALKED TO the Council Hall, a magnificent stone
structure that was a harmonious mixture of straight lines
and rounded curves, of soaring domes and high ceilings. A
structure built to inspire awe and reverence and fear. A place
few Monère ever entered, other than those who ruled here,
and those who were to be judged by them.

Other warriors talked of their time at High Court with
wonder and admiration. The few times Stefan had come
here, however, he had arrived in the company of one queen
tiring of him, and had left in the company of a new queen
tempted by his beauty. Old patterns churned Stefan's stomach, even though he knew this to be different. And thrown
into the turmoil was the wonderful, awful occasion of meeting the Queen Mother. Not that they would meet her per-
sonally. Lucinda would no doubt speak with her while they
hovered in the background. But just to be in her august
company . . . the prospect fair shook his knees.

Lucinda spoke of the Queen Mother so casually. With
reverence, yes. But no fear. Much like the way she spoke of
her brother. The Princess was at ease in these surroundings,

and expected them to be as well. It was here, with this difference of attitude, that set Lucinda apart from the rest of
them. Not her skin. Not those lethal nails. But the noncha-
lance with which she walked among the titans of their world.
And of the world beyond.

Nice. She had described the High Prince of Hell as
nice. And no doubt he was to some. But Stefan had heard
of occasions, more than one, where Halcyon had been not
so nice.

Much as Lucinda spoke of her brother with fondness, it
was Stefan's most ardent wish never to meet the powerful,
deadly prince of darkness.

They passed two royal guards stationed at the entrance
who nodded respectfully to Lucinda and eyed the rest of
them suspiciously. Especially Talon whose black skin shone
with dark luster against their lighter complexions, making
even Lucinda seem pale in comparison. A creature of such
utter blackness they had never seen before and would likely
never see again.

A distinguished gentleman with salt-and-pepper hair
met them within. Had not his power given him away, power
greater than any Stefan had ever sensed before in a male,
the gold medallion he wore, proclaiming his status, would
have. Before them stood one of the few men in their long
and bloody history to have ever reached that rare and most
coveted status of Warrior Lord. Someone with enough
power to sustain himself, able to prolong his own life inde-
pendently, free from a queen and her Basking. Able to rule
his own territory, if he so wished, or stay here and serve
the Queen Mother, as this man had chosen to do.

"Warrior Lord Thorane," Lucinda murmured, smiling.

The Warrior Lord swept a courtly bow over her hand,
and placed a light kiss on the back of it. "Princess Lucinda.
As beautiful as always."

"In my brother's ill-fitting clothes?" Lucinda's dark
brow arched. "You lie, Lord Thorane, though it is a gallant
one."

Stefan almost choked over the insult she had just casually

given the Warrior Lord. But Lord Thorane simply smiled. "It only enhances your natural beauty." And he told nothing but the truth. Truth that Lucinda brushed away with casual disregard.

The Warrior Lord turned to them. "Your weapons, gentlemen."

They passed him their daggers and he handed them to a footman, who stored them in a side room that apparently served as the weapons check-in chamber.

What, no ticket or receipt? Stefan wanted to ask, but bit back the giddy, nervous impulse.

"The Queen Mother awaits you," Lord Thorane said. He escorted them not down the wide hallway that led to the circular chamber where the Council officially met, but down another narrow corridor, stopping before a simple closed door that was only remarkable because of the two royal guards stationed before it. He gave a perfunctory knock then opened it. "Please enter. She is expecting you."

Lucinda stepped inside the room. When Stefan moved off to the side, as if to wait outside in the corridor, Lord Thorane looked at him and said, "You, too, gentlemen. She is most eager to meet you all."

Such piercing eyes, Stefan thought, as Lord Thorane ushered them into what appeared to be the Queen Mother's private study, a room lined wall to wall with books, with the scent of leather and old pages filling the air like a faint perfume.

But if Stefan had thought Lord Thorane's eyes piercing, the ones that met his now caused him to quickly alter his opinion. Here was piercing. They were blue like a sunlit sky, a sky most Monère never saw. And they were just as vast, as endless, as impersonal. Eyes that looked down deep into your soul and passed judgment.

Only a brief glance from those all-seeing eyes, and it left Stefan shaken.

Other details came to him once those eyes passed over him and moved on to the others. Lines of age creased the

Queen Mother's face. Wrinkles looked upon with reverence because they were almost unheard of among the Monère, a people whose skins remained unlined up until their very last days. The rare marks of age declared that she wasn't just old, she was ancient.

The children of the moon lived up to three hundred years. The Queen Mother was the sole exception among their kind; she had lived far beyond that allotted time. How much beyond it, no one was certain. Those soft wrinkles only enhanced the weighty power emanating from this small woman who dressed simply but sat so regally in a chair set behind a mahogany desk. A large bejeweled ring upon her finger was her only adornment. A book was in her hands, and a pile of scribbled notes stacked neatly to the side.

"Lucinda," the Queen Mother said. Her voice resonated with an almost aching age. "How good to see you again, and only months after your last visit instead of waiting your usual century or two."

Lucinda knelt. They followed her example, falling to their knees behind her, their heads bowed, Talon's so low that he was almost kissing the ground.

"Venerable Queen Mother," Lucinda said and rose. Uncertain of what to do, the rest of them erred on the cautious side and remained kneeling as Lord Thorane came to stand beside the Queen he had chosen to spend the rest of his life serving.

"I am told that these are your men, child," the Queen Mother said.

Child? Stefan thought. A demon who had existed for over six hundred years?

Lucinda's next words caught his attention. "That is only partially true."

The Queen Mother's brow lifted. "Is it? Pray tell what part is true, and what part is not?"

Lucinda hesitated, and unease trailed down Stefan's spine like a ghostly finger. "What I would speak of, perhaps, might be best for your ears alone, revered Mother."

The revered mother waved Lucinda's request aside.

"The room is bespelled, Lucinda, as you know. No ears other than ours shall hear what you say, and Lord Thorane serves as my right hand. He is aware of all matters pertaining to the Court, which my instincts tell me this will fall under."

"Your instincts are correct." Lucinda gestured behind her. "This is Nico, the rogue that the High Council requested my aid in returning to Queen Mona SiGuri."

What might have been wry amusement in another flashed in those sky blue eyes. "Is that what you are doing, Lucinda, bringing the rogue here to return to her?"

"No, I have done that already. Returned him to her," Lucinda clarified.

"Did you? Then why is he here now with you?"

Stefan's nerves were jangling now, his instincts—instincts that had never failed him before—warning him of some impending danger. Nico, however, knelt in calm peacefulness, in utter trust.

"I returned him, Queen Mother," Lucinda said. "Then I claimed him as my own. And Nico has accepted my claim."

A movement passed over those lips, smoothing out before they had a chance to form. "Rise," she bid, "all of you," and they did.

Those piercing blue eyes studied Nico for an intent moment. "Is this true, Warrior Nico?"

He replied calmly, "Yes, revered Mother."

She pursed her lips. Said mildly, "I'd imagine Mona SiGuri was far from pleased."

"She tried to stop me from leaving," Lucinda informed her.

"Did she?" the Queen Mother murmured. "Silly girl."

Lucinda smiled sharply in agreement. "Her treatment of her people leaves much to be desired. But that is a minor issue compared to what I discovered in her attempt to detain me. I took another from her besides Nico." Turning, she drew Talon forward, a quivering arrow of darkness. He'd begun to shiver again. "This is Talon. He is a creature from my realm, secretly brought here as an infant child over twenty-six years ago by another demon and placed in Mona SiGuri's hands to raise."

"Over six and twenty years . . ." Those blue eyes sharpened. "I was not aware of this."

"No, Queen Mother. No one was. What this rogue demon did violated many of our rules, for which he must be punished. The matter is further complicated by the fact that he was once the guardian known as Derek."

"I met him before," the Queen Mother murmured. "He still roams free?"

"Unfortunately, yes."

"So I was mistaken," she said abruptly. "It is a demon matter."

"You were not mistaken, revered Mother, though you are correct that Halcyon will want this matter investigated and handled by our people. He will want Mona SiGuri and her people questioned."

The Queen Mother waved her ringed hand and said in a cool voice, "He has the Court's permission to do anything that he wishes, short of killing Mona SiGuri."

Lucinda inclined her head. "Thank you, Queen Mother. The other matter that I bring before you, however, is very much a Court matter. Or so I would hope."

His instincts clamoring now, Stefan turned and looked at Lucinda, willed her fiercely to look at him. But she didn't.

"The other warrior here at my side is Stefan, another rogue that I came across. And the Mixed Blood is Jonnie, his ward that he raised among the humans." Lucinda paused, uncharacteristically hesitant.

Look at me! Turn around and look at me, Stefan silently commanded.

She didn't. She took a breath—a sign of agitation—and continued on like a disaster that could not be averted. "I had claimed these two as mine, also. But I did so hastily, with thought only of my needs, not theirs. Until this rogue demon is captured and terminated, they will not be safe anywhere other than here at High Court."

"And after the rogue demon is captured," the Queen Mother prompted gently.

"I still cannot Bask," Lucinda said with a slight catch. She sank down on bended knee. "Blessed Queen Mother, I ask most humbly that you consider taking Stefan and Jonnie into your service. I know that it is an honor few warriors are granted, but I would ask this of you as a personal favor."

No! Stefan's screamed silently. *Don't do this!*

The Queen Mother looked at him, those piercing blue eyes weighing him for a brief timeless moment before she rose and walked around the desk. Gently she grasped Lucinda's hands and pulled the demon Princess back onto her feet.

"Lucinda," she said, that lined face softening. "The debt we owe you and your family can never be fully tallied or repaid. Were it my choice alone, I would grant you your request."

Lucinda looked up, stricken, confused. "What do you mean, revered Mother?"

"I mean, child, that such service requires a willingness from both parties. I would be most willing to accept them, but I fear that is not the case on your man's part."

"My man?"

"On Stefan's part," the Queen Mother clarified. "The warrior you are trying to give away. He does not seem to want to leave you, child."

Lucinda looked up into Stefan's face and flinched at what she saw in his eyes.

"What do you wish, Warrior Stefan?" the Queen Mother asked, not unkindly.

Stefan didn't just kneel. He fell to his hands and knees, prostrating himself before the Queen Mother. "Most revered Queen Mother." His voice trembled. Not with fear, but with the rage he could barely contain. "You honor me most greatly. But it is a position I cannot accept because I am already bound in the service of another."

"I release you," Lucinda said faintly.

He lifted his face from the ground and speared her with eyes that burned raw and intense.

"But I do not release you," Stefan gritted, almost biting off the words as he rose to his feet to tower over the diminutive demon like an angry storm cloud ready to burst, his hands clenched at his side. "All other ladies I have served selected me, I had little choice. But I chose you! And you accepted me. I hold you now to that bond."

Lord Thorane moved protectively between them. An ironic gesture, Stefan noted, as what he tried to protect— Lucinda—could have easily ripped him into bloody pieces with a few quick slashes.

"It's all right," Lucinda murmured. She stepped around the Warrior Lord to put her hand on Stefan's arm. To plead openly with him. "Stefan, please. It's a position few warriors are ever offered in their lifetime."

"I have the position I want," he repeated.

"The position you want will kill you in thirty years if not sooner! Here at High Court you can live for the next ninety-five years with honor and respect and the satisfaction of worthwhile service, returning to the Monèrian way of life: Basking. Regaining your vitality."

"No," he said stubbornly.

"You are a fool!" Lucinda spat, her dark eyes flashing fire.

"Yes, I am!" He leaned down until his face was only a breath away from hers. "I want only you."

Her face crumpled. "Stupid, foolish rogue."

"Yes," he said hoarsely, his hands coming up to frame her face. "But I am *your* stupid, foolish rogue. You accepted me and I will not let you go."

Lucinda shook her head helplessly, her eyes swimming red with tears.

Lord Thorane cleared his throat.

Brought back into awareness of their audience, Stefan's hands dropped away from her face.

The Queen Mother's voice broke into the awkward, appalled silence. Awkward on Lucinda's part over her display of emotion. Appalled on the part of the others over Stefan's rejection of a position most warriors would give their left and even right nuts for. And his presumptuous insistence— not request, but insistence!—on holding Lucinda to her word. In claiming her and not letting go. *Way* overstepping his bounds.

"I do not think he will allow you to give him up, my dear." A smile played upon that wrinkled face. "A most un-Monère attitude, but then he has been long away from us."

"Forgive me, Queen Mother, if I offended you," Stefan said, forcing calm into his voice. "That was not my intention."

Another wave of that ringed hand. "Don't be silly, my boy."

Coming from someone whose hair was completely silver white, Stefan let the "my boy" comment pass by. Who was he to complain when she called Lucinda "child"?

"Lucinda, dear," the Queen Mother continued. "There are other options that you perchance may not have considered."

"What options, Queen Mother?" Lucinda asked in a ragged voice.

"I would be most happy to have you and your men—" She stressed the two last words with a little smile. "—here as our guests for as long as you need stay. Until you are assured once more of their safety. During that time, they may Bask here with me. Afterward, if need be, they can return here each full moon. Although by that time, I suspect that you will have found another queen closer to your province willing to share her light with them . . . without your sacrifice of giving them up."

The generosity of the Queen Mother's offer left Lucinda reeling. Her eyes lifted to Stefan. His blue green eyes were a swirl of beseechment, of demand. Of a hard, fierce glittering hope.

Accept it! those eyes cried. *Accept me!*

With an inner sigh, she did.

"Thank you, Queen Mother," Lucinda said, bowing. "I accept your generous offer."

TWENTY-EIGHT

⁂

LORD THORANE HIMSELF noted the service contract entries down in a ledger. Stefan, Jonnie, Nico, and even Talon signed beneath my bold flourish. They were officially mine now, and I was their lady, whom they had pledged to serve. For how long, no one knew. Maybe only for the next few minutes.

I requested that Lord Thorane inform my brother, Halcyon, of all that had occurred if I did not return in the next few weeks.

"I will, Princess," Lord Thorane assured me outside in the corridor. "But you will likely be able to tell him yourself first."

One could only hope.

The same footman who had taken our weapons retrieved them and returned them to us, and we bid Lord Thorane farewell.

"Where to, now?" Nico asked quietly as we departed the Council Hall.

"So eager, Nico?" I asked.

"No," he said honestly. "But neither would I delay you."

"Always so aware of ticking time." I led them down a path that wound behind the Great House. When we were near enough to the forest edge, I stopped.

"Do you feel it?" I asked Talon.

The Floradëur closed his eyes, turning in a half circle. Through our link, I felt his senses expand. The gathering of it first like a tight lasso around him, then casting it out in a wide, arching radius. Spreading, searching, seeking. And finally finding.

Facing the southwest rim of the forest, he opened his eyes. "There," he said.

"Take us there," I said, and he did, leading us with silent sureness deep into the woods. A mile in, Talon stopped suddenly. "It's here," he said quietly, eyes fixed on something the others could not see.

"Yes, that's the portal that will take you home." *Perhaps.*

With a touch of my power, I brought the portal forth. It shimmered into visibility, a white wall of mist the size of a doorway.

Jonnie gasped.

I threw a cone of silence about us and turned to Nico. "You have a choice," I said. "You do not have to come with Talon and I."

"The choice that you speak of will only allow me to die here." Nico shook his head. "I have a chance of surviving this. Slim, but still a chance. Correct?"

I inclined my head. "Yes, you have a chance, and not as slim as you believe. I told you before that no Monère has ever survived the trip down to Hell. What I did not say was that a Mixed Blood Queen recently did. She survived the trip, not just once, but twice."

"A Mixed Blood," Jonnie said with surprise.

"Yes, but she was three-quarters Monère. Only a fourth of her was human. I would not advise that you ever risk the trip, Jonnie."

The young man's lips kicked up into a crooked smile, just like Stefan's. Not genetics but the natural emulation of the man he admired and patterned himself after. "Don't worry, Princess. I'm happy where I am."

I turned once more to Nico. "It's the heat, I believe, that kills the Monère. They cannot withstand it. Mona Lisa, the Mixed Blood Queen, was able to, though. And I believe you may be able to, also."

"Because of our bond," Nico said.

"Yes, because of our bond. Your skin is warmer, no longer cool. You were comfortable in the heat Talon and I generated beneath the blankets."

"Didn't even break a sweat," Nico said with a little smile. It was odd hearing such a human phrase coming out of his mouth, especially with that Continental accent, but no odder than the other strange things the poor warrior was experiencing because he'd tried to save me. He'd succeeded, and I hoped I could do the same for him.

"Hold on to me," I said, "both you and Talon. Do not let go until we emerge from the portal."

"Because?" Nico queried.

"Do you really want to know?"

He smiled mockingly. "Unfortunately, yes."

And so I explained. "Portals come in various strengths, and require a matching strength in those who would use them to traverse the realms. The older portals require the most power. The newer portals, those only a few centuries old, need less power to travel them, thus are more frequently used."

"And this portal?" Nico asked.

"Is one of the most ancient. To my knowledge, only Halcyon and I, the High Lord, and one or two rulers before him, have ever used this portal."

Stefan finally asked the question the others were wondering by now. "What happens to those who don't have enough power to safely traverse a portal?"

"We never see them again."

Nico blew out a breath. "Ah, hell," he muttered, then grinned. "Which is where we are trying to go. Is it safe for you to use this portal, Princess?"

"I've used it several times before," I said, skirting a direct answer, because I could not answer his question with certainty anymore. I did not know if our bond had changed things for me. And I didn't have the luxury of time to seek out another, safer portal.

Nico didn't notice my slight evasion, but Stefan did. His eyes focused on me. I feared he would say something, but he only gripped my shoulders lightly, bent down and brushed his lips against mine in a kiss so fleeting and soft, we barely touched. "Promise me," he said. "Promise me you'll try to come back."

"I promise," I said, looking up into his eyes.

"Safe journey, Princess," he said, releasing me. "Safe journey to you all."

I held out my hands to the other two. Talon and Nico stepped to my side and folded their palms around mine. If their grips were uncomfortably tight—and mine was painfully so around theirs—no one said a word as we walked into that misty wall.

With unhurried deliberation, we stepped into that powerful field of energy, and I prayed as I had not prayed in a long time. *Mother of Darkness, Mother of Light. Please help us.*

The mist enveloped us and swept us away.

TWENTY-NINE

I GASPED. NOT with fear but with surprise because it hurt. Blood of a cursed troll, it hurt! A prickling pain like a swarm of bees buzzing over your skin, stinging you.

"Holy night, that's uncomfortable," Nico muttered, beside me. "Is it always like this?"

"No."

Anxiety filled his eyes. "In this case, it might have been better if you had lied."

"Oh!" I gasped again at the stinging discomfort, and looked to the other in our triad. "How are you doing, Talon?"

"It hurts," he said quietly. Only his eyes betrayed the pain he was experiencing.

"Your body's relaxed," I said, gritting my teeth.

"It doesn't help if you tense up. Only makes the pain worse."

What had Talon gone through to have learned something like that? *Derek, you bastard. You have a lot to account for.* And Mona SiGuri. Her, too, most definitely.

We arrived, less smoothly than I would have liked, but

we made it, tumbling out of the portal onto hard ground, a tangle of bodies and one loud pounding heartbeat.

I rolled us free of the portal, and slapped a sound barrier around us, praying that nothing nearby had heard that one thumping beat of life that had so loudly disturbed the stillness of Hell's hot air for a trembling moment.

I glanced anxiously at Nico. Found him staring back at me. "Are you okay?" I asked.

"Yeah. Hot, a little hard to breathe, as if the air is heavier here, more dense. But I seem to be fine."

I relaxed. Prematurely.

Talon began to shake, faint tremors that quickly grew in force, as if each one that followed didn't just double in intensity but magnified ten times. He shook like a glass of water jarred by the footfalls of a large and heavy creature. Just a ripple at first, then growing successively stronger and more violent until it was like waves slapping against the shore, pounding it. I swiftly untangled us and laid Talon flat. Tried to straighten his limbs as best as I could. But I had to fight the stiffness, the almost harsh rigor that gripped him and shook him mercilessly.

"Talon, what's happening?" I asked. But if he knew, he was unable to tell me.

"What's wrong?" Nico asked, laying his hands over mine, connecting us all. But the open ties between us did not help Talon. He continued to shake. And not just shake, but spasm.

Then the sound began: the crackling of bone. That wet and familiar sucking sound of flesh slowly changing, distorting, bones reshaping. The sound a new demon made when he shifted slowly into his demon beast form for the very first time. Talon, though, was not a demon. Yet he was shifting. Or doing something similar.

His black skin rippled, and the snapping and crackling of bone beneath our hands was as sickening to feel as it was to hear. His body shuddered and spasmed with such force that he almost shook us off. I would have called it convulsions in a human, but Talon was awake, alert. Poor bastard. It would have been kinder had he not been.

Talon's mouth jerked open, and I slapped my hand over it. Told him in a rush, "Don't scream. You can't scream. Not with the sound barrier around us. It'll reverberate back on us, and maybe kill us or, even worse, knock us out, and break the cone of silence, letting Nico's living heartbeat call everything to us like a dinner bell."

I didn't know what to do if Talon screamed. Keep the cone of silence intact or release it? He didn't make me choose. Eyes brimming with agony, he held back that awful echolating screech he was capable of generating, and let sound escape from him in a high keening wail instead. A sound that raised the hair on the back of my neck.

It was the noise that a creature being beaten horribly would make; something tied with nowhere to run, only able to quiver and bear the blows that pummeled it. A high, hopeless wailing of something that could only take the pain and try to endure it.

"Sweet merciful Mother," Nico muttered.

But whatever held Talon was far from merciful. In great shuddering jerks, as if invisible hands gripped him at both ends, he slowly, agonizingly stretched out. His bones cracked, lengthened and widened, and that dark form grew longer in powerful wrenching spurts. His shoulders widened and his length increased until with one last painful snap and crackle of bone, one last high keening shriek ripped from his throat, it stopped and silence reigned.

He didn't move, he didn't breathe. Then he stirred and turned toward me, and what I saw stunned me. It was like looking into the face of another person.

His skin was still like darkest night, his eyes the same jet black. But all else had changed. That unfinished look, the look of youth not fully grown was gone, and in its place was the final product as nature had intended it. Maturity marked his face now . . . a broader, wider face. The nose was taller, the mouth wider, fuller, the cheekbones more prominent, beautifully sculptured. All in perfect proportion to a body that was longer now, without that stunted shortness.

"Can you sit up, Talon?" I asked.

"I think so." His voice, too, had changed. It had the same bell-like melody, but was an octave lower in register, a deep baritone instead of a high tenor. His eyes rounded at the sound of his new voice, and he sat up cautiously, looked down at his body with surprise.

"My hands are bigger." He spread his fingers wide then measured them against mine. His fingers overlapped mine completely, almost obscuring the tips of my inch-long nails.

"My feet. They're bigger too," he said.

With Nico's bracing support, he stood. To everyone's surprise, he was taller than the Monère warrior. Just an inch taller, but it was a shocking reversal when just a moment ago, he had stood a whole head shorter than the other man.

"I'm taller than both of you," Talon said, looking down at me with astonishment. Hearing himself again speak in that new, deeper voice, he started to laugh almost hysterically. Then sank to his knees as if they no longer supported him, and began to cry.

I took him into my arms, held him against me. "Shhh. It's all right."

"What happened to me?" Talon asked, bewildered.

I wondered the same thing myself. "I think your body changed once you entered this realm. Became what it should have been, what it was meant to be. You were stunted, unfinished before."

"I know." He pulled back, wiped the wetness from his face. "What does the finished me look like?"

"Like a man," said Nico.

"A beautiful man," I said.

No longer did his head seem overlarge atop a smallish body. The delicate features and build that marked all of his kind were still there, but now with everything in proportion, it was striking rather than frail looking. He was true Floradëur. A graceful stem of a flower.

Talon gave that half sob, half laugh again. Scrubbing his hands once more over his eyes, removing the last trace of tears, he gazed about him with awe and curiosity.

Hell was shadowed in dim twilight darkness, and the heat was oppressive. Overhead, an egg-yolk colored moon hung in the black velvet sky like a giant elliptical pupil, casting not silver rays but a yellowish light.

"Is that your moon?" Talon asked.

"Yes. Kantera, our second moon. It marks our midday."

"You have more than one moon?"

"We have three. Sumera, a gray color closest to your Earth's moon, rises in the beginning of the day. Rubera, our third moon, shines at night, red like the light Nico glowed with."

"Where are we?" Nico asked.

"Not far from where we need to go. Can you walk, Talon?"

He nodded. "Oddly enough, I feel almost energized."

"Stay close to me," I told Talon, and held out my hand to Nico, ensuring that he remained within the cone of silence. His warm skin felt almost cool against the heat of my skin, which had risen several degrees higher upon arrival.

"Don't worry, Princess," Nico said with that mocking smile of his. "I plan to remain glued to your side."

I led them across a tract of grassland onto an old, narrow path almost completely overgrown now, and tried to view the surroundings as Talon and Nico would see it. There was a hushed quality to the air as we traveled across the land, but signs of existence stirred every once in a while. A roco-rat scurried away when we stepped too near its hiding nest. A green serpent, soaking up the heat atop a rock, hissed at us with a red forked tongue when we disturbed its slumber. It flew off, carried by large iridescent wings like that of a giant dragonfly. A small furry animal hopped across our path, then stopped and eyed us curiously with big brown eyes, its long fluffy ears upraised, and stubby nose twitching.

"You have bunny rabbits down in Hell?" Nico asked, smiling.

"Hell hares. Not quite the same thing as their earthly cousins."

Nico crouched down, extending a hand out to the fearless little animal. "Oh? In what way?"

"I wouldn't do that," I warned.

He turned back to look at me. "Why not?"

"Because they . . ."

The Hell hare moved, striking so fast it was just a blur. Its long razor-sharp teeth snapped closed an inch away from Nico's fingers, missing him only because I yanked him back, sprawling him onto the ground.

"What the hell?" Nico sputtered, eyeing the creature's sudden transformation, from innocent bunny to scary predator, with shocked startlement.

"Exactly." I flicked a mental warning at the hungry hare, and it darted away to seek easier prey. "That cute looking ball of fluff eats other little things down here like that serpent that just flew away." I pulled Nico to his feet. "If you want to keep your fingers, I'd suggest that you don't offer them up as an easy meal."

Nico looked a bit pale. But then he would, compared to Talon and I. We continued down the path without further word or mishap until a black edifice loomed up before us, its twin towers reaching mournfully for the sky like dark stretching hands.

"What is this place?" Talon asked, his voice a hushed whisper even though, had he shouted, no one would have heard us, shielded as we were by the sound barrier.

"The High Lord's private residence." I halted and gazed up at the black stone structure. Memories both good and bad were associated with that towering construct. Much like my feelings for the man who lived there.

"Your father?" Talon asked.

"That is a matter debated by many." I took a step forward and was brought up short. Nico stood on the grassy path, unmoving.

"Come on," I said, urging him forward.

"Lucinda." Nico's eyes were fastened on the rising black monolith before us. "You just said that this is the High Lord's private residence."

"Yeah, I know."

Nico swallowed. "Could we not go see your brother instead?"

"I would have preferred that myself. But this is closer, and we have arrived here safely. I need to tell someone about everything that has occurred."

"All right," Nico replied. But still he did not move.

I felt exposed standing like this, out in the open, flanked by a black Floradëur and a pale, living, breathing, heart-pounding Monère. Both were rare, never seen before by many. Wanted by all who saw them. We'd been lucky that no one had come upon us yet. But then, few demons dared trespass on the High Lord's private lands, another reason I had chosen that portal.

With great reluctance, Nico allowed me to lead him to the front door made of a blue black metal alloy. I knocked. The door opened immediately.

A demon dead male of imposing height and freakishly lean build loomed over us like a physical echo of the mournful edifice he cared for, wearing his usual attire: starched white shirt, waistcoat, and duck-tailed jacket.

"Hello, Winston," I said. He was close enough so that he was within the sound barrier and could hear us.

The tall demon took in everything in one quick glance: my presence and that of my strange companions, my sound shield. His eyes widened only a tiny fraction.

He swung the door open and gestured us hastily inside without a word.

"Who's Winston?" Nico whispered as we stepped inside.

"The butler of Darkling Hall."

The interior was immaculately clean, furnished in heavy wood tones, accented with dark forest green and gold trim, unchanged from the four centuries since I had last set foot here. We watched as the gawkishly tall butler closed the heavy door. He pressed something, and the walls trembled and ground quaked . . . soundlessly. Winston's mouth moved.

"What did he do? What is he saying?" Talon asked fearfully, his tall body pressed up against mine. It was a little disorienting to have to look up to him.

"He set the wards. Now nothing can enter or leave here until they are released. As for what he's saying . . ." I dropped my shielding. "I think he was just telling me we can speak freely now, that no one can hear us."

"Correct." Winston bowed, stiff and formal. "Princess Lucinda, you and your guests are welcome here."

"Thank you, Winston. Is the High Lord up?"

"Yes. I no longer sleep away the days," a voice said from the grand staircase. As he slowly walked down, it was as if a deity descended from heaven. An odd thought to have for the ruler of Hell. But then Blaec had always seemed bigger than life—or death—to me. Others might see a simple man of average height and lean build, dark of hair except for the solid silver wings flaring at his temples. It was in his eyes, however, where the true weight of his years rested. Eyes dark brown like Halcyon, like myself, but with a chilly remoteness, an impartiality, a blankness. Disengaged eyes that had slowly withdrawn from me and the rest of the realm, coldness filling in the space where emotion had once been. A seeping chill that had begun with my mother's death, her final one, and become icier as the years passed, and I had lost what I had once loved most, a warm and happy man, the loving father that he had been, both in life and in death.

Power made Blaec what he really was. It leaked from him, trailing behind in his wake like a fine fragrance, a weighty essence that drifted down to you in invisible waves as he neared. Nothing that he did consciously. It simply exuded from him and pressed down upon your skin like a heavy blanket, power so ancient and so vast that it made your bones literally ache.

He reached the bottom of the stairs and stopped, his

eyes sweeping over us. "Lucinda," he said. And something inside of me took a breath, for his eyes were no longer remote, no longer frozen in icy withdrawal.

"High Lord." I bowed. Beside me, Talon and Nico went even further; they dropped to their knees.

With an elegant wave of a finger, he bid them rise. "Who have you brought to me?" asked the High Lord of Hell.

"These are my men." Something flickered in Blaec's eyes at my words. "The Monère warrior is Nico, the rogue that the High Council requested our help in returning to Mona SiGuri."

He didn't ask how the holy hell Nico was able to exist here. He simply inquired, "You returned him?"

"Yes, and then I took him back once my duty was accomplished. I claimed him for myself."

"That is not what a guardian usually does." No rebuke in his words, just a statement of fact.

"I know. That is why I wish to resign my position."

Those dark eyes drifted quietly over us. "Come have a seat." He led us into the sitting room and sank down gracefully into an armchair. "I have a feeling this will take some time."

I perched on the chaise longue across from him, bracketed by Talon and Nico.

"Finish your introductions, please," Blaec said.

"Talon is a Floradëur that I found kept in secret by Mona SiGuri." I went on to explain how Derek had brought Talon to that other realm as an infant. And how the former guardian had tried to take back from me what he considered his property. Of how we had fought, how I had almost died. And why Talon had bound us—the three of us, accidentally. To save my life.

"So that is how the Monère can walk this realm," Blaec said. "An old Indian burial site. You are more reckless, Lucinda, than I ever was." And though the High Lord's tone was mild, his eyes were not. A flicker of power thickened the air for an oppressive moment before it ebbed away.

He inclined his head first to Talon, then to Nico. "You

have my deep gratitude for saving Lucinda, although in doing so, you have complicated all of your lives."

"Can the ties be undone?" I asked.

Nico drew in a sharp breath. Talon tensed beside me.

The High Lord's answer came after a thoughtful pause. "What you have done, this binding, between three and not two, has never been done before. Therefore I do not know if it can be undone. What we know of the bond a Floradëur can share with a demon is scarce little. The last bond to exist ended before you were born."

"Born as a demon, or on Earth?" I asked.

"Your Monère birth."

"Then over seven hundred years ago." A long time ago, even for us.

"Why are there no longer bonds like ours?" Talon asked.

"A most pertinent question. The answer to that, however, is not so easy to tell." The High Lord's voice deepened into a smooth, flowing cadence, almost like that of a storyteller. "Your people once mixed freely with ours. We existed in harmony. Things began to change, though, in Xzavier's reign, the ruler of this realm before I. A rumor spread among the demons that drinking the blood of a Flower of Darkness—if you drank enough of it—could restore a demon back to life. A new name was coined for you: the black flower of life. Your people became hunted by mine, and were slaughtered by them. The Floradëur withdrew to Hell's outermost lands, and the demons that ventured out after them oft never returned. What used to be bonds of friendship has grown into a harsh enmity."

A profound silence filled the room.

"So Floradëurs and demons are not friends but enemies." Talon bowed his head. "Is the rumor true, that we can restore life to a demon?"

"I have never known it to be so," said the High Lord, "but mayhap you can tell me that best. Derek drank of your blood for over six and twenty years, did he not?"

Talon's head dipped in affirmation. "His power would

increase for a short time, but his heart never beat, nor did he change in any other way I could discern."

"Then you have your answer."

"What about separation?" I asked. "If the ties cannot be broken, what happens when those who are bound are kept apart from one another?"

Blaec fixed his enigmatic gaze upon me. "When the bond is as fresh and new as yours, I do not know. All I know is that the ties grow stronger with proximity and time. That the longer the bond exists, the more likely that when one dies, the other does as well."

"I promised Talon that I would return him to his people, that I would see him home. I intend to keep that promise."

"It was a promise made before we were bound," Talon said.

"We cannot be together," I told him gently. "You are just as rare down here in Hell as Nico is with his beating heart and white living flesh. You cannot reside among the demons. Only with others of your kind. Do you not want to see your people? Be with them once more?"

Talon was unable to deny that yearning. "Yes, but I want to be with you and Nico, also."

"You cannot. Not safely. You can only be safe among others of your kind."

Talon stared at me as if I had betrayed him, and perhaps I had by not telling him this sooner. But what could I have said to him: *Oh, by the way, we demons hunt you Floradëurs and eat you up. Why don't you come with me and trust me to return you safely back home?*

"I promised to return you home, not to stay with you. Nico has to be with me. He has no choice if he wishes to live. But you can sustain yourself apart from me. You have a choice."

"Not true," Talon said. "You're not going to give me a choice, are you? You're going to bring me back to my people and leave me with them whether I wish it or not. I can feel that in you, that you've already decided."

He had read me accurately. "You are correct."

"Then you are no better than he was, the demon you call Derek. You allow me no choice."

"I am a demon," I told him harshly. "You should know by now not to trust any of us. To just fear us." But it was not fear I saw in those black eyes. Just anger and sadness.

"It's partly because of this," Talon said softly. "Because I can read your emotions. Because I can *feel* you. You want free of our tie. If it were possible to break our bond, you would do so."

Another truth I could not dispute. I turned back to the High Lord and made my request. "My lord, I would ask that you keep Nico here, safe and protected, while I bring Talon back to his people."

Those dark, intelligent eyes considered me for a moment. "In return," Blaec said quietly, "I would ask that you allow two of my men to accompany you, to keep you safe."

He didn't try to make the request a command. No need to. He knew he had me. That was one of Blaec's greatest strengths: knowing his position, and the position of those around him. He knew, unfortunately, that I had nothing to bargain with. And that I dared not risk the short journey to Halcyon's residence with Nico's white pulsing flesh and Talon's tempting darkness so vulnerably visible.

"Very well," I said, "if that is your condition."

"It is."

"Then so be it. But I will be in charge, not your men."

"Agreed," he said, and our bargain was sealed. With a nod from the High Lord, Winston left the room. A moment later, the foundation shuddered and the house groaned with a loud and terrible sound.

"What was that?" Nico whispered.

"The house ward released," I told him. The sound of an arrow *whooshing* into the air filled our ears. "The High Lord's guards will arrive here soon."

"Will they have to fight off all the demons who are going to come running when they hear my heartbeat?" Nico asked. His breathing and the resonant pulsing of his heart were the only sounds in the room.

The High Lord leaned forward. With a languid wave of his hand, Nico's life sounds suddenly ceased.

"Shit," said Nico, his hand flying up to cover his heart. To feel its reassuring thumping beneath his hand.

"I did not kill you," the High Lord said with a slight smile. "Just muted the sounds of your body."

Nico relaxed his hand, took a deep breath, and turned to me. "If he has muted my life sounds, then I can go with you."

"No, it will last only a few hours before he will have to renew it. Our journey will take one full day, perhaps two."

"I don't have a choice, either. Do I?" Nico asked.

"No," I said, making it an even consensus. Both of my bond-mates were unhappy with me now.

"It will be best for Lucinda if you remain with me here, Nico," the High Lord said. "Your well-being is tied to hers now, and she is more prudent with your care than she ever has been of her own. You will be a good incentive for her to return in one piece."

I doubted Nico and Talon realized that Blaec meant the words literally. His comment, though, made me remember something else. "There are two others that I have claimed, High Lord. Another rogue, Stefan, and the Mixed Blood ward he raised among the humans, a young man named Jonnie. They are officially registered under my name in High Court records. I would wish to have them listed in our ledgers also, along with Talon and Nico. If anything should happen to me, I would ask that they be protected and cared for."

"For once you think of the future, Lucinda," Blaec said, "and you no longer cut yourself apart from others. What has brought about this change?"

"She fell in love with Stefan," Nico said. "The rest of us are just accidental accruements."

"Indeed?" said the High Lord, noting the spots of color darkening my cheeks. "First Halcyon and now you, Lucinda. It seems my children are showing a sudden, unusual fascination with Monères."

My children. His casual words made me bleed inside.

"Your son, at least," I said roughly. "I am not your daughter."

"You have never stopped being my daughter," Blaec said, with something horribly like compassion in his eyes. Compassion mixed with aching sadness.

I shook my head, opened my mouth to refute his claim when a knock sounded on the door. It swung open and five demon warriors walked in.

A score of them resided in a guard house situated in the north corner of the estate, the closest distance the High Lord allowed, and they patrolled the vast boundaries. It was a twenty-minute leisurely stroll from the guard house and outer perimeter; a five minute sprint if haste was required. They had more than sprinted to have arrived here this quickly. Yet they had remained totally silent and undetected until that knock. I'd known they were formidable warriors, some of Hell's best fighters. But I had forgotten the impact of seeing them in full battle readiness, fangs fully emerged, claws lengthened, eyes red and flashing. Even I wanted to flinch beneath those hard, fiery stares.

Talon began to shiver. Nico went utterly still beside me.

Only when the demon warriors had assured themselves of the High Lord's safety did that brittle battle-ready tension begin to ease. Well, as much as possible, having five big royal guards gathered together in one room. They seemed to fill the space, and it had been a generous one before they had entered. Now with their presence, their naked, violent threat permeating the room, it didn't seem so large anymore.

Three guards were new to me, their skins without my golden darkness, younger than I. But two I knew from my earlier days, their skins darker than even my dusky gold, closer to the deep bronze of the High Lord's. Ruric and Hari of the dragon clan; the High Lord's ancestral lineage. They were the last of that long-lived line, along with my brother Halcyon and the High Lord. Only four left. Once I, too, had been considered a part of that noble line, but no longer. My name had been removed from the records after my mother's claims.

Both warriors were tall but there their commonality ended and the contrasts began. Ruric, which in the Old Language meant rock, was appropriately named, for that was what he resembled. He had an almost brutal ugliness to his looks, his face craggy, features rough, lips too thick. His jawline was jagged and blunt, his deep-set eyes a little uneven. The coarse heaviness of his features was reinforced by the hulking massiveness of his body. But it was his eyes, a light eerie pale green, hard, cold, and flat, that made one want to shiver as Talon visibly did. At two and one-half times my width, and almost twice my height, he was one of the few demons I hesitated to tangle with.

Whereas Ruric was brutally ugly, Hari was painstakingly handsome in a sulky bad-boy way. With sharp-bladed features and hooded eyes, both dark and cynical, he was arrogant and abrasive and as clever as the monkey he was named for. Tall, but almost wiry thin. As quick to smile at you as he was to snap off your hand, almost never still. Ruric, on the other hand, was like the rock for which he was named—motionless, until action was called for. Then he could move in a blur of blinding speed. They were both fast, both deadly, savage fighters. And I knew before he spoke, who the High Lord was going to choose to accompany me.

"No," I said.

"I agreed that you would be in charge. Not who would go with you," Blaec said calmly, while I cursed myself for that lack of foresight.

Ruric and Hari were the only guards whose stares did not linger on Talon. They focused instead on Nico, on the movement of his chest as he took in and released breath, though no sound was heard.

"Is he a new demon?" Hari asked. A reasonable assumption. The newly dead sometimes still made the unconscious motions of life, and only those fresh to the realm were so pale.

"No, he is Monère still," Blaec said. "I just muted his life sounds."

The two senior guards took the High Lord's statement with an unblinking calmness I would not have been able to manage were I in their place.

"How can that be, High Lord?" Ruric asked in a low coarse rumble, his voice pitched almost painfully deep.

"Nico is bound with the princess and the Floradëur. That is what allows him to walk this realm and survive it."

Five sets of eyes studied the three of us even more intently.

"I am declaring the demon Derek, a former guardian, an outlaw for attempting to end the Princess's existence," the High Lord said with silky menace. "I want Derek hunted down and brought back before me. I do not care what condition he is in so long as he is able to talk. Nico will remain with me while the Princess returns Talon to his people. Ruric and Hari, you will accompany them on their journey. I am entrusting you with her safe return, keeping in mind that her well-being is now tied with the other two."

"We will do our best to ensure her safety, my Lord." Hari bowed.

"High Lord," Ruric rumbled. With an impact that shook the ground, the big man knelt before the man he had served for so long. "I would ask to remain behind, and that one of the other guards go in my stead."

The High Lord placed a hand on the big demon's shoulder. "Old rock, I trust none other to keep safe what I treasure most dearly. And only you and Hari remember what it was once like to walk among the Floradëur. I trust in your control. Do not fear, I will be safe enough here."

"Things are changing in Hell, my lord," the big demon said, gazing upon the three of us—Nico, Talon, and I.

Blaec smiled. "Indeed, and that is a good thing."

The stony expression on Ruric's craggy face said that this demon thought otherwise.

"I have molded, grown stale here in the last few centuries, and you along with me, Ruric. Change is good for us all. Go now and prepare quickly for the journey. You will depart as soon as you are ready."

"Yes, my Lord." Ruric lumbered to his feet, bowed deeply, and left the room. Hari and the other demons followed behind, leaving as silently as they had entered.

THIRTY

WITH HIS FIRST step outside, Talon felt something inside him shift, grow, expand. Like taking a breath for the very first time, though nothing in him moved.

They left as Kantera, the second moon, disappeared down over the far horizon and the third moon, Rubera, rose on the opposite end in full scarlet glory, elliptical, much closer and larger than the Earth's moon.

Rubera was an impressive sight that only Talon seemed to marvel at. Had Nico been there, he would have marveled, too, for he carried those reddish rays within him. But they had left Nico on the doorstep of Darkling Hall, a pale forlorn figure watching them until they disappeared, the High Lord standing beside him in his twin role as warden and protector.

"Will he be okay?" Talon asked.

"Yes," Lucinda replied, knowing intuitively who Talon spoke of. "If Nico falters, if they need us, a signal arrow will flare in the sky." Which explained why she had been looking upward so often.

Then all thoughts and worries about Nico disappeared

as the first red rays fell on them. "Oh," Talon gasped, as something unseen but felt, definitely felt, entered him. It filled him like a gentle, spreading tide, washing over him and through him, filling every part of him like a soft, sighing breeze. "What is that?"

"That is our version of Basking," Lucinda said because she had felt it, too. "Only here, under our moons, are we renewed. Each demon is renewed most strongly by one specific moon. For me, that is Rubera."

"Is that true for Floradëurs?"

"I don't know. I would have thought so once, but you were able to exist on Earth all those years without being renewed by our moons."

"The Flowers of Darkness gather their power through the plants and natural environs. They are renewed through nature." This little gem of knowledge came from Hari, who spoke without turning his head. He led in front while Ruric followed behind, guarding our rear. Even with his increased height, Talon felt dwarfed by the two demon warriors. But even so, Talon felt more comfortable with them than the other three demon guards they had left behind. At least these two did not look at him with hunger in their eyes.

"Then why did I feel that just now?" Talon asked.

Lucinda shrugged. "You must have sensed it in me, through our binding."

"Or it is an ability that you have gained from her," Ruric rumbled from behind. "To be renewed by our moons."

Talon turned back to gaze at the brutal features set so hard and unemotionally that they seemed an inanimate mask. "You seem to know much of my kind."

"Only a few basic things," Ruric said, falling back into a stony silence.

They traveled at a brisk pace for the next several hours, and though Talon marveled at the new sights he encountered, he did not talk any further, conserving his energy instead for keeping up with the others. While he and Lucinda carried only a light rucksack strung over their shoulders, the two guards carried heavy packs strapped across their backs. Yet they moved effortlessly as if they weighed nothing. Remarkably enough, Talon was able to keep up with them. Gone was the fatigue of the past, that ever-present physical weakness. And while he would not go so far as to say his energy was boundless, it was indeed plentiful, as he had never felt before in his life.

He soaked in the heat. Soaked in the energy that seemed to constantly replenish within him as soon as it was lost, and pondered over this amazing new state of physical well-being.

The journey would have been wonderful were Lucinda not giving him away at the end of it. For his own good; Talon understood that. And he realized it was more her issue than his. Her self-image and sense of self-worth was pitifully low. Something he could relate to but did not know how to correct. He, himself, had only reached out once for something he'd wanted—her. And it had resulted in the binding, their current sad mess. Other than that, he had known nothing but fear and weakness within himself, and obeying others' orders. No wonder the Princess did not wish to be bound to him.

But still, as they trekked across the increasingly wilder and more desolate land, he could not help but feel astonished at being here in this realm, something he had not even known existed. He had thought himself odd and alone, a misfit all his life. And could not help but thirst to see others of his kind. Others like him.

When Rubera had marched across the sky and began to dip down over the land's rim, they stopped in a small clearing, a bare strip of land with nothing but hard, dry dirt and a few stunted bushes here and there.

"We stop here for the night," Hari said, dropping his pack, letting it thud heavily down to the ground, kicking up a puff of dust.

"Why are we stopping?" Talon asked.

Lucinda answered. "Because it will be dark soon."

An odd thing to say, Talon thought, when it had been

nothing but dark in Hell so far. The orange-yellow rays of the second moon had cast only a dim glow, and Rubera's red light was more dusky than bright.

Ruric began to yank up the brush, pulling the scrubby growth out by its roots. "Why is he doing that?" Talon asked.

"Ruric," she said, "tell Talon why you are doing that."

"As the Princess commands. I do this so that there is no place for others to hide," Ruric rumbled.

Talon didn't think the poor stunted bushes were big enough to conceal a mouse, much less a demon, but he held his tongue, not wanting to anger the big, intimidating demon.

Lucinda felt no such obvious constraint. "My father is not here, Ruric," she said, her voice sounding terse and annoyed. "There is no need to call me by a title you do not believe true. My name will suffice."

Ruric's face and tone did not alter in any way, staying remote. "It is what your father calls you."

"He is not my father," she snapped.

Ruric simply walked away to dispose of the brush he had uprooted.

Hari cast them an oily smile. "Ruric is a demon of few words and simple belief. The High Lord's word is law to him."

"And to you?" Lucinda asked silkily.

"To me as well," Hari said with an easy smile.

Congenial words, but Talon did not like how the demon lingered his gaze upon Lucinda. He looked at her like a man watched a woman he wanted to fuck. Not as a warrior should look upon a princess he was supposed to be protecting.

"Are you interested in me, Hari?" Lucinda asked, her lips curving up into a lazy come-hither smile, her voice taking on a deliberate, rich stroking sultriness Talon had never heard before.

Hari's smile widened. "I would not be averse to some pleasure."

"Nor would I," she said with biting sweetness. "But it would be my pleasure, not yours. In case you were delusional enough to entertain other hopes, let me make clear that I have no interest in you, whatsoever."

Hari's teeth flashed white in the shadowy bronze of his face, a pirate's smile. "Perhaps I can change your mind."

Lucinda slowly shook her head. "When Hell is ablaze in sunlight. I'd forgotten why I'd never quite liked you, Hari. That vanity and heavy ego of yours. It must be quite a burden to carry around."

"No burden at all," Hari smirked. "And that ego comes from the cries of many a satisfied demon lady."

Lucinda sneered. "I am not one of those sheltered, giggling aristocrats."

"I know," Hari said, his words a soft and sultry, vibrant sound.

She gazed at the handsome demon guard with unveiled disdain. "Then you know that if you touch me in any way, I will cut off your limbs and then your balls and leave them here for the hellhounds to feed upon."

"Careful, Princess." Hari's eyes narrowed. "Your hellhound bitch is not around this time."

Lucinda curled her lip contemptuously at him. "No need for Brindle when I can so easily take care of you myself."

Their hostility swirled like a dark thundercloud, thickening the air around them with the brittle tension of violence ready to be unleashed.

Ruric suddenly reappeared, his impassive face closed and hard. "You take watch, Hari. I will stay here with them."

"Says who?" Hari snarled with ready aggression.

"Says Ruric," growled the bigger demon, his face looking as if it were carved from sharp jutting stone.

Hari threw a murderous glare at Lucinda, then, snatching up his pack, stalked off. After he left, Ruric sat down on the ground. Opening his bag, he pulled out a leather drinking pouch. The tang of blood filled the air as he twisted it open, and a small pang of hunger gnawed at Talon as he watched the demon gulp down the liquid.

"Sit and rest and eat, Talon," Lucinda said, once more at ease, as if nothing untoward had happened. She rummaged through her rucksack.

Talon examined the contents of his own bag—two leather pouches similar to the one Ruric drank from, and strips of dried meat.

"What are these?" he asked.

"Challo," Lucinda told him. "A mixture of sheep and cow's blood mixed with wine. The jerky is yaro, similar to venison."

"I only drink blood," Talon said.

"On Earth. Our metabolism slows down in that other realm; you cannot digest solid food. Here, though, we eat. Try it."

Talon did, cautiously biting off a small piece of the yaro jerky. It felt strange to chew and swallow. And it felt weird going down his throat. But his stomach did not revolt and spew it back up. It tasted surprisingly good. He took another bite and washed it down with a gulp of challo. The blood wine was sweet, while the meat was salty and tough.

As the red twilight darkness ebbed and grew dimmer, as Rubera slipped down over the edge of the land, Lucinda murmured quietly to him, "Stay by my side."

"I was not planning on leaving it," Talon said.

She looked at him. "You are not angry at me anymore?"

He avoided a direct answer. "I understand why you are doing this."

"Do you?"

"Yes."

The last burgundy ray of light disappeared. Like a light switch suddenly flicked off, they were abruptly swallowed up by darkness so complete, a blackness so overwhelming, that Talon could not see for one frightening moment. Then his eyes adjusted and the fear gripping him lessoned as his senses expanded out in a new and wondrous way. It was as if he became the ground itself, the air that swept over it. He was aware of the insects scuttling across the ground, of the small trill of birds sheltering in trees just beyond the clearing. In an unfathomable way, he knew every rock and blade of grass that tenaciously sprang out of that dry, hard soil.

He could see Lucinda beside him. Not clearly as normal eyes would see, but rather the outline of her energy and that of Ruric's. And he knew where Hari stood watch a short distance off. He even saw himself sitting beside Lucinda. But the force that he sensed in the others was absent in him, for some reason, as if his energy had left his body. That absence alarmed him, made him flow back into himself, and as he did so, he saw vitality flicker and outline his form, too. He sat there in darkness, once more in his solid body, shook by what had occurred.

Lucinda's voice reached out to him like a lifeline, something to hold on to. "Don't be afraid of the darkness, Talon. It will soon pass."

"I'm not." And he wasn't afraid. Not of the darkness, but of what had just occurred to him in that darkness. Of what he had touched, become a part of for one brief instant. Out of everything that he had seen so far, this utter absence of light seemed the most natural to him. Almost comforting.

What am I? Talon wondered. But said nothing as darkness cloaked them like a heavy shroud.

Perhaps had he been less reticent, less frightened, he might have sensed what next approached them and warned them of it before it struck.

THIRTY-ONE

I SAT THROUGH Hell's darkest moment with my senses
flung wide open, screamingly acute. But even then it was
as if I were blind. I could smell—that distinctive tang of
demons, a sensing more psychic than physical. I could
hear—the wind blowing, the leaves rustling. But I could
not see. Even my highly acute eyes could not pierce this
utter blackness. I could have also sensed movement, but
there was none. Ruric sat unmoving, and even Hari remained still in the outer perimeter. But Talon . . . I only
detected Talon because he sat right next to me, so close
that I could feel the warmth of his skin. His presence,
though, that distinct feel of another's force brushing against
your own, dimmed. Disappeared for a brief moment. I almost reached out my hand to him, to touch him and reas-
sure myself that he was still there beside me, when I felt
that faint presence return once more to him. Had I imagined it, that absence? That brief instant when he had been
gone? The question hovered on the tip of my tongue, but I
bit it back, not wanting to ask it in the hearing of the others. And I could not risk erecting the cone of silence around

us to speak for fear of how it would affect Nico, our third.

So we sat in silence, letting time slowly crawl by until the gray rim of Sumera, our first moon, crept reluctantly over the edge of the land and shed its first dim rays, casting us once more in faint light.

Most people equate darkness with danger, but it is not always so. Danger can strike at anytime. It did so now when the tension had passed and we thought ourselves safe.

The ground groaned and trembled, surging wildly beneath us as if the solid soil was fluid water. I had only a moment to see the alarm in Ruric's craggy face. To hear him shout, "Run!"

I did. Or at least tried to. I grabbed Talon's arm and rolled us backward, away from the heaving ground. Before I gained my footing, the earth broke where we had sat just a moment ago, and a giant gaping mouth with sharp serrated teeth broke through the soil.

It was a Gordicean, a massive wormlike creature. But like most of the things that existed down here in Hell, it was much bigger than a worm, and had sharp teeth. And it ate meat instead of dirt. It was a fully mature male, denoted by the long deadly spikes rimming its head and neck. With a trumpeting cry, it thrashed its giant head to the side, smashing the ground near where Ruric stood. The spikes missed him by mere inches. The smooth, wrinkled hide of the creature's neck actually brushed the demon's leg for a moment on the jerky upstroke. It heaved back up and down again in a fast whiplike motion, trying to find Ruric. To either pummel him with its body or pierce him with its deadly spear points. Ruric rolled and the creature followed him for two more ground-thudding strikes. Two hair-raising near misses that occurred in such quick, battering succession, that Ruric had no time to spring to his feet, only to keep rolling.

"Here," I shouted, then leaped with my hand locked tight around Talon's arm. The ground trembled and shook as the blind Gordicean turned its attention to us, alerted by my call, smashing the area we had just jumped from. Our feet touched the ground and I sprung us into the air again as the air *whooshed* behind us, the ground trembling from another body-ramming strike and the resonating roar of the hungry beast's angry cry.

When we touched aground again, Talon stumbled and took us down. I desperately rolled us, heavy battering thuds rocking the ground in our wake, heaving the earth beneath us, showering us with sprays of rock and clods of dirt.

With Talon and I entangled, I could not roll us as fast as Ruric alone had been able to move. The Gordicean came closer to us with each striking attack. It thrashed itself again and the ring of spikes sank into the ground, missing my leg by a palm's reach. Had I stretched out my hand, I could have touched it. Talon cried out in fear and the creature jerked its spikes free of the ground and rose up above us.

As it reared to strike, something sprang atop its head. Something dark, with skin bronzed. A clawed hand struck down with a force that made the creature shudder and give a fierce, bellowing cry. It heaved and shook its massive body above us, trying to dislodge its rider. Thick powerful hands suddenly grabbed us and tossed us out from beneath the beast, sending us flying in the air. I had a glimpse of Ruric's fierce face, his familiar ugliness almost beautiful to me; it had been he who had thrown us. He stood below the giant worm creature, and above him, perched atop the Gordicean, riding it like a wild bronc, was Hari.

We hit the ground with jarring force and rolled. Coming to our feet almost at the same time, Talon and I sprinted away from the thrashing beast. But his legs were longer than mine now, and this boy could move. It was he who gripped me and pulled me along now, so fast that my feet barely touched the ground. When we'd gained enough distance, he stopped, and we turned back to watch the ensuing battle.

Hari had shifted into his demon beast shape, which meant that he'd doubled his size and tripled his weight. But even then, he seemed a tiny thing on top of the Gordicean. Hari lifted his curved talons and plunged them deep into the creature's head where the braincase was located. It shuddered and screamed with a rage-filled, echoing cry. With a sudden dipping maneuver, it relinquished its attempt to dislodge its demon rider, and smashed its head and body down on the ground instead, twisting and rolling on the rocky soil, trying to flatten the demon with its weight instead. Hari hung on, gripping the twisting, giant worm despite the punishment his body took.

Down below, Ruric had shifted also. If he was massive before, he had to be even more so now. But from afar, he seemed almost doll-like next to the enormous creature. He was a deadly doll, though. Blood the color of fermented grapes spurted out from where Ruric hacked at the giant worm, cutting it almost in half. He continued to slash and rip at the creature as it writhed and twisted on the ground, with less force and strength now. It was in its death throes. But Hari wasn't happy with letting it die slowly. He sank his talons into the creature's skull once more and gave a massive heave that strained his bulky muscles. The skull cracked open with a loud splintering sound, and those clawed hands reached down inside and pulled out the creature's brain, a wet, shiny, oblong mass the size of a watermelon. With a last blasting cry, the Gordicean stopped writhing, stopped moving. It gave one giant convulsive shudder, then stilled. Ruric continued to hack away at it down below.

"Is it dead?" Talon asked.

"Yes."

With a final powerful slash, Ruric severed the body into two pieces. At the head, sitting triumphantly atop his vanquished foe, Hari began to drink from the cracked skull, the bloody brain he had ripped out dangling from his claws. Below, Ruric sliced open the chest, sank his arm deep down almost to his armpit. Squishy noises were heard as he rooted around. A few more wet sounds, and he pulled out a foot-long organ.

"What's that?" Talon whispered.

"The heart." I watched as Ruric sank his fangs into his prize. Heard the wet slurp as he gulped down heart's blood, his face totally savage, as beastly as the creature he fed upon. His eyes glowed red, as did mine, I knew.

I watched them feast. To tear into the flesh after they were done drinking the blood. Savage, fierce creatures, no different than I.

"Do you want to join them?" Talon asked.

I shuddered. "No. I did not shift. Nor had I fought. I do not need to replenish energy lost in battle. Besides, it is their kill." I sat on the ground, with Talon beside me. The Floradëur was braver than I would have been in his place, surrounded by this realm's most ruthless predators. We patiently waited until our demon guards were done sating their bloodlust and replenishing their energy.

I rested my head on bent knees and closed my eyes, knowing that the other wild creatures here would wait until the ones who had brought down the prey were finished eating their fill. We had a short time, at least, before other animals moved in.

I felt a shimmer of power as Ruric and Hari shifted back. Heard cloth ripping as they tore off their ruined clothes. Wet splashes as they washed themselves free of the blood, and dressed in new clothes. Then no more sound. I sensed their approach. Felt their thrumming energy, battle-fresh, strong and vital.

"You should drink some of its blood," Hari said.

"No." I opened my eyes to see Hari and Ruric standing before me, and discreetly assessed them. They appeared calm, their eyes no longer hazed red.

I realized I had seriously misjudged his mental state when Ruric grabbed my arms and lifted me to my feet, his face no longer impassive.

"Do not," he growled, his eyes flickering with dangerous sparks of red hot rage. "Do not *ever* endanger yourself on my behalf again, Princess."

"Release me." My voice was deadly quiet, with an ice so pure and biting he had to have felt its warning frost against his skin.

Ruric dropped his hands and took a step back, his huge fists clenching.

"I do as I choose. *I* am in charge," I enunciated with cold hauteur, every inch the Princess he called me.

Ruric pierced me with those deep-cut, asymmetrical eyes. "Not if you ever do anything like that again," he rumbled in a menacing timbre. "I will *not* return to your father with news of your final death."

"Nor will I return to the High Lord to tell him that the last two demons of his dragon clan were killed when I could have prevented it."

"We were more than able to look after ourselves, Princess," Hari said with a conqueror's arrogant smugness.

I may not like the egotistical bastard, but I owed Hari gratitude for what he had done. "My thanks, Hari," I said stiffly, "for coming to our aid."

"It's my job," Hari returned offhandedly. "And I agree with Ruric. It would be easier to accomplish our duty if you did not take unnecessary risks, Lucinda." *He*, apparently, had no problems dropping my title.

I gazed at Hari coolly. "Your definition of unnecessary differs from mine."

Ruric was back to being his rocklike self, and even more frightening because of that stony control. In those uneven eyes glinted an implacable will. "Your word, now, Princess. You allow us to guard you and the Floradëur as we have been so entrusted. Or we will turn back now and return to your father."

I didn't bother arguing with how he titled my relationship with the High Lord. Nor did I try bargaining with him, knowing it would be useless. "I agree."

Ruric drilled me for a moment more with those deep, piercing eyes, and finally grunted. "Then we continue on."

When Sumera was a hovering oval mass straight above

us, casting its gray light across the realm, we reached the distant shore of the North Sea.

We had arrived. As far as we would travel.

I wanted to hold Talon's hand, to feel that connection flow between us one last time, but kept my hand down by my side. "We leave you here," I said.

"Here?" Talon looked around, gazing at the peninsula snaking straight out to sea a mile away. "Is that where my people are?"

I nodded. "We cannot venture safely beyond this point."

"And I?"

"You are one of them. You will be safe."

"And if I wish to return to you after I have seen them? After I have learned of my kind?"

I shook my head. "The trip across the wild lands is too dangerous to attempt, Talon. Even if you somehow make the journey safely, the demons that await you at the other end are even more dangerous. There is no future for you and I together."

"Not just you and I, but also Nico. The three of us. Separating us will not break our bond."

"But neither will it drain you of your power, trying to support one or the other of us. With time, perhaps the ties between us will fade." I backed away from him. "Good-bye, Talon."

He said nothing. Just watched as we drew back into the tall rushes that grew along the beach, leaving him a stark black figure standing alone on the dark sand. He looked abandoned. Desolate.

Determinedly, I shook the impression away from me. I was returning him to his people, not abandoning him. *Are you not?* a voice inside me whispered.

Ruric gestured for us to go, but I shook my head, resisting. I wanted to wait until I saw Talon greeted and accepted. Ruric's big hand clamped down on my shoulder and drew me forcefully back. I went because I had no other choice, seething, ready to fight him if he tried to draw me completely away, but he stopped at the outermost fringe, in a sparser area of growth. I turned back to see four black figures in the gray twilit sky, winging above Talon. They looked like big birds, but I knew that was not what they were. They were Floradëurs in their animal form. They glided down and landed softly on all fours on the sand, surrounding Talon, their shoulders reaching to Talon's waist. With their wings folded up, no longer distracting the eye, you could appreciate the sleek, graceful animals they were. Unique, with delicate, triangular faces. Not quite cat or dog or fox, but a blending of all three. A small creature the size of a lynx, with erect ears, a small pointed snout, and sharp claws. Entirely black. Creatures once worshipped by early Egyptians and ancient Babylonians. But the primitive carvings left behind by these people failed to capture the regal grace and elegance. And these creatures were winged. With wings like a bat, and in some ways they resembled one, but only if bats were beautiful instead of ugly; large and graceful instead of hideous.

Three of them disappeared. There one second, vanished completely in the next. Only one Floradëur remained beside Talon.

Hari grabbed my shoulder—Ruric still gripped the other one—and they both turned me to go. But it was too late. The small bush to my right, the thin sapling to my left, and the flowering shrub before me morphed and changed shape. They grew, stretched out, distorted. And in their place stood the three Floradëurs, surrounding us. One of them clicked its teeth together. A split second later they opened their mouths and blasted us simultaneously.

It was like the sound Talon had made, but weaker, almost melodic cries rather than his harsh, terrible screech, without his hammering force. The combined blow from all three, however, was still enough to stun us a little despite our mental shielding; here in Hell, our shields were always in place. It swayed us back, stopped us in our tracks. Ruric was the first to recover. He lunged forward, swiping at the creatures with his claws.

"No!" I cried. "Don't hurt them."

But I need not have worried. They vanished and we ran once more, Ruric and Hari on either side of me, almost carrying me between them. Two Floradëurs appeared, blocking our way. The third popped up behind us. We sprang up over them as that warning click sounded, airborne when that combined echolating cry hit us. Faltering, we fell to ground. When we rolled to our feet, it was not just three of them surrounding us now, but over a dozen.

Shit, I had time to think as I heard the menacing click again. Their percussive blast hit us again, their cries beating down upon us from all sides with a synchronized force that wasn't just quadrupled but increased maybe forty times more. They overwhelmed our mental shields by sheer brute force and numbers.

"No," I gasped, clutching my pain-splintered head. "We brought him back . . . Not here to hurt you."

They hit us again with another echolating cry.

A sharp pain burst in my head, and then nothing.

THIRTY-TWO

THE SOUND OF beating waves, a sound not hyperacute but distant and filtered, pulled me from the void I'd been shoved into and sent spinning down. The climb back up into consciousness was a painful, arduous one.

My head ached. So did my body. My arms and shoulders were sore, my wrists and ankles tender and abraded . . . and restrained. The familiar warmth of metal alloy against my skin told me before I opened my eyes that I was bound with demon chains. And the splattered drops of wetness across my cheek, along with the muffling of my senses, told me that I had been doused with the oil of Fibara. Neither was surprising. It was the Floradëurs who had invented both, after all. Once our closest allies, they were now one of our most feared enemies. Not so much because of their warrior skills but because of their fierce intelligence, their skills as artisans and craftsmen, and their packlike approach to battle. They were small, slight creatures, easily overpowered if you managed to corner one. That, however, was the greatest challenge—capturing one before they slipped away from you. They were ferocious fighters, once banded together, as aptly demonstrated. But alone, the vocal blast of one was more of a painful annoyance, not an overwhelming force, Talon being the exception. And that ability to slip away . . . to meld their energy with a plant, a bush, and emerge from it, or disappear down it . . . only a few things hindered that ability, pregnancy being one of them.

My lashes swept up and I found a multitude of black eyes filled with hate and loathing fixed upon me. Several hundreds of them, women and children scattered among the males, their eyes as hostile as their menfolk but filled with curiosity. We were at the other end of the peninsula, if I guessed right, farthest away from shore. And perched on top of a cliff with nothing but the sea below, if my muffled senses informed me correctly. I lay in what seemed to be their punishment circle. A dozen yards to my right, the land dropped away.

My arms were stretched out upon the ground, my legs likewise secured, demon chains holding me simply and effectively in a splayed X. Hari and Ruric, who had apparently returned to consciousness before I, if they had even lost it, were likewise restrained; Hari was to my left, Ruric opposite me, closer to the cliff edge.

Our capture was no surprise. What surprised me— shocked me—was that Talon was restrained with us, just beyond Hari, completing our little circle. And not just restrained, his mouth was gagged.

"You are awake, demon."

I turned to the voice that spoke, and looked up into a black angular face standing over my head. It was a little disorientating to look at him like that, upside down. He frowned, and seemed to think so as well. He walked between Hari and me to stand in the open space between my hip and outstretched arm. He was an older Floradëur with white hair sprinkled among the midnight blackness like specks of dust. He moved with the fluid, lithe grace of their kind, carried the same musicality in his voice. But authority cloaked him, was borne by his proud and erect carriage, in the way he spoke. Stripes of gold lined his cloak, denoting his higher standing. Just how high, I didn't know, but could guess at.

"Why have you chained Talon?" I asked.

Those black eyes narrowed down at me. "Do you speak of the Floradëur you have turned against us?"

"Yes to the name. No to the rest of it. I have not turned him against you."

"He injured our guards, trying to come to your aid." Those black eyes bore down into me as if he would unearth my darkest secrets. "You have enhanced his cry, turned it into a powerful weapon."

I wanted to close my eyes, pinch myself, to wake up from this horrible nightmare. How the holy Mother of Darkness had we managed to screw up so badly something that should have been so simple?

I opened my mouth and attempted to repair some of the damage. "Talon is a Floradëur that was taken from this realm by a rogue demon six and twenty years ago when he was an infant, and raised up among the Monère."

A heated murmuring rose up among the watching Floradëurs.

"We were returning him to you and leaving," I said. "Why did you attack us?"

"You ventured onto our lands." His words stabbed at me like knives.

"To return one of your kind back to you."

"To spy upon us!" He barred his sharp teeth, and his nails, retracted until then, sprang out with his anger, sharp black pointy things.

A woman stepped out from the crowd of onlookers. "He is Sarai and Jaro's child," she said firmly. She was slender and graceful, wrapped in a flowing tunic the color of ivory. Her hair was long, black, and loose. She approached Talon, looked down at him, her voice trembling softly. "We thought him dead, lost to us. He has Sarai's features."

"Step back, Mesa. He is dangerous."

"He will not hurt me, Deon." Her hand reached out to touch Talon's face.

"You will obey me!" Deon thundered, his voice crack-ing like a whip. "Step back now."

Reluctantly, Mesa did as he commanded. Talon's wrists flexed against his restraints as he followed the female Flora-dëur's progress back to the perimeter, blending once more into the ring of onlookers.

"Who are you?" the man called Deon demanded, crouch-ing down beside me. "A female demon who wears the Demon Prince's clothes?"

That confused me until I remembered that I wore Hal-cyon's shirt, pants, and belt. I wondered if I could bluff.

"The Prince has made it a popular fashion that other demon's imitate." A blatant lie. None others dared wear his exact colors and style.

Deon's black eyes drilled into mine. "They carry his scent."

So much for bluffing. If he was familiar enough with our kind to know Halcyon's scent, then he had to have at least a suspicion of who I was. There were few demons with my distinct hair and skin color.

"Tell us now," Deon said, "or we will simply kill you as we should have done already."

"Why didn't you?" I asked.

"I was curious."

His reply made me wonder what would happen once his curiosity was satisfied. I watched those black eyes flicker as I answered, "I am Lucinda, Prince Halcyon's sister."

The murmuring rose, grew agitated, swelled up in vol-ume.

"Princess Lucinda roams the other realm as guardian. She is rarely seen down here in Hell."

That's what you get for telling the truth—doubt that you were telling it.

"It's how I found Talon, roaming that other realm. And why I am bringing him back to you. I sought to do nothing more than that, my solemn oath on it."

"What is a demon's oath?" Deon sneered, a world of bitter cynicism in his voice, making me wonder how old he was.

"Respected elder," I said in a voice loud enough to carry to all ears. "If you are knowledgeable enough to know Halcyon's scent, then you know there is at least a fifty percent chance I am who I claim to be, Halcyon's sister. Factor in these two royal demon watchdogs the High Lord sent with me . . ." Another rustling of whispers among the watching throng. "Demons you know by their skin color that have lived almost a millennium of afterlife faithfully serving the High Lord. If you know enough about us, you know who they are: royal guards that my father"—stretching the truth a bit here, but taking any advantage I could—"would be very unhappy about losing, for they are the last two that carry the blood of the dragon clan, other than the High Lord and Halcyon. Take in all these facts—my golden hair and skin, my long centuries of age, and the two legendary demon warriors that accompany me—and those odds rise up closer to ninety percent that I am who I say I am. That is why you did not kill us. Because you suspected our identity and realized that you had bitten off more than you could chew. Because if we just disappear, the High Lord is going to send an army of demon warriors out here to your lands to find out what happened to us and avenge our deaths."

Those cold black eyes glittered. "If you are who you say you are, and these two are indeed the legendary *drakons*, Hari and Ruric, then it makes it even more tempting to kill you. To strike such a heart blow to the High Lord. To kill his daughter as he killed my son. To kill his men as he has slaughtered so many of our people, our women and our children." Sheer malice glittered from those dark eyes, telling me that I had badly miscalculated. He wanted to kill us now with a deep-seated urge that was almost maniacal.

I tried to reason with him still. "The High Lord is the one who made it law forbidding the killing of your people. Who prohibited the hunting of Floradëurs and the unsanctioned taking of your blood."

"Yet so many still do," Deon said with chilling coldness.

In a swift movement, he unsheathed a short sword. Made of a precious alloy even stronger than demon chains, it gleamed purple under Sumera's gray light. A pall of silence overfell the multitude as they watched their leader tremble. You could not tell what he trembled from, rage or restraint. If it was the latter—restraint—it was not enough. I looked up into those anger-maddened eyes, and knew that bloodlust was going to overpower good sense. He was going to kill us. Chop us up and throw our pieces into the sea. Feed us to the sea beasts that dwelled in the dark waters at the base of the cliff.

"We are bound, Talon and I," I said in one last desperate bid at reason. "If you kill me, you will also kill one of your own kind."

Mesa gasped from where she watched among the crowd, but Deon's eyes glittered with eerie triumph. As if I had just given him the perfect reason to do what he so badly wanted to.

"By his own actions, he is not one of us," Deon declared. "He cannot even flow from flower to flower, from growth to growth, but is held down by chains, just like you are. If you are bound together, then even more reason to kill you. To free him of that perversion, that evil condition that enslaves him to you."

He raised the sword high above his head, and I saw my death in those black burning eyes. Words that should have spared Talon's life had ensured the ending of it instead.

Perversion, he had called our bond. Evil enslavement, when it was far from that. I'd run from it. Pushed it away from me. But no longer. Now bound by chains, with my power smothered by the oil, with not just my death but of all our deaths a moment away . . . I no longer fought that bond.

I dropped all resistance and didn't just open myself to it, I ran down that invisible line binding us together, and found it open. Talon had never closed himself away from me; it had only been I throwing a block between us. A barrier that was no longer there, an impediment that I smashed down in my need. I roared down that mental pathway and cried, *Talon, help me. Give me power.*

I felt the confusion in him, and then a sea of calm amidst the confusion.

Take what you need. The words rang clear, so clear in my mind, as if he had spoken them aloud.

With that invitation, that willingness, I didn't hesitate. As the sword swung down, as Ruric and Hari roared and fought to break free of the restraints, I took the energy, gathered it all, and thrust it entirely into my voice.

"Stop," I commanded. And Deon did, against his will. The wicked, purple sword screeched to a trembling halt a bare inch away from my neck. He fought that command, and fought hard, but could not go against it.

The power of that compulsion was a familiar use. What I did next was not. Talon drew his power from nature, from the very elements. And in the short time he had been here, he had soaked in much of its abundant force. It seemed to have poured into him, filled him up like a bucket too long emptied. That rich reservoir of power was there, so full and abundant, completely open to me, to my emotions, which were no longer calm and not entirely controlled.

Rage roared through me and filled me up. That beastly monster that had always dwelt within me stirred and breathed to life, my beast and something more. Destructive fury flashed through me, vibrated my entire being. And this time I did not try to control it. I loosened all restraint, and the heavens rumbled with my anger. The wind picked up, began to moan. Lightning flashed, illuminating the dark twilit sky. The air grew dense and heavy, and a jagged bolt struck the ground a body length away from me. Thunder shook the air with a dramatic rumble, and four more powerful lightning bolts cut down from the sky, striking the ground in a perfect, symmetrical circle around us, sending the guards that had surged inward lurching back, crying out in fright.

I pulled against the restraints. The chains held. I was strong mentally, but not physically. Channeling the energy as I was, I did not have enough power to throw off the blocking effect of the oil and feed both mind and body. Almost, but not quite enough. I knew, though, where I could get that added punch of power.

My gaze locked upon Deon, still frozen by my command. I gave him another one. "Come to me."

His eyes widened, and the fanatical hatred burning there turned to fear as he shuffled forward in jerky motion and bent down to me.

He resisted. With everything he had, he resisted, pulling upon the deep reserves of his own power. It was enough to stop him. To halt that forward, bending motion. To keep him from me that last final foot.

I laughed and it was as if the wind took my breath and echoed my amusement, swirling it around us in rough, windy play.

"Come," I commanded.

A powerful whip of wind ripped the sword from Deon's hand. A second lifting draft picked up his slender form and threw him to me.

He fell on top of me, his sharp claws digging painfully into my skin as he tried to push away, but it was too late. He was within my reach and I struck hard, sinking my fangs deep into his neck, gulping down his rich blood. It blasted through me, that sweet, singing energy. With a snap, I broke free of the chains and seized his wrists, yanked his claws out of my flesh. Another hot swallow of that hot energizing blood and I pulled my mouth from him. Didn't rip out his throat like I so badly wanted to do, only because two others needed his blood.

I rolled to my feet and dropped him between Ruric and Hari. Tore their chains off as they tore into Deon with sharp, ripping fangs. Deon cried out, his dark, slender body jerking and shuddering under the dual impact of their bites, Hari into his thigh, Ruric plunging deep into his neck. I left them to feast on the rich blood as I freed Talon.

Amidst the confusion of whirling wind and chaotic cries, I heard that warning click, the signal that preceded a unified cry. Turning, I saw that we were surrounded by a circle of Floradëurs. The women and children had fled beneath the moaning wind whipping around us with screaming frenzy, and the sizzling bolts of lightning I had called down from the sky. It was warriors only now.

The ebony warriors opened their mouths and I had a moment to think, *Forgive me, Nico*, before I threw up a cone of silence around us. I put all my power into that barrier. So much power that I saw it visible for the first time: a shimmering force that encircled upward, tapering to a point above my head. It flared bright for a moment as the percussive force of all those cries—hundreds of them—hit the barrier.

It held.

We heard nothing within, felt nothing inside that protective cone, while miles distant I knew that Nico faltered, cut off from us. Cut off not just from I but Talon, too. No one to sustain him. My fury swelled and burst from me, and that shimmering force, that protective cone swelled out as I released it. It struck our encircling attackers, roared over them. Swept them up and flung them violently away.

But even as I unleashed it and watched them scatter, I knew it wouldn't be enough. It would only stun them for an instant. Then they would regather and hit us again, and I would be forced to erect that barrier once more. I ran down that third line that bound us together and found it weak. Only seconds, and how it had weakened him. We needed to escape quickly.

My beast felt my need and answered it, wanting out. I did not fight it. I embraced it. But what emerged was something other than my familiar demon beast.

All my life, and the entirety of my afterlife, that was what I had fought most: to keep that control so necessary to a demon, or else a bloodbath would ensue.

But if that's what it took to leave this place quickly, then so be it upon their heads. That was my last thought before the change took me violently. Not the quick morphing transformation into my demon beast form, but something else. My clothes didn't just strain and rip, they tore completely from my body as I swelled, grew, and kept growing. My spine enlarged, lengthened and curved, and I fell to all fours. I watched as my skin melted away and scales—gold, glistening scales—took their place.

I heard Hari's whisper, "Dragon," and turned to look down upon him and watch the astonishment slacken his face. To see his tiny body so far beneath me, both him and Ruric . . . big, bulky Ruric looking so little, Talon a slender black curve beside them.

Sounds and movement whipped my head around to see the fallen Floradëurs regaining their feet, to hear their frightened cries as they gazed up at me. That click, that annoying, ominous click sounded again, and wrath like I had never known before burned hot within me, churned my gut. It grew and grew and built like quicksilver within me until it spilled out, could not be contained. I opened my mouth to scream, but what came spewing out was not sound but heat and fire. A roaring flame that flashed toward where that hateful click had originated. Floradëurs screamed and scattered beneath the fiery blast, the stench of singed hair and burning flesh mixing caustically with their cries. My tail, a weighty rear appendage, swept out behind me and knocked even more Floradëurs down like pins, flinging them wide into the air.

I bellowed my savage glee, stamped my feet, shook the ground, and toppled more of them over—my own men, included, unfortunately. I stopped, and another click sounded. Another stream of fire shot from my mouth, burning them. Another shift and scattering swipe of my tail. But as fast as I dispersed them, they reassembled around us like an unending wave. My tail whipped up and down, catching a few, pounding them, dispersing them. But I knew it was only a delaying action. We had to escape. I arched my back, and the tightness there along my back unfurled. Wings expanded, so long they extended beyond the punishment circle.

I dipped my head down to my men. "Climb on board," I said in a booming grumble so deep that the words were almost unrecognizable.

They did with a hop and a spring, Hari onto my back,
Ruric astride the base of my neck along with Talon who
the big demon had grabbed.

"Hang on," I growled. Another scattering sweep of my
tail, and I pounded toward the edge of the cliff. I could see
the ground fall away, and gathered up even more speed. I
leaped, soared in the air, and the waters spread black blue
beneath us. Rushed up at us as I flapped my wings desperately, slowing our fall, but not stopping it, burdened and
unbalanced by the weight I carried.

I felt a shifting of the heaviest weight atop me and knew
what he intended to do.

"No," I roared, a stream of heat hissing from my nostrils.
"Do not jump, Ruric, or I swear I will dive into the water
after you."

"I am too heavy," he said.

"No! Do not!"

Madly I struggled to keep us aloft, beating those virgin
wings with desperate strokes. By my will, my almost maddened will, we lifted and dipped. Lifted and dipped up
and down. The cold sea water splashed my feet, soaked my
dragging tail. My wings surged, a powerful beat, and we
rose up into the air, out of the water. Another powerful beat
of those wings and we flew higher. I wanted to laugh. I
wanted to shout. I wanted to trumpet my joy to the entire
realm as I cut through the air. Up and up, higher and higher,
soaring through the air, the wind rushing by—what I had
always yearned to feel and never had as a Monère. What I
had dreamt of in my deepest, most secret dreams.

But my floating joy was short-lived. A cloud of dark
wings swarmed down after us like a hive of angry bees,
pursuing us.

"Protect your ears," Talon warned us. He shifted
around, gathered himself, and let loose his fearsome cry. It
spread out above us and hit our pursuers, stunning them
like a hammer's blow. A few recovered enough to continue
flapping, but a dozen fell into the waters below, where they

floated, dazed or unconscious. I looked down, glimpsed large moving shadows in the water.

Two floating Floradëurs were suddenly yanked down beneath the surface. Jaws yawned wide as another creature broke up through the water and chomped down on a third Flower of Darkness. More creatures broke the surface. More frantic splashes, more screams suddenly cut off.

And then complete, dead quiet. Utter calm. The violence occurring in a heartbeat suddenly gone beneath the waves. Nothing. Only the blood that swirled the surface of the dark waters with crimson stains.

Our winged pursuers fell away, returning back to the safety of land, and we flew on.

"I didn't know," Talon said, shaken. "I didn't mean to kill them."

"They would have done that to us," Ruric said. "Chopped us to pieces and fed us to those sea beasts, or downed us with their cry had you not struck first."

Ruric had known what had awaited him down in the sea; he had been willing to jump to his sure death to lighten my burden. But he hadn't because he had heard my conviction. I would have followed him down into the cold depths of the waters and tried to save him. I would have done the same for Hari had that handsome, sullen demon toppled into the sea accidentally . . . and it would have been by accident. No self-sacrificing, that one.

I would have gone in after them because they were the last of their kind. The last of that ancient blood, the *drakon*.

As was I.

Tears welled up in my eyes and blurred my vision for a moment, because in the surest, most telling way, dragon blood flowed in me, too.

"I didn't know you could become a dragon, Princess," Talon said, hugging my neck tight, his claws delicately anchoring his hold.

I had not known, either, and the discovery was a momentous joy, altering everything in me, changing my world.

I felt the pieces of me that had been broken, broken by my mother's falsehood, being mended now by truth. And I felt myself becoming whole once more. The fabricated burden I had carried for so long drifted away from me as my beating wings lifted us up.

"Why didn't you and Hari take dragon form, also, Ruric?" Talon asked.

"Because we cannot." In his deep bass, Ruric explained the miracle that had just occurred. "Once we become demon dead, we lose the Monère ability to shift into pure animal form. We have only our demon beast shape."

"But Lucinda changed—"

"Because of your bond," Ruric said.

"And likely because of the Monère included in your bond," added Hari.

My thoughts went to him, Nico. And to my other Monère, Stefan, as we drifted in flight.

What required over two moons to walk, took only an hour to fly. Oh, the freedom of the air. But exhilarating as it was, by the time Darkling Hall spiraled up before us, I was feeling the weariness in my wings and along the muscles of my back.

Shouts were heard as they caught sight of us. We could have landed nearby and walked in, but we sailed in boldly because I was anxious to see how Nico fared. We landed under the eyes of the full troop of royal guards, which had sprinted out en masse. Were it not for Ruric and Hari's presence on my back, some, no doubt, would have unleashed their weapons upon me. But Ruric's bulk and Hari's wiry form were perched aloft, along with Talon's dark self. And not only was I a dragon, a creature of the High Lord's blood clan, but my scales were golden. That distinct coloring alone would have made some of them wonder at my identity, unlikely though it might be.

The High Lord himself watched, standing on the steps of Darkling Hall, and my heart ached with both sadness and happiness. We landed and it was a rocky touchdown, with a few stumbling steps before I steadied. If my riders were jolted, at least they did not fall off. They sprung down, and with a shimmer of energy, still abundant, I changed back into upright form.

Pure shocking silence met me, broken by Winston's tall gaunt form moving forward in silent approach.

"Welcome back, Princess," the butler said, his mirror-dark eyes twinkling with amusement and relief, pride and other unnamable things. He swung the High Lord's cloak around me, covering my nudity, which I had completely forgotten about.

Then the High Lord made his way down to me, and I met him halfway. I ran to him, feeling as if my heart had squeezed up into my throat.

"Father," I said, standing before him.

Those eyes blinked, grew moist, and the air vibrated with a wave of emotion he could not fully contain.

"Lucinda," he said in a voice that trembled. "I had given up all hope of ever hearing that word from your lips again." Then I was in his arms and we both were crying, red tears rolling down our cheeks.

"Father," I said again, tasting the word with joy. "I truly am your daughter."

"You always have been."

"She lied." The malice of it was hard to comprehend. My very own mother. She had chosen a lie that could not be proved or negated. Even my long years of existence had proven nothing because my mother descended from the phoenix clan, another long-lived line.

"Yes, she lied," Blaec said softly, then put aside the hurtful past and concentrated on the future. "How can this be, that you can take dragon form?"

"My bond with Talon and Nico." I looked around for Nico and did not see him. "Where is Nico?"

"I am here." He came out of the house and down the steps, alive and well, his skin stunningly white amidst the guards' darkness. "I could not stay inside," Nico said to my father—how sweet those words were upon my lips, and in my heart. *My father.*

"Nico," I cried and laughed and launched myself at him.

He caught me with laughter of his own, a beautiful white pigeon among all the dark-skinned wolves.

"You are well," I said, running my hands over him, needing the tactile proof of what my eyes beheld.

"Yes."

"I had to shield."

"I felt it. It staggered me for a second, but then I was fine. I seem to be stronger."

"We all are," Talon said, standing beside us.

"Hey, you returned," Nico said with a grin.

"Yes, it seems that she cannot get rid of us, no matter how she tries," Talon said. To all of our amazement, he grinned also.

Nico reached out and pulled Talon in, then we were all embracing and touching and laughing, our triad complete. And it felt right and whole.

"Enough theatrics and emotion for the day," the High Lord said gruffly. "Into the house before all creatures far and near come panting after Nico's white, tender flesh."

"And your delectably naked one," Nico murmured.

I raised a haughty brow. "Are you leering at me?"

"Absolutely."

"Good." I swung one arm around that white, tender flesh, the other around Talon's dark slenderness, and together we walked into the house.

I TOLD MY father of all that had occurred. Hari and Ruric confirmed my report. At the end of our tale, Blaec sighed.

"So much death and bloodshed of both demons and Floradëurs. It will be hard to overcome, but your bond . . . perhaps that will do what my laws do not. To start to heal the rift between us. It will take time, but that is one thing we seem to have. And speaking of time, I have sent out word on Derek's rogue status, but none have seen him, and no word has come of his whereabouts."

"It has only been a day," Nico said.

"That is all it should have taken to locate him," I explained to Nico. "Justice is swift here. When you are decreed outlaw, no one dares help you or render aid. To do so will mean their own death. That we have not found Derek yet means that he is not here in this realm."

Nico frowned. "Where else could he be?"

"In the lower realm or the upper realm," I said.

"There is a lower realm?" Nico asked with surprise.

"Yes, though not many Monère know this. Many consider Hell as the lower realm, but in truth, Hell is just the middle kingdom. We have a lower realm called Nether-Hell."

It was Talon who grasped the situation. "So we are not safe until Derek is captured."

"Correct, dark one." Blaec looked at me. My senses tingled, and like before, I suddenly knew what was coming.

"No," I said, raising my hands.

"Yes, daughter mine."

"I see where you get your autocratic ways now," Nico murmured. I snarled at him before turning my attention back to the implacable rock that was my father.

"You are tied to both Hell and Earth now," Blaec said. "With this rogue demon at large, your Monère warriors will not be enough. You will need demon guards who can be trusted to protect you and your people, and traverse the two realms. Who can control themselves around a Floradëur and among the living Monère." A weighty pause that was lessened somewhat by the laughter shining from those dark chocolate eyes that now I could see were so much like my own. "And most crucially, who can keep a demanding, unruly demon princess in line."

The High Lord turned to his two most trusted guards. "Do you know of any that I can entrust with such a task?"

Ruric knelt before his ruler. "I know of none other than Hari and I, my Lord, who could fulfill all of those requirements. Especially the last."

My eyes narrowed. Blaec smiled and slapped his right hand on the big demon's shoulder. "Thank you, old rock."

"I pledge to keep our Dragon Queen safe," Hari said, kneeling beside Ruric, his handsome, dark face uncharacteristically grave.

"I'm not a queen," I said. *Not anymore.*

"But you are," this new and serious Hari said with not a trace of his usual sullen, leering self. "You are our Dragon Queen."

He said it with utter belief in his eyes, with a reverence and devotion that shook me. That made me want to shout at him: *Don't look at me like that. As if I am your sun, your moon, your earth, your sky.*

I would have preferred his old snarkiness, but it seemed to have been wiped away.

"Thank you, Hari." The High Lord's left hand came down to rest upon the wiry demon's shoulder.

They knelt there before him like two knights of old—surely an odd thought to have for demons. And they looked at me as if I were their holy grail.

Holy shit, as the humans were so fond of saying.

"Keep her safe. And try to keep the peace above while you're at it," Blaec said, his dark eyes twinkling. In a voice almost too low to hear, he murmured, "Things are going to be different up there."

What a hellish understatement that was. I didn't know whether to feel sorry for myself or for the Monère Court I was about to unleash these two demonic watchdogs on.

Yup, things were going to be very different.

Goddess help us all.

Dear Reader,

For more about Lucinda, please pick up Over the Moon, *where the demon princess makes her first appearance. And* On the Prowl, *her second cameo.*

If you've developed a thirst for more about the delicious Monère and the series that began it all, Mona Lisa Awakening, Mona Lisa Blossoming, Mona Lisa Craving, *and* Mona Lisa Darkening *await your dark reading pleasure.*

Till then—
Sunny
www.sunnyauthor.com

ABOUT THE AUTHOR

SUNNY is a physician by training, and an author by lucky happenstance. A graduate of Vassar College and mother of two, this PRISM Award–winning author lives with her husband, author Da Chen, in New York's beautiful Hudson Valley. Please visit her website at www.sunnyauthor.com.

KEEP READING FOR A PREVIEW OF THE NEXT BOOK
IN THE DEMON PRINCESS CHRONICLES SERIES
BY SUNNY

LUCINDA, DANGEROUSLY

AVAILABLE OCTOBER 2009 FROM BERKLEY BOOKS!

THEY SAY THAT you get wiser as you get older. I don't know about that. In my opinion, sometimes you just get dumber.

A Queen saw us and screamed. A Monère Queen garbed in the usual long black gown denoting her status. As if you couldn't tell by the feel of her presence alone. She took one look at the seven of us and let loose a wail of terror as if the Wild Hunt itself had spit out of Hell and come here to hunt her.

It wasn't really her fault. But, really, she was old enough to know better. She was close to three-quarters of a century, as far as I could tell. But then again, you could argue that I also should know better. I was over six hundred years old. Over seven hundred if you counted my other life before this, my Monère life. What I had been before I died and became demon dead. I lived in Hell now. Or at least I had before I was booted out due to circumstances entirely of my own making.

Those circumstances stood beside me now, cringing as the young Queen screamed her silly head off, the two I had bonded with. One was a demon creature as black as night. No, I take that back, he was even blacker. The entirety of him a charcoal shimmer of hair, skin, and eyes. No whites in those eyes, just darkness against darkness, a pure absence of light. Talon, my Floradëur, which literally meant *flower of darkness*. A poetic name aptly describing him, a tall willowy wand with delicate features that edged over into feminine prettiness.

On the other side of me stood my other bondmate, Nico, the Monère warrior who had been intimately sheathed inside my body at the time when Talon had bonded us. The supernatural tie had linked all three of us together, accidentally. It had been like, *Oops, didn't know* that *could happen*. That something dead—Talon and I—could be tied to something living. We were bound together now, the three of us, two creatures from Hell and a former Monère rogue. Former because now Nico was mine, officially recognized as such by High Court, where we presently were. Bringing us back to the screaming ninny before us.

It wasn't so much Nico and I who upset her. Demon dead that I was, I was a petite woman, not too threatening in appearance . . . unless I wanted to be. And trust me, I wasn't trying to be at this moment. Nor was it Stefan— beautiful Stefan, the Monère warrior who I loved—or his human-Monère Mixed Blood ward, Jonnie, a young man of eighteen or nineteen years of age. Nope. It was the last two of our group that had struck terror into the woman's heart and made her cause such a ruckus. Ruric and Hari. My royal demon guards.

Yup, royal. I was a princess. Daughter of the High Lord of Hell, and sister of its current ruler, Prince Halcyon. I was Princess Lucinda. It was an empty title, really. The only thing I had ruled over had been the occasional wayward demon I had caught over the last few centuries while roaming this earthly realm. As a guardian, it had been my job to find them and bring them back to Hell before they wreaked more havoc.

Another problem, a big one, had been that my paternity had been called into question. No longer. I had proven true that I was the High Lord's daughter in a most indisputable way. And Daddy dearest had, in turn, sicced his two oldest, most trusted demon guards on me. They were supposed to watch over me and keep me out of trouble. Whatever my father's intentions may have been, they seemed to have backfired. One look at Ruric, and your instant gut reaction was to let out a wail of terror. Ruric meant *rock* in the old language, and that was what he happened to look like—one great big pile of hardness. Massive not so much in height, which was just over six feet, but more in width and depth. He was one great hulking mass of muscles. His impressive physique alone would have made him intimidating, but it was the startling ugliness of his face that took your breath away. His coarse, heavyset features were rough, brutal, his deep-set eyes slightly uneven. He was ugly as none of the Monère ever were. Even the plainest child of the moon caught a human's eyes, and we had all been that once—Monère, supernatural creatures descended from the moon, blessed with her gifts. Ergo, those who became demon dead afterward were usually still blessed with pleasing looks. Not so with Ruric. He was one big block of pure ugliness. He was also one of the oldest and strongest demon warriors, one of the last two existing descendants, other than me and my family, of the *drakon*. The dragon clan.

The other last existing *drakon* stood next to him. Hari. As handsome as Ruric was ugly. Their skin was the color of light bronze, even darker than my golden hue, because they had existed longer than I down in Hell. The only one darker than they was my father Blaec. His skin shone the color of dark bronze after existing for over a millennium in our realm. I'd put Ruric and Hari's age at close to that: greater than my six hundred years, less than the High Lord's one thousand years of being. Other than the skin color, you couldn't tell that Hari was that old. Besides being handsome in a bad-boy sulky kind of way, he was arrogant and abrasive. His name meant *clever like a monkey*. But if that was so, it was in a spoiled, infantile manner, as was oft the case with those who looked as he did and scored well with the ladies. He was tall and lean with sharp-bladed features that were curled now into a sneer. Or maybe closer to a snarl. Not too handsome now with that look of distaste distorting his face, casting it more, well . . . demonically.

We were an odd assorted lot, and of everyone standing before her, I guess it was Hari, Ruric, and Talon who were causing the Monère Queen to scream in such a panic— pure gut reaction. Hari and Ruric because they were exactly what they looked like: big, bad demon predators. Talon because he was something she'd never seen before, a creature of absolute darkness, as if he had been distilled from the very bowels of Hell. Of course, only someone who didn't know Hell very well would think that. There were much worse things than the lovely Flowers of Darkness.

"Shut up," I said. *My* instant gut reaction. Because the loud noise was not only embarrassing me, but hurting my ears. She shut up. Not because she wanted to, but because she had no choice. My command, verbal for the benefit of her guards who had all drawn their swords, and my even stronger mental one, had left her unable to do anything but obey me. One of the reasons why we demons were so feared. Not only for our greater physical strength but for the frightening psychic power that becoming demon dead granted us. But hey, you had to have some compensation for dying.

"Leave us," I told her coldly. "Go away." And it wasn't so much my shooing motions but the unheard mental command I issued again that had her and her men doing just that, leaving us in great haste.

Running toward us in their place were other guards, a whole slew of them, official guards, those belonging to High Court. We hadn't poofed out of thin air to appear in front of them, although their extreme reaction almost made it seem so. Nope. We'd arrived the usual way via the portal situated in the woods behind Halcyon's place here at High Queen's

Court. We'd stopped at Halcyon's quarters, reunited with Stefan and Jonnie, and then all of us had walked like normal people onto the path that wound around to the front of the central manor house where our paths had crossed with that dim-witted Queen who, from her frightened reaction, seemed as if she had never seen a demon before.

I sighed. She probably hadn't. Most Monère didn't unless they came to High Court and caught a glimpse of my brother Halcyon. And he was like me, not that intimidating to look at. That certainly could not be said of Ruric and Hari, who were intimidating even to other demons. And add to that the startlement factor of a midnight black Floradëur. But, come on, most of the guards knew me, or at least knew *of* me. I'd walked here, quite civilized among them, only a few days ago, and they had seen Talon then. But—memory kicking in belatedly—he had been a short, stunted thing. Now he was as tall as Ruric, and more strikingly lovely, his head in proportion to his body now. I guess the change in him was, well, startling. And one look at the two new demons, Ruric and Hari—with the Queen's terrified screams on top of that (that had to have really harried their nerves)—and the guards approached us with wide eyes and drawn swords. Exactly what I had wanted to prevent. A situation.

I tamped down my urge to command them mentally as I had that Queen: *Put away your silly swords.* I didn't, out of respect for the Queen Mother—these guards belonged to her. But my teeth ground together, and my fingers instinctively curved clawlike in irritation at being treated like the dangerous predator that I was.

"Hold, men. Put your swords away. It's Princess Lucinda," called out a voice that I recognized. Captain Gilbert coming to the rescue. Not of me, I thought sardonically, but of his men.

Well-trained guards that they were, they obeyed their captain. He strode up to us, and if his eyes were a bit wary as they swept over Ruric and Hari, they warmed as they came to rest upon me.

"Princess Lucinda," he said, bowing. Taking up my hand, he pressed a kiss to the back of it, his sweeping mustache lightly brushing against my skin. He was one of the few men I allowed such privilege—to touch my hand like that. One of the few men who wanted to do so. I allowed it because of a genuine liking for the man. And because he had been my willing blood donor the last few times I'd visited High Court.

"Welcome. We weren't expecting you back so soon," said Captain Gilbert. For good reason. I hardly ever came here. Maybe only once every century, if even that. Now I'd put in three closely spaced appearances, the last two only days apart. Days that seemed to have wrought quite a change at High Queen's Court. Whereas it had been quiet, tranquil, and empty the last time we were here, now it was overflowing with people.

"Is Council in session?" I asked.

Captain Gilbert's eyebrows arched up. "Yes, is that not why you are here?"

I had done that several months ago. Sat in Halcyon's seat on the Council, representing my brother when they had called that special session to question Mona Lisa over the death of another Queen. Halcyon had been too weak to do so, had still been recovering from the violation that dead Queen had dared inflict on him, and he'd asked me to go in his place. I'd done so because the only other person who could have gone would have been the High Lord himself. He'd been the one who had actually killed the Monère Queen after she had broken one of our greatest taboos, and was recovering himself from his recent trip to the living realm, exacting his revenge. I'd gone because there had been no one else to go. Otherwise I stayed far away from Monère politics. I was the least civic-minded demon in my family. Halcyon had been raised up in that tradition, and swam the political waters well in both realms. I didn't. I usually didn't give a damn. I'd had no ties, no interest. Now I was loaded down with them: five people who seemed to belong to me now, for different reasons. Why I was here.

"No," I replied. "I've come to see the Queen Mother on another matter. A personal one."

The captain's gaze flickered past me. Polite demon that I was—at High Court, anyway—I made the introductions. "Captain Gilbert, you've already met Talon, Nico, Stefan, and Jonnie."

He inclined his head, acknowledging them. They politely nodded back.

"The two new demons are Ruric and Hari, my father's royal guards whom he has assigned to me."

Captain Gilbert's gaze sharpened. "Are you in danger, Princess?"

I answered yes, indirectly. "There is a rogue demon at large—one of the things I have to speak with the Queen Mother about. Until he is captured, Ruric and Hari will be at my side."

"A rogue demon?" said Captain Gilbert.

"Yes, Derek. A former guardian."

A whole new onslaught of worry filled the captain's eyes at my pronouncement. A rogue demon in itself was reason enough for concern. They targeted humans—much more plentiful and easier prey—but nothing was as sweet and powerful as Monère blood. There had been slaughters in the past, entire territories wiped out when wayward demons found their way into this other realm and glutted their thirst on Monère blood. Incidences that were almost unheard of now due to demon guardians.

A new demon with poor impulse control was easy enough for a guardian to deal with, but a former guardian—by definition one of our more powerful demons—going rogue . . . Captain Gilbert had good reason to be alarmed.

He was in a pickle, the good captain was. Common sense dictated that he report this immediately to the Queen Mother, who ruled High Court and was the ultimate authority over all the Monère on this continent. Common sense also dictated that he not let me or any of the other demons out of his sight. Nor could he risk bringing me and my new demon bodyguards into the Queen Mother's presence, not when the captain's whole purpose was to protect her. What to do? And who to dispatch with carefully worded news of our arrival?

Captain Gilbert was saved by the arrival of Lord Thorane. The Council Speaker's familiar authoritative presence and warm smile was a relief to both the captain and me.

Lord Thorane greeted me with a low bow. His eyes took note of the two new demons looming beside me, but he didn't seem overtly alarmed. "Princess Lucinda. Your return is most welcome. But the timing could have been better."

"When the Council is not in session, you mean?"

"It's the Lunar New Year," he said, shedding much light and great dismay over me. Oh! So that's why so many people. Of all the days to return, this had to be one of the absolute worst: when High Court was packed with thousands of Monère gathered to attend the holiday festivities.

"So much for trying to see the High Queen," I muttered. The presence of not just one but three demons here at High Court—two of them highly threatening, unknown entities— would send all the Monère into a panic.

I glanced surreptitiously at the two demons by my side to see if there might be any way to part them from me. Ruric returned my look with a slight frown while Hari looked amused. The mocking laughter in Hari's eyes, however, did nothing to hide the steely message in them. *Don't even think of it, Princess. Wherever you go, we go.* Ruric *looked* like the greatest threat, but appearances, as I quite well knew, could be deceiving. Hari, to me, was the one to watch out for, the less predictable one.

Nope. Separating me from them here was not going to happen, which left me with the idea of trying to soften their appearance. Ruffles and lace popped to mind for some ridiculous reason, and my lips curved in sly amusement.

Which wiped the smirk off Hari's face and replaced it with a wariness I was much more comfortable with.

Lord Thorane cleared his throat. "The Queen Mother has put her private jet on standby, in case you should happen to return during this busy time." No need to say where to. I had no other place to go to other than my small territory. And no need to say when. It would be now, of course.

"We'll be happy to escort you there now," he graciously offered, confirming what I already knew: that the sooner we were gone, the better. Our presence here in the midst of the New Year celebration could only cause disruption, if not outright panic. Not the sort of demon diplomacy my father would have encouraged.

"Our luggage?" I asked, though in truth it was only just what Jonnie and Stefan, and Hari and Ruric had brought. We had left their things at my brother's cottage. Talon, Nico, and I had nothing other than what we wore.

"My men will transport your luggage down to the plane," Lord Thorane assured me, and led us discreetly away to a back lot where two vans were waiting for us.

"Three demons, one black Floradëur, two Monère rogues, and a Mixed Blood whisked away from sight in under two minutes. Now that's true magick," I said dryly once we were seated and on our way to the private airstrip. Hari sat in the back, while Nico, Talon, and I took the middle row. Lord Thorane was seated in the front passenger seat beside the driver. Ruric, Stefan, and Jonnie followed behind in the second van.

"The Queen Mother holds you in great esteem and the highest regard," Lord Thorane carefully returned. "Indeed, she looks upon you with deep fondness. And those feelings, and respect, extend to your men as well. She does not see you as mere categories," he said, softly chiding.

"I know. I'm sorry," I said, apologizing. "I just wish I could have seen her. But I can tell you everything just as easily." And I proceeded to relate to him how my father and brother had hunted for Derek down in Hell, but hadn't been able to find and apprehend the rogue demon. Derek had tried to end my afterlife, and had almost succeeded in doing so. "We've already spread the word to the other guardians," I told him, "and they'll be on heightened alert until he is caught."

"As will we. So that's why your father assigned you bodyguards," Lord Thorane said thoughtfully, glancing back curiously at Hari.

Belatedly, I introduced Hari to him.

Lord Thorane's eyes lit up. "A true pleasure to meet you," he said to Hari. "Is Ruric the other demon guard?"

"You know of them," I said with surprise.

He nodded, looking quite delighted. "Yes, I have indeed heard of the last two great warriors of the dragon clan. The Queen Mother's regret at missing you will be even keener with this news."

"We'll be around. I'm sure we'll have a chance to see her later." Indeed, I was going to be spending a lot more time topside in this realm.

The jet's engines were already primed when we arrived. And our luggage arrived three minutes after we did. In a surprising short order of time, we were in the air, hurtling toward Arizona. Our new home.

HIS NAME WAS Vandar, and he was a creature from an ancient nightmare. A creature who had lived for centuries relying on his psychic powers, his cunning.

Now he lifted his massive head and roared for the pleasure of feeling his slaves cringe.

In his present incarnation, he was a huge, scaled being with glittering red eyes, a reptilian body, and wings shaped like those of a bat—only infinitely larger. But he was just as likely to take human form.

Leaping into the air, he circled his lair, looking down with a feeling of satisfaction as he churned up the chemicals in his belly, then spewed out a blast of fire that singed the already blackened landscape below.

His huge mouth stretched into a parody of a smile as he looked down on the circle of destruction. It was a warning to any enemies who dared approach this blighted place. And a warning to the slaves who lived in the huge cave he had blasted out of a mountainside. If any tried to escape, he would turn them to ash as easily as he charred the land spread out below him.

In his long life, he had seen many changes. The world of men had climbed from primitive existence to a rich civilization. Then, in the space of a few years, everything had spun out of control when thousands of people had developed psychic powers, throwing civilization into chaos.

Governments had been wiped out as the ordinary people fought the psychics. And when the fighting was over, the people were left huddled together for protection in city-states.

He had almost lost his life during that terrible time. But he had learned to use the new order to his advantage, sending raiding parties to the cities and bringing back slaves to serve him—and supply his food.

Just as he began scheming to widen his circle of influence, his adepts told him that virgin territory existed for the taking—in a world parallel to this one. A world where the old rules still held sway, and the people who lived there would be helpless to fight a powerful being who could dig his mental claws into their minds and bend them to his will.

But he hadn't lived for close to a thousand years by leaping unprepared into the unknown.

As he flew over his territory, he thought of the tasks that must be accomplished before the invasion. He had already started his preparations for the assault by sending spies to the other universe, men who had stayed for a few days and come back to give him a sense of the place. Now he must send someone else who would give him a more detailed report.

Who should it be?

Someone with psychic powers that would give him an advantage over the people in that other universe.

But not a man.

The spy should be an attractive woman because she would seem weak and vulnerable, yet her pretty face and sexy figure would disarm the men who ruled the place. As he thought of who it should be, the perfect candidate came to his mind.

But before he called her to him, he would feed.

Circling back, he landed in the ceremonial site fifty yards from the mouth of his cave. Lifting his head to the skies, he roared out four notes. Two long and two short. A signal to the people who did his bidding.

While he waited for them, he pictured his three hundred slaves instantly dropping what they were doing and hurrying to answer his call.

One by one and in groups, they stepped outside the cave, blinking in the morning sunshine.

He watched their stiff posture, their wary eyes as they stood in their color-coded tunics. White for adepts. Gray for house servants. Brown for those who did the dirtiest jobs like washing the floors and mucking out the toilets.

They knew what was coming, and they cringed, even as they came toward him with hesitant steps.

Standing before them, he began to change his form, his wings folding into his body. His claws retracting. The shape of his torso shrinking and transmuting to the incarnation he used when he walked among his minions.

He was vulnerable when he changed, but they didn't know that, and they trembled as he transformed from a silver-scaled monster to a tall, dark-haired man. He stood before them naked for several moments, letting them take in his well-muscled body with its impressive male equipment.

Satisfied that they had had enough time to contemplate his magnificence, he snapped his fingers. Two blond-haired women clad in white tunics came forward and walked to the carved wooden chest where he kept a set of clothing. From its depths, one of them removed a long black tunic of fine linen edged with gold braid. As he held out his arms, one of them slipped the garment over his head and the other knelt and strapped a pair of supple leather sandals onto his feet.

When he was dressed, they stepped back into the crowd. He turned and smiled at the waiting throng, feeling the waves of tension rolling toward him.

They knew he would feed now. On one of them. He could have done that in his dragon form, of course. But this was so much more intimate, and it impressed upon them that even when he looked like a man, he was as far above them as an eagle was above an ant.

Long moments passed as he let them sweat, let them wonder which of them he would select. And why.

A man or a woman?

They didn't know he had made that decision. In his mind, he kept a running assessment of his slaves' deeds— of the times they pleased him and of their transgressions. One man above all the others had earned the privilege of starring in this ceremony.

Finally, he raised his voice. "Bendel, come forward."

The man gasped. Everyone else breathed out a sigh of relief.

For long moments, nothing happened. Then Bendel broke and ran.

Vandar was ready for the man's futile bid for freedom. His tongue flicked out, lengthening like a whip, catching the man and pulling him back.

The man's face had turned white. His eyes were wide and pleading.

"Were you foolish enough to think you could outrun me?" Vandar murmured, his voice silky. "And foolish enough to steal food from the larder?"

The man's jaw worked, but no words came out of his mouth.

Vandar spread his lips, baring his teeth as he sent out his fangs. His gaze never leaving the man's terrified eyes, he grabbed Bendel's hair and arched his neck before sinking fangs into pale flesh.

The first draft of blood sent a burst of warmth through Vandar. He felt the life-giving liquid flow into his mouth, down his throat, and into his stomach.

The nourishment brought him a satisfying glow of energy. In his childhood, he had subsisted on a human diet, and he could still eat small amounts of food and drink.

He had tried wine made from grapes and other fruit, and to his taste buds, the wine had a tang that was similar to blood.

He could have spared the man's life. He didn't need to drain any one individual to quench his thirst. He didn't even need to drink human blood. An animal would do. But an animal could not fear him with the intellect of a man, and that was part of the pleasure for him. He loved feeling a victim's terror swelling as his life force slipped away.

When he had drained the last drop of sweet-tasting nectar, he cast the husk of the body onto the ground and wiped his mouth on his sleeve before raising his head to stare at the other slaves.

Searching their faces, he let the moment stretch, prolonging the little ceremony and impressing the gravity of the occasion on the group of terrified watchers. Then he selected two men to take out the garbage.

F EELING AN UNACCUSTOMED restlessness, Talon Marshall exited the former hunting lodge where he lived in the woods of rural Pennsylvania and walked to a stand of pines that he'd planted years ago. In maturity, they formed a tight circle, shielding him from view. After pushing through the branches, he pulled off his clothes, stowed them in the wooden box he kept in the clearing and stood naked among the pines, enjoying the feel of the humid air on his well-muscled body.

Then, in a clear voice, he began to say the ancient words that had turned the men of the Marshall family into werewolves since the dawn of time.

"Taranis, Epona, Cerridwen," he chanted, repeating the phrase and going on to another.

"Ga. Feart. Cleas. Duais. Aithriocht. Go gcumhdai is dtreorai na deithe thu."

The human part of his mind screamed in protest as bones crunched, muscles jerked, and cells transformed from one shape to another.

No matter how many times he changed form, it was never easy to feel his jaw elongate, his teeth sharpen, his body contort as muscles and limbs transformed themselves.

The first time, he'd been terrified that the pain would kill him—the way it had killed his older brother.

But he'd willed himself to steadiness. And once he'd understood what to expect, he'd learned to ride above the terrifying physical sensations.

Thick gray hair formed along his flanks, covering his body in a silver-tipped pelt. The color—the very structure— of his eyes changed as he dropped to all fours.

A magnificent beast of the forest.

With animal awareness, he lifted his head and dragged in the familiar smells of the forest—leafy vegetation, rotting leaves, and the creatures that made their homes here.

Racing past a stand of oaks, he caught the scent of a fox and automatically corrected his course to follow the trail. The animal gave him a good chase, taking him to a patch of wilderness that he hadn't visited in months.

As he stopped for a moment, breathing hard, a scent came to him. Not one of the familiar odors of the forest. Something that didn't belong in this wilderness environment.

Slowly, he walked around the area, sniffing, until he came to a place where the forest floor had been disturbed. As he pawed the earth, he found it was soft, with leaves brushed back into place over an area of fresh dirt.

The wolf dug down several inches, sure there was something buried here that didn't belong in the woods. A body?

He dragged in more of the scent and decided it wasn't anything living. But that was as far as he could go in wolf form. He needed hands to get to the bottom of this mystery.

Raising his head, he looked around at the silent forest. He considered himself the guardian of this natural area, and he knew someone had been here—invading this place.

The visit had been long enough ago for the man's scent to fade, but he had left something behind him.

Turning, Talon raced back the way he'd come, to the circle of pine trees where he pushed through the change. As soon as he had transmuted from wolf to man, he pulled on his clothing, then strode to the five-door garage where he kept his outdoor equipment—some of it for his business, leading wilderness expeditions, and some of it for maintaining the property around the lodge.

Selecting a short-handled shovel, he slung it easily over his shoulder and strode back through the forest toward the place where he'd stopped in wolf form. After looking around again, he began to dig, scooping out the dirt and piling it to the right of the hole so he could easily refill it when he was finished.

When the shovel scraped against something hard, he dug around the object. Using the shovel as a lever, he pried up a metal box, which he hauled out and set on the ground beside the hole.

Obviously, the box was private property. But it was buried on public land. With the shovel blade, he whacked at the padlock securing the top of the box until the hasp broke. Then he knelt and lifted the lid.

What he saw inside made his breath catch.

The darkly sensual Monère novels
by national bestselling author

SUNNY

"A refreshing, contemporary urban
erotic horror thriller."
—*The Best Reviews*

MONA LISA AWAKENING

MONA LISA BLOSSOMING

MONA LISA CRAVING

MONA LISA DARKENING

"Sizzling... [An] intrigue-filled
erotic paranormal."
—*Publishers Weekly*

M338AS0509